THE
AMAZON HEIST

KIMBERLY M. GRIMES

ILLUSTRATIONS BY MARCO A. HERNANDEZ

PAGE PUBLISHING, INC.
New York, NY

First originally published by Page Publishing, Inc. 2015

ISBN 978-1-68213-613-3 (pbk)
ISBN 978-1-68213-614-0 (digital)

Printed in the United States of America

For Peter and Brandt

CONTENTS

ACKNOWLEDGMENTS

While this is a work of fiction, many of the characters and events are based on ethnographic fieldwork I conducted in the Amazon. I chose to transform my notes into a novel in order to share people's experiences in this part of the world with a wider audience and, hopefully, in a more amusing way than a traditional ethnography.

My sincere and deepest appreciation goes to everyone in the village where I lived and my dear friends in Iquitos and Lima without whom I could never have implemented a study abroad program or written this book. Abrazos mis queridos.

A big thank you to Joan Gero and Marcela Vasquez for their insightful reading of an earlier draft. Their comments improved the book in many ways. I am grateful to have two such fine anthropologists as colleagues and friends in my life. Gracias, amigas del alma.

I want to thank Michael Yarnell and his team at Page Publishing. A pleasure to work with, they made the publishing process smooth and provided helpful suggestions.

A special thanks to Kitty Mac who supervised the writing and editing process – paws always touching the keyboard and body curled around the laptop—inspiring me to keep at it. He died two weeks after I finished. I guess he thought his work was done. Descanse en paz, mi hijo.

My lifelong gratitude and love goes to Marco Hernandez. I hope his wonderful drawings bring to life some Amazonian images for the reader. Again none of this work would have been possible without him by my side every step of the way. Te quiero siempre, amore.

Chullachakis appear in the jungle after the sun sets. Protectors of the rainforest some say. Evil acts happen at night, and chullachakis take those responsible. Others fear they are a form of the devil with one foot human and the other a hoof. Horns growing on their heads. The misfortune of getting stranded in the forest after dark either lost or homeward bound after a long day deep in the jungle result in mysterious disappearances. Parents warn their children not to venture beyond the village at night. Everyone knows of a family member or friend who has vanished.

1

ELIZABETH

The plane bumps and jerks as it passes over the Andes. Descending below the clouds, the green blanket of the jungle spreads as far as the eye can see. The Amazon, Elizabeth's second home for the last ten years. Her students squirm in their seats, excited and nervous at the same time, wondering what experiences await them for their winter semester in Loreto, Peru. Loreto is Peru's largest state yet the least populated, at least if one means humans. Snakes, on the other hand, are a different story.

The plane drops suddenly from the sky like a pelican diving for a fish and lands on the short runway. The professor, her husband, and students grab their luggage from the conveyor belt in the open-air Iquitos airport. The humid air smells like rich organic topsoil mixed with exhaust fumes from the planes and the *mototaxis*, three-wheeled vehicles with a seat strapped across the back two tires. The vehicles are the main form of transportation around the city. Reached by air or river, Iquitos is the largest city in the world not accessible by road, so cars are a rarity.

"Jump in, two per taxi, and hold your backpacks tight on your laps," the professor instructs. Her two friends who have served as her most trusted guides over the last decade check that all the suitcases are in the back of a makeshift pickup, a modified mototaxi with the back two wheels supporting long wood planks that serve as a truck bed to haul larger cargo. The students fill seven mototaxis, two more with Elizabeth, her husband and the two guides. The drivers rev their engines and take off. Looking like a long boa weaving in and around the traffic, the students squeal with delight. The professor in front instructs the driver to take them to the main port where they have reservations on the *Eduardo IV*, a large ferry boat that travels upriver from Iquitos to Pucallpa and back. The port is chaotic with travelers, animals, cargo, mototaxis, and people hawking everything: food, clothing, hammocks, toothbrushes and whatever else one could possibly need for a long trip up the Amazon.

Eight short, stocky men appear beside the mototaxis. Without a word they hoist two of the students' suitcases up on their shoulders making themselves almost disappear. Elizabeth shakes her head. She asked her students to pack light. The people in the village basically have two sets of clothes: the ones they are wearing and the ones being washed or dried in the sun. Most of the students listened, carrying just a medium-sized duffle and a backpack but several have suitcases the size of a refrigerator. Even these enormous bags are not a problem for the muscular porters who quickly carry the bags up the three flights of stairs to the top deck of the *Eduardo IV*.

Elizabeth Long and Bob Marquez are a team with no need to voice what each needs to do. This is their fifth trip with students to the Amazon. Elizabeth heads to the top floor where she has rented a cabin to store the luggage. A small indigenous-looking woman leans on the rail across from the cabin's door. "What a luxury," the woman's eyes say. The Americans even have beds for their bags. Elizabeth smiles at her and she smiles back.

Bob pays the taxi drivers and checks to make sure no one left anything behind. Even though the students are twenty and twenty-one years old, one has to constantly look after them. Sure enough, a pair of sunglasses has fallen on the seat. Last time, Jen left her camera. It is not a good way to start a trip. Bob pays the drivers and shakes hands. They pat one another firmly on the shoulders. Each wishes the other, their families and friends well as they depart; a custom he has always enjoyed.

Once the luggage is secured, Elizabeth sees thirteen pairs of eyes anxiously staring at her. "Let's get our hammocks hung. Make sure to tie them tight. You don't want them falling down in the middle of the night." Rey, her most trusted guide, shows how to tie a timber hitch knot. The students struggle but with the locals' help, the hammocks are strung, taking up most of the starboard side. More people arrive stringing their hammocks on the port side curious as to why so many gringos are aboard. Some students try to maneuver sitting in the hammocks excited as their adventure begins.

A barefooted petite lady passes along one side of the ship with a tray of sandwiches balanced on her head. Her hair is wrapped in a turban, which helps balance the heavy tray. She wears a kitchen apron whose pockets are full of napkins. A passenger requests two sandwiches. She aptly holds the large wooden tray in one hand while using a napkin to remove each sandwich. Minutes later another woman follows with a tray of fresh yucca empanadas on her head. "*Tres soles.*" Three soles or about a dollar each the woman announces.

"What is she selling?" Sarah asks. Elizabeth explains and buys the whole tray of empanadas for her students to try. The warm soft yucca dough encapsulates a piece of chicken covered in a spicy sauce. Delicious. "We'll learn to make these in the village," Elizabeth tells her students.

"Look over there at that boat." Mike points three boats to the east. The closest two are similar to the *Eduardo IV*, sturdy ferry boats that carry people and cargo up and down the mighty river every two or three days. The second appears to be docked for a major overhaul. But the third boat looks like something out of a romance novel. A beautiful, dark-stained wooden ship with freshly painted white carved trim and handrails graces the port. On top is a bar and lounge chairs for an excellent view of the jungle and its waters. The restaurant below has chandeliers, crystal glasses, and china. Only twenty cabins, most with a little balcony jutting over the water.

"That's how to do it," Ed smirks. A tall lanky student, Ed seems a little out of step with the rest of the students making his attempts to be cool more obvious. He fidgets with the zipper on his backpack and finally pulls out his iPod.

"Nah, I'll take the hammock any day of the week. Who wants to be in one of those stuffy little rooms?" Mike replies.

"I bet they're air-conditioned."

"Even so, can't imagine anything better than sleeping in the open air in a hammock. Why come here if you don't live like the folks here do?"

"I agree, Mike, but you have to admit the ship is beautiful, a wonderful artifact of a bygone era. I'm glad it is being preserved," Sarah adds. She is a double major in history and anthropology and loves old relics.

Mike nods in agreement. They walk to the stern to join Jane. The three are mesmerized by the Amazon. It's like a dream. They can't believe that they are really here. The sun hangs low in the afternoon sky, casting beautiful orange and red hues across the horizon. The river mirrors the sky. Flecks of colors shimmer on top.

Jane points to lower left side of the antique riverboat. Two women sit on planks of wood with two ropes attached to the sides and wash the porthole windows. It's quite a balancing act to exert enough force to clean without pushing the body off the ship and then swinging back into it. Two foreign-looking men are on the top level directing other workers in preparation for a new tour.

The *Eduardo IV* ferryboat is scheduled to leave at 4:00 p.m. That hour passes and another. And another. Boats come and go on the wide, swift brown river, skirting logs and other debris that poke out of the water. The jungle begins to darken. People scurry about finishing a few more tasks, ready to be home after a long day of work.

After the sun sets, a loud and deep blast of the horn readies all for departure. Eduardo IV's motors begin pushing the boat away from the dock. Black smoke billows from its stacks. Thick ropes splash into the water as the deckhands pull them onto the boat. The lights of the city of Iquitos fade as the ship heads upstream into darkness. Without a full moon, only the lights from stars above sparkle and cut the obscurity. The land is so dim, it disappears. The ship's searchlight illuminates the water just ahead. Tree branches and other foliage floating in the river part as the boat moves steadily.

Many of the locals are already asleep, swaying gently in their hammocks to the sound of the waves lapping against the boat. No storm that evening, so the river is fairly calm. The students fumble around with their flashlights. Some write in their journals. Others are too excited to settle. Soon exhaustion takes over. Elizabeth checks on everyone and then lies in her hammock next to Bob. "Another adventure, Lizzie," he says. She smiles at her husband, grateful he is always by her side.

* * *

Roberto Marquez was born in Chile but his family moved to Mexico when he was seven due to the brutal military coup in the early 1970s. His father had worked for the assassinated Allende during his presidential campaign, so he feared his family would soon be killed. Pinochet eliminated anyone he thought would oppose his dictatorship. Roberto's grandfathers were both folk musicians and were murdered days after the coup. In the dictator's mind, Andean folk music represented populist ideologies, and all who played that style must be eliminated.

Roberto doesn't remember much of his early years in Chile, just the frantic departure, but he did inherit the gift of music from his grandfathers. He honors them by playing all types of folk music but mostly music of the Andes. He taught himself to play string and wind instruments in junior high school. By his twenties, his band played in cities across the Mexican republic. It was during one of his tours that he met Elizabeth. She was living in Oaxaca, researching her doctoral thesis that summer. They both happened to stay in the same little hotel near the *zocalo*, the main plaza. While working in the Bolivian Andes the previous summer, Elizabeth heard panpipes, *quenas*, and other types of bamboo flutes played for the first time and fell in love with the music. A year later when she saw Roberto carrying the same bamboo panpipes, she struck up a conversation, curious as to why people play music from South America in a country rich with its own musical traditions. It was love at first sight even though Elizabeth never believed in such a thing. But the connection between them was undeniable, and the rest of the summer, they became inseparable.

Twenty-five years later, they still shared a deep passion and a love of travel. Roberto became Bob, a gringo nickname that long ago began as a stupid joke but then stuck. After their first trip to the Amazon, they both knew that they would return for the rest of their lives. Elizabeth's department of anthropology accepted her proposal to bring students for winter term abroad. Never traveling apart, Bob began a fair trade project upon seeing the Amazon villagers' need for cash income.

Amazon communities live for the most part in a cashless economy. Villagers farm, hunt, and collect from the rainforest almost all their essentials. But salt, cooking oil, plastic buckets, and school books cost money. They turn fallen trees into charcoal, yet a canoe full brings only a few *soles*, not nearly enough to purchase everything. Some years, they have extra rice and melons to sell, but they can't count on them from one year to the next.

Sacha inchi is a funny name to English and Spanish speakers alike. It is a legume that grows on a vine like a peanut in the low jungle. Throughout Bob and Elizabeth' second trip, a buzz about the plant permeated the air. A possible savior for the weak economy in the state of Loreto. Discovering its high concentration of omega 3 oils, government officials promoted it as the next great superfood to export to developed nations' peoples with their high-cholesterol problems. A French company had already begun contracting local growers to transform the legume into cooking and salad oils. Unfortunately, they insisted on growing it plantation-style, clear-cutting the forest to plant neat rows, resulting in more rainforest destruction and dramatically reduced yields by the third year. By the fourth year, the owners had to abandon the insect-infested plantation.

The locals know better, cultivating it in their abandoned yucca and banana fields while the forest recovers the land. The vines wind around the bushes and climb up the sides of trees, preferring to meander in complete disorder rather than be forced up a straight stick. Compost made from plant-waste materials fertilizes the plants and pest control comes from birds and beneficial insects that live in the abandoned fields. It takes about a dozen years for a field to return to its natural state, about the same amount of time a sacha inchi plant will produce its "nuts" before dying. The plant offers the potential to provide food and income while reforesting deforested areas but only if grown this way.

After many long discussions, Bob and the farmers in the village that hosts his wife's students decided to make sacha inchi brittle using the sugar cane they grow also to export to the US. The project has taken time to come to fruit. What are normally simple tasks become more complicated when working in a place without any basic infrastructure. One year, Bob devoted to sourcing plastic bags to package it and to find a way to get the bags to the farmers without costing an arm and a leg. A talented friend in Baltimore designed a beautiful label, knowing how important packaging is for sales. Getting nutritional information and meeting USDA requirements to import the brittle into the US also took time. Two years ago, everything seemed in place to export, all major issues had been resolved or so they thought. That year, the Amazon rose higher and faster than ever anticipated. The floodwaters wiped out the crop. A few farmers gave up. The others stuck to their guns.

Bob is hopeful that this is the year, everything comes together, and he will leave with a couple of boxes ready to export. The farmers trust Bob unlike many foreigners and government officials who seem to appear only in election years. Both promise so much and, in the end, deliver nothing. Bob always returned as he said he would. He sent money to buy the necessary supplies. He finds solutions as an unpredictable environment throws out challenges. Yes, this is the year, Bob thinks to himself as the ferry gently rocks from side to side. "We have to make it work this year," he murmurs to no one in particular.

The ferryboat pulls into Nauta, a town of some ten thousand people, just before the sun rises. A long string of canoes onshore flanks both sides of the boat. A crimson orange stripe sits between the dark green of the jungle canopy and the dark blue sky above. Elizabeth rose a half hour earlier treasuring her favorite time of the day, just before dawn. Everything is so quiet, you can hear the earth rotate she always says. She feels sharpest in the first hours of the day, the time she does her best writing and thinking. It is a clarity that fades and disappears by late afternoon. Maybe that is part of the bond, the connection she feels with people here. They too rise before dawn with energy and vigor to complete many of the days' tasks while the air is cool. At home, most folks are snoozing soundly at that hour; just the few working the late shift are out shuffling around town.

One by one the students stir. Some fall out of their hammocks, forgetting where they are before fully waking up. Bob joins Elizabeth on the stern, watching the action below. All kinds of supplies are carried off. One stubborn cow refuses to walk the plank until his owner waves grasses in front of his nose. Slowly the cow moves. A few more people balance possessions on the top of their heads and come aboard. The ferrymen scramble to buy a homemade meal from the women waiting along the shore in makeshift restaurants. Carrying wood tables and some benches from home, the women place them on the muddy banks near where the boats dock along with their cooking pots full of steamed fish and rice bundled in banana leaves. The banana leaves give a wonderful sweet flavor to this typical dish. That day one woman has stewed a duck, a special treat if one can afford the extra centavos. Two long pulls on the horn signal that the boat is ready to leave. Men stuff the rest of the food in their mouths and run to board. "In a couple of hours, we'll be the next stop. I better get everyone moving." Elizabeth kisses her husband on the cheek and strolls down the deck.

* * *

The students line up on the front of the large ferry boat with their luggage. A water buffalo shuffles to one side away from them. Several goats tied to a pole strain their necks, trying to chew on luggage tags. Frustrated that they cannot reach the tasty treats, they bray and stomp their hooves.

"Get ready with your bags. We'll hop off just ahead," directs Elizabeth. "See the fellows in the white shirts waiting, we'll pass our bags to them one at a time."

The students can't quite figure at first how they will hop off but soon remark on the amazing job the captain does, parking a boat that large so carefully in the exact spot, a small opening in the jungle next to a set of stairs. Men shove long wood boards about two feet wide and thirty feet long to the men standing below. One by one the students pass their suitcases to the men and then descend, teetering and joking about walking the plank.

Their home for the next several weeks appears discretely on the horizon, lush and green, green, green. A world of green. Grass shoots, palms, and tiny yellow, pink, and blue flowers surround the bungalows and communal hut. On the edges of the complex awaits the unfettered jungle, spreading its wild tentacles of luscious growth as far as the eye can see. The students follow the long boardwalk from the river to the communal hut where Juan and Juanito greet everyone with a big smile and a glass of camu camu juice made from the delicious fruit loaded with vitamin C. Another long boardwalk on the backside of the hut leads to small thatched roof bungalows where the students head to unpack their suitcases.

While the group settles in, brushing their teeth after the long boat ride, a scream and then running feet is heard by all. Elizabeth whose bungalow is in the middle of the students huts yanks her door open to catch Charlene running by.

"Whoa. What's up?" she calmly asks.

"A snake," Charlene gasps, "on the boardwalk at the end."

"Breathe, sweetie. It's fine. There are lots of snakes here. This is the real jungle. Not some supposed reality show on TV. I'll call one of the guides and see what kind it is." Seeing the other students are roused out of their huts, Elizabeth tells them to go back inside. "There's a snake, and we need to get rid of it. Just close your doors. You'll be fine," she reassures them while inside her heart is pumping a mile a minute. She has bad luck coming into contact with fer-de-lance.

She sees Rey walking with Pedro, the cook, outside the communal hut. Elizabeth has worked with Rey, her number one guide, for the last three trips. She yells to get their attention and waves vigorously for them to come. Together they rush toward her but stop abruptly when they see the long, brown-leaf-patterned snake slithering toward them.

Rey holds steadily his machete in his right hand. He instantly knows it is a fer-de-lance, one of the most dangerous snakes in this part of the Amazon. Without the anti-venom, one bite and you are a goner. Elizabeth always brings anti-venom from the Santa Ana Clinic in Iquitos yet, so far, hasn't had to administer it. She always jokes how she enjoys taking students to the Amazon because, with no cars and bars, she won't have the typical problems other professors have on study abroad. Only has to watch out for snakes. Ha ha. Now that joke doesn't seem funny.

Rey quietly studies the snake's movements. Fer-de-lance aren't as dangerous as bushmasters, if one of them spots you it will hunt you until it bites you, but the vipers do command respect. *Swoosh, swoosh.* The fer-de-lance's head spirals off to the ground below. With two swift swings of his machete, Rey eliminates the danger. The snake's body slithers and flops as it slowly dies.

"Thank you, Rey," Elizabeth says. "I can't believe our first day, our first minute, really, and here we already see one. And here on the boardwalk, not in the agricultural fields where we have seen them before."

"It's the river rising so fast. You see how much higher it is this year than in previous Januarys when you have come. The icecaps on the Andes are melting, and we are getting all the water. It forces all kinds of critters to seek higher dry ground. We must keep our eyes out for more. There could be a nest," Rey warns.

As if saying it makes the possibility come true, in the late afternoon after the students return from their first jungle hike, Elizabeth hears two other students outside her room.

"Look, it's a little a baby snake all curled up. How cute. I'm going to get my camera."

Elizabeth opens her door to see the two young women in flip-flops less than a foot from a baby fer-de-lance.

"Stay perfectly still. Remember the snake Rey showed us this morning? Well, that must have been mama because that baby is a fer-de-lance also. I'm going to get Rey or one of the Juans." She runs to the kitchen. In less than a minute, Juanito is by her side with a large piece of wood that he uses to pound the snake's head flat. He pounds it over and over to make sure it is dead.

Juanito tells them that a baby snake's venom is actually more powerful than an adult's although they can't bite as deeply. He shows them a bulge in the middle of the snake's body. Some small prey. The girls were lucky because, after a snake eats, he is sluggish and less likely to attack. And it makes them easier to kill. He places the snake into a garbage bag like his mama.

Bob enters their room all sweaty after his long walk to inspect the sacha inchi fields. He sees Elizabeth sitting in the hammock out on the porch and starts chatting about the condition of the crop while striping to take a shower. Cool water pumped from the river flows over the body, one of the few ways to refresh in the hot and humid environment. Rubbing the towel over his head, he walks onto the porch and notices the concerned look on his wife's face.

"What happened? You look worried," he asks.

"Not one, but two fer-de-lance today," she pauses and runs her fingers through her hair. "Both on the boardwalk."

"Shit, Lizzie."

"I know. Not a good way to start a trip. There must be a nest. Juanito and Juan have gone to search for it."

"They'll find it. Everything will be okay. Maybe you should do what Rey told you last trip. Kill one yourself and eat it to gain power over them. You do have a way of attracting them," he teases. He looks at her and realizes that now is not the time for jokes. Instead, he sits in the hammock and wraps his arms around her. "That will be the last one, you'll see." She sighs and relaxes into his arms.

2

THE SISTERS

The name of the antique river cruise boat, the one that the students so admired, is the *Grand Amazone*. It was established by a French couple, Pierre Duval and Breton Dubois. Pierre and Breton toured the Brazilian part of the Amazon River a few years ago on a ship that claimed to be as elegant as the Silversea Cruise Lines. They fell in love with the jungle but not the riverboat. They know better than most what comprises excellent service and exquisite food paired with perfect wines having owned a four-star restaurant for years in their beloved Provence. In their early fifties, they decided to abandon everything familiar and sink their savings into a new venture. A lovely, three-tiered riverboat for small group cruises was up for sale in Iquitos, Peru. Although their previous travels had always been in Brazil, Breton speaks a good bit of Spanish. He apprenticed in a restaurant in Madrid what now seems like ages ago. Their neighbor in Provence was originally from Arequipa. He spoke about the ease of starting a business in Peru and was thinking to return to his homeland especially now that Toledo had won the presidential elections. His excitement was contagious.

After a few months of lawyers and paperwork, the French couple were convinced that their dream to provide a vacation combining the lure and excitement of the wild rainforest with all the comforts of home, or actually better than home, could not fail. Pierre was clever at marketing. Breton talents lie in service. The two had the *Grand Amazone* ready for service in less than a year. Reservations were coming in steadily.

The cruise begins in Iquitos and heads upstream to the Pacaya Samiria Reserve, Peru's largest national park equal in size to the country of Costa Rica. The reserve holds claim to having the largest biodiversity of any area in the Amazon. The International Nature Conservancy funds projects in the reserve with a Peruvian partner, Pro-Naturaleza, to rescue fish, turtles, and monkeys from the brink of extinction. Together they campaign against the selling of protected species through the black market. Pumas, jaguars, ocelots, and other wild cats are rapidly disappearing. Educate the children first is the philosophy of Pro-Naturaleza, they in turn can teach their parents. Anti-black-market programs are now in most schools and universities throughout Loreto and are causing quite an impact. Many of the animals are indeed making a comeback. Only time will tell if their hard work has prevented extinctions before the tipping point was reached.

In recent years, the conservationists have expanded their education programs. They first focused on people living in the Pacaya Samiria Reserve. Now they have begun work in the communities bordering the reserve, including San Jorge, the village where Elizabeth takes her students to live for the month of January. One of the most important parts of her study-abroad trip is to provide students the opportunity to see firsthand what the conservationists' programs are accomplishing, such as teaching local people to protect, rather than hunt, most mammals in the forest. The fact that parents rarely see troupes of monkeys swinging in the branches as they did often when young makes most locals concerned about their children's futures.

Pierre and Breton support Pro-Naturaleza. When they mapped out the cruise's schedule, they decided to spend two nights in the reserve, and pay the fees that provide financial assistance for education. Some cruises or tour guides skirt the park rancher's office at the main entrance of the reserve and sneak in passengers via smaller boats on one of the many creeks, a practice Pierre and Breton find despicable. After two days in the reserve, the ship turns around and returns to Iquitos. Seven days on board, two nights in Iquitos, top quality promised. Pierre markets the cruise to older Europeans, Canadians, and Americans who hung their backpacks in the attic many moons ago but still want some adventure in their lives.

Edith Cambry is just one of those people. Traveling all her life, she toured the great pyramids of Egypt on camelback, flew in a tiny seaplane to the fjords in Scotland, lived in a canvas tent in Rajastan, and crossed Tanzania in a jeep. She saw Pierre and Breton's advertisement in the *London Times* and then again walking by a travel agency on Hadley Street, but with her and her sister's financial situation, the dream cruise to the Amazon must remain a dream.

The next week, walking to the store for a few groceries, a glimpse out of the corner of Edith's eye changed everything. The Hadley Street travel agency had a new poster in the window announcing a free cruise on the *Grand Amazone* through a raffle. Two lucky winners would win a week cruise, a promotional tool Pierre designed to get their new venture off to a good start. Edith quickly entered the agency, a rare entity these days now that most people book vacations online. Printed brochures with a picture of a gilded era riverboat surrounded by dark green vegetation captured Edith's heart and soul. She took her only ten pounds, what she had to spend for the groceries, and bought five tickets. Five, her lucky number. And sure enough, three weeks later, she got the call that she had won a cruise for two on the Amazon in January. Warm, sunny skies; away from the cold, gray, winter drizzle in London. Away from the boring tea parties that her sister made her attend with pretentious ladies blabbing about issues that did not concern her. Edith was ecstatic. Her sister would not be.

Edith began dropping hints subtlety to her sister, suggesting the Amazon as a fantastic travel destination. Helen never liked getting her hands dirty, not even when gardening, so it took a while to convince her that the trip would work out. Maybe even be exciting and more pleasurable than their previous sightseeing tours. Tours that attracted travelers who seemed to take no real interest in the place they visited, excited only by buying souvenirs at a bargain and taking pictures of everything to bore folks back home, never remembering any names or interesting facts. No, forget fun. To convince Helen, Edith would have to focus on the trip being prosperous.

* * *

"First time on the Amazon?" asks the tall man with the long grey ponytail for the second time.

"Yes. Remember, we met earlier? Helen Count. As I said, my sister and I love cruises, but after taking a few on European rivers and the Mediterranean Sea, we became uninterested in seeing yet another medieval church. They are beautiful sights, but after you have seen a dozen or so, you know. And yes, always delicious food, but at our age, we need to be careful not to keep adding extra pounds. Edith suggested that we need more adventure. 'What's life without it?' she said. She can be quite persistent. So here we are in this godforsaken land, cruising the Amazon. I must admit though it isn't as bad as I thought it would be. They actually have adequate service on board." Helen keeps fanning herself.

"Me, I've crossed many a dangerous mile here in this jungle. Started young at sixteen. I was looking for adventure myself. Ah, that was when this place was really wild. Savage. Few white men. Natives would shoot a white man on the spot if you didn't know how to control them. Of course, I always knew how to talk to them. They do know the jungle. Good to try and make friends by trading something. The problems with trading," he pauses, "is finding something they want. They don't seem to want things we know are useful. Got caught in quicksand once. Most people panic and struggle to get out, which makes you sink deeper. No, I kept my wits about me, stayed perfectly still until I could slowly move one leg at a time straight up, like climbing a staircase with deep, deep steps. I grabbed a vine to pull myself the rest of the way out. Must admit I was scared."

Helen sighs. Oh for goodness sake, he's repeating the same story he told me this morning. Edith must have had the same thought at the same moment because, in unison, they raise their eyebrows and shake their heads. They know when he starts talking about himself, he won't stop for hours. One of those men whose talk is mostly wishful thinking at best. Must nip this in the bud today, Helen decides.

"Sorry, dear. My sister and I must pop off. Nice speaking with you again," Helen says as she helps her chubby sister out of the chair. They go in search of a quieter spot on the other side of the boat.

"Yeah, sure. Next time I'll tell you how I wrestled an anaconda and..."

"Mmm hmm." Helen waves him off, pulling her sister along. She pushes her short, tight curls away from her face. Tall and thin, Helen walks with perfect posture.

"Good save, sister dear. We could have been saddled listening to that rattle all afternoon. Besides, I like this side of the boat better. You can almost touch the luscious foliage." Edith adjusts her chair so she can look straight into the jungle canopy. "So thick. How can anyone live here? You can't see two feet in front of you. It's a miracle they survive," she adds.

"Yes yes, dear." Helen's mind is focusing on something else. "Now let's think about our activities this afternoon. We are cruising up this smaller river, and I'm sure the captain will stop along the way when the guides spot some tiny creature that only they can see. Afterward, we visit another native village. I can't remember the name, but I do hope this time they wear enough clothes. Yesterday at that other village, I had to keep looking up to avoid starring at all the women's naked breasts, and I have a terrible crick in my neck from it," complains Helen. "Anyway, you go off first. Grab a hold of that macho fellow. He'll like that."

Edith looks up, and for a moment of utter clarity, distinguishes the intricate details of the largest leaves she has ever seen. Stunning, she thought. She turns back to her sister to share the beautiful vision she just beheld but thinks again. Her sister wouldn't care. "Why do you have to be so contrary?"

Helen ignores her question. "Pay attention. You can be so absentminded. Really, sister, you know if it wasn't for me, you'd be wandering off with some naked native fellow, lost forever."

"Poppycock! I just have a more curious mind than you," responds Edith.

Helen finishes going over their plans when they hear the boat's motor slow. As the boat nears an opening in the forest, faint sounds of drumming grow louder. Jose Antonio, their Amazon guide, calls the passengers to gather on the bow of the boat and starts narrating. "You hear the drums? The Bora Bora uses them to communicate to each other. They are saying, 'Come. A boat is arriving. Let's welcome them.'"

A group of half a dozen children suddenly appear on the path in native garb made of bark cloth. The smallest child is naked. He clings to his sister's hand to keep his balance while walking toward the boat. The children watch intently as the white elderly people precariously walk down a wooden plank to come ashore. Swatting the mosquitoes buzzing around their heads, the visitors are glad to wear long pants and shirts to fully cover their bodies. The insects are merciless, especially along the shoreline. The children giggle at these funny-looking people wrapped up like grubs in their cocoons. As the group gets closer, the kids sprint back to the protection of their parents. Even though they look funny, the children know strangers can be dangerous.

The cruise passengers pause a minute to catch their breath and regain balance before resuming on the wet, slippery clay path. Edith stops suddenly when she announces that she forgot her hat. "Oh dear, I have left my hat, and the darn mosquitoes won't stop biting my scalp. I must go back."

Helen shakes her head. "I'll get it. I'm quicker than you."

Two of the other visitors mumble how Edith is always forgetting something, poor soul. Helping one another, the group walks carefully over some roots and muddy puddles. The path is rough, virtually disappearing at times in places the trees have fallen, pulling their mighty roots into the air and leaving deep holes. Trunks and branches crisscross the narrow path.

A large thatched roof, circular building with palm fronds as walls is the communal hut where the Bora Bora receives visitors. The group ducks to enter the hut where the older Boras await. The white people shuffle inside and sit on a long wooden bench built specifically for visitors. The men and women begin singing in their native tongue. They wear painted tree bark skirts and seed neck-laces adorned with piranha teeth or macaw feathers on their chests. Stomping their feet to the rhythm of the drumbeat, they move forward and backward as if in a trance. They stop. No clapping, the guide said. These are their holy songs, not entertainment.

"Aye, my neck. At least some of the women have sense enough to cover their jingling breasts with their long black hair," whispers Helen.

"Shh. This is sacred, sister. Have some respect. When did you get so prudish?" Edith turns her head quickly so Helen won't respond. The second song comes to an end.

Jose Antonio tells the group that during the next song, the Bora will invite them to join in their dance. The song is not a holy one but, rather, a happy tune about digging yucca, the Boras main source of food now that they rarely eat monkeys and wild boar. Edith grins. Helen rolls her eyes. A young Bora woman offers her hand to Helen, posturing for her to dance. Helen starts to shoo her away, but Edith, embarrassed, quickly grabs the woman's hand and lets her help her stand.

Edith closes her eyes and lets the drumbeat take her back to her youthful days when she danced all the time. She gets winded yet keeps moving, slower and slower, while the other dancers swirl around her. She gestures to her sister to join in the dance, but Helen feigns not to see. Several other passengers rise and dance. When it ends, they all clap since it's not a holy song.

As the visitors catch their breath, the Bora women instantly surround them. Their hands are full of necklaces and bracelets they made to sell to tourists. A meager yet important source of cash income to the families. A dozen teenagers appear out of nowhere, hawking tree bark paintings, blowguns, and coconut carvings. Seed of various colors strung as necklaces or bracelets, some with fish bones or carved tagua nuts are their best sellers. Most of the visitors buy something while a few wander over to the big *manguare* drum to listen to Jose Antonio explain how it was made and played. As the group walks back to the boat, the kids hug their sides, still offering their wares, determined to make one last sale before the boat leaves. Who knows when another one will arrive?

* * *

Edith puts her feet on a stool the cabin boy brought her. The warm sun and the soft waves splashing on the sides of the beautiful *Grand Amazone* make her sleepy. She can barely believe that she managed to persuade her sister Helen to travel to the Amazon. Helen is not an adventurous person and is often anxious. She rarely shows any positive emotions—stiff upper lip and all. The cruise boat is perfect although Helen worries it won't be as copious as other cruises they have taken together. Edith sighs at the thought of her dear sister always concerned about something. She wishes Helen could just relax and be happy. If anyone in the family has a reason to be mad at life, it should be her, not Helen although Edith must admit that she has been blessed with the love of two wonderful men while her poor sister never took a chance on love.

Edith smiles when she thinks of her first love in college, Henry. They met at a concert on the quad. Henry grew up in many countries as his father's diplomatic service required. They started traveling during summer breaks, young and free with only the packs on their backs. The first summer, hitchhiking across Europe, they made love every day, drank good cheap wine and laughed. The next summer, they ventured into more unfamiliar territory—Southeast Asia. They loved eating exotic foods they couldn't identify from street vendors. Not having a clue as to any of the languages, the trip was difficult, but the beauty of the peoples and places made the challenges worthwhile. Her addiction to Asian dumplings has never ceased.

At the end of their college careers, they thought to marry but were still too immature to handle differences in opinion well. They began arguing more, both digging in their heels about who was right. At first the arguments weren't personal; they focused on political, economic, or social issues, big picture topics. In time they came to be about petty, insignificant things. The next year, they went their separate ways, but the love they shared in their hearts never ended, only retreated to live deep inside. The memories radiate like a warm soft light on a summer's eve, soothing in times of need.

Edith always wonders how her life would have turned out with Henry. She continued with her passion to travel that he inspired in her. She realizes now that it was that pure and innocent first love she was trying to replace when she fell so hard for Lazaro in Rome. Rome became home after college. An art history major, Edith worked at a small gallery, earning enough liras to pay the bills and to visit every little Italian town nearby. On one of her bike excursions, she met Lazaro, and he showed her the sights only locals know. Lazaro was the most charming man Edith has ever met in her life. The result was baby Sally, the greatest joy in her life. When Sally died five years later, Edith died as well. How cruel life can be. To give such a precious gift only to have it taken away moments later.

Edith wakes up from her memories and readjusts the back of her chair. That was a long time ago, she reminds herself. She looks to the jungle, to the abundant foliage to recoup her earlier sense of contentment and peace. At first everything just looks green, but when one pays closer attention, a rainbow of colors pop out. Fiery orange and red heliconia, bromeliads, and monkey bush flowers. Delicate rose and yellow orchids. Purple and red passion flowers. And the famous giant water lilies with their aromatic white blooms, *Victoria regina*, named after the new Queen Victoria in 1837. Sister should like that. She is a true royalist at heart.

The palm trees have a wide variety of fruits, not just coconuts as Edith had always assumed. The boat glides by men and women in dugout canoes, paddling from the front to better see the floating branches, trees, and other pieces of the jungle brought into the river by the rising tide. She waves, and the people always wave back. Wouldn't it be nice to live this simple, beautiful life without all the hustle and bustle of city living, she wonders? Her romanticized view of the jungle, similar to most tourists, neglects to see or understand the struggles Amazon people confront. Maybe because the people face adversity with such resignation. Flying in for a week or two, tourists use the people as a backdrop for the vacation pictures. If they do visit native villages, no relationship can develop with the time so short. The people remain as faint romantic images.

Edith settles into the chair, straightens her floppy hat to keep the sun off her face, and falls sound asleep. Her mind drifts back to the day she met her husband, only in her dream, he's an angel. A loud crackle, crunch sound breaks through her reveries. Another tree, only this one some six meters long, hits the boat. An angel, yes, she agrees, in a way he was. She remembers how he rescued her from a depression that enveloped her mind and soul like the long black veils widows used to wear, blocking sight and smell, muffling one's hearing. Edith was so disconnected from life unlike her sister, Helen who always had her students. Never wanting to marry, students were Helen's children. Born with an amazing facility for languages, Helen taught both French and Spanish. So dedicated, when traditional language acquisition techniques failed, she invented new ways to get the kids to pronounce the foreign words correctly.

"If it hadn't been for her physical care of me," Edith stirs awake and whispers, "I would have died on the streets and not cared so heartbroken after losing Sally. Helen saved me first, and then Ralph, my soul mate for forty-one years saved my spirit, my heart. I was physically alive but emotionally dead. Ralph resuscitated my will to live. No one can understand how every cell in my body loved that man. Helen complains that he didn't save a penny; he should have thought about what would happen to me, now old, widowed, and poor. But I ignore her. We lived in harmony and knew the best life was a generous life." Edith grins at the bright red-and-yellow butterfly resting on her lap, both bathing in the warm sun.

* * *

"Johnny, *sientate*." Helen stands over Johnny's desk, grips his shoulder, and presses him down into the chair. As a young female teacher, Helen knows that she must maintain discipline or her class of rambunctious eighth graders will take over and no learning will be possible.

"This week in class, we will learn how to order food in a restaurant. No matter where you are in the world, you have to eat. Johnny, since you cannot sit still, you can be the waiter." A soft moan is heard. "Marge and Peggy move your desks together like a table." Helen continues with instructions, giving each student a role. She worries that the principal may not approve of her abandoning the standard Spanish text from which she is supposed to teach. Page after boring page. The text is based on the theory that repetition, repetition, repetition is the best way to learn a foreign language. Reciting vocabulary words ad nauseam. Boring. It almost puts Helen asleep, so why wouldn't it her students?

Helen pursued a different method, one in which she made her students enact real-life situations in the classroom, focusing on communication rather than translation. She got the idea from Edith's memory scrapbooks of her travels although she never told Edith this. Before the tragedy, Edith traveled like crazy. Funny stories about her inept attempts to order food, get train tickets, find cheap lodging and so forth in Europe, Africa, and India made Helen realize how out-of-date secondary school language acquisition methods are. She decided to experiment on her own. The worst they can do is fire her. With no children of her own to provide for, she could afford the risk, now that Edith has moved out.

Helen had to admit that Edith married a kind and compassionate man but a dreamer. Hopefully, he'll get a steady job soon to provide for them now and in the future. Helen thought that she would never see her baby sister smile again. Pale and withdrawn, Edith gazed out their living room window day after day ever since that godforsaken spring morning. It was as if all her sister's blood drained out of her body and into the hole where they laid little Sally to rest. Mixed in with the soil on top of the coffin, the grave contained two souls instead of one. Ralph was a welcome surprise indeed. Now Edith smiles every day. If only he would stop giving away all his coins in his pockets to any Joe Blow who asks. They'll need those pennies when they get older. Helen proudly remarks on how much she has saved thus far from teaching no less – a terribly remunerated profession – but they seem to have yet taken the hint. "Generous to a fault is one of the things I most love about him," Edith always says. "You don't understand because you have never been in love."

Helen does know what it is like to fall in love, contrary to what her sister thinks. Edith never knew of Helen's affair while studying for her Spanish proficiency exams in Almeria, Spain. Her favorite teacher, mentor really, recommended that Helen live with a Spanish family and submerge herself in Spanish culture for a summer before the fall exams. She told Helen that the experience would be inspiring, invigorating, and with it, there would be no doubt that Helen would pass the exams with flying colors, easy as pie. The teacher arranged a suitable family with whom she could live for free.

The remote town of Almeria on the Mediterranean Sea, a beautiful spot in the rocky, semi-desert Almeria province of Andalucía was a perfect choice. Although the town has over one hundred thousand people, it still retains the laidback atmosphere of closeness and beauty of many Andalusian coastal towns. Helen explored the ancient Alcazaba. She took a morning dip daily in the sparkling sea. Her favorite activity of the day was to walk along the shore, collecting shells in late afternoon when the sun hangs low in the sky, producing a multitude of colors above the water. It was on one afternoon stroll that she literally bumped into Mr. Wonderful. No exaggeration. He was perfect: well-read, kind, funny, handsome, and worldly in an interesting traveler way, not in a pretentious snob-like way. They talked and talked. She had never spoken to anyone in her life like that. Not even her sister with whom she had to be protective and a bit more guarded in discussions. They dined. They danced. They loved one another that summer. That marvelous, perfect summer.

Helen said she would return after her exams, and she believed it herself. She never did. She wanted to. She cried reading his letters asking of her return. She never did. How could she explain? Once back in England, the summer seemed like dream or a fantasy. How could she abandon all her hard work, her years of dedication, her saving and scraping together money to get her degree? She could not let go and fly in the wind. She was too sensible. Sensible people don't believe in silly girls' summer romances. Her exams grounded her. She received the highest score and several job offers followed. Security and respect—two things she lacked and so desperately wanted all of her life.

Life on the farm in Arkansas. Parents dirt poor, Helen remembers those winters when all they had to eat was turnips and more turnips. If their parents hadn't died in that car accident, they'd probably still be on that farm eating turnips. Edith was too young to remember, a baby, no, she was around three years old. Edith was walking, Helen is sure. Her long blonde curls used to bob up and down when she ran. Helen remembers leaving the US as if it were yesterday, holding little Edith's hand, boarding the enormous ocean liner. Arriving on the doorstep of an aunt they had never met and who begrudgingly took them in her home. Over a decade earlier, the aunt, her mother's only sister, was whisked away by a good-looking chap with a funny accent who visited Arkansas on business. The aunt was euphoric and expected a romanticized version of living in Europe like the Hemmingways or Fitzgeralds she had come to know through books—parties, glamour, the nightlights. Instead, she has had a dreary, hard life with an unfaithful, philandering, drinking British husband.

Childless, the aunt adopted Edith as her own. Edith attended elementary school, took piano lessons, wore new clothes, and played in the gardens and neighborhood park with the other children. Helen learned to serve. Good training, the aunt said. "Plus, can't afford two of yas. One of ya has to help out," she would say with a scowl. "Life ain't easy." At thirteen years old, Helen wasn't a child any longer. Many children start working younger than thirteen her aunt had said as she accompanied Helen on her first day to be a kitchen girl in a fancy house across the river. She had to earn enough to pay for her clothes, food, medicine, books, anything she needed. At least her aunt didn't charge her rent.

Helen didn't mind that her baby sister had the good life while she toiled. If it had to be one of them, Helen preferred it was her. Edith always shared everything with her anyway, even giving her most of the precious chocolates she was given twice a year. Helen soon learned how to skim a few pounds of her pay before giving it to her aunt and hid their nest egg in a coffee can stuffed in the back of the closet. She feared one day their world would be forever changed like that day in Arkansas when Preacher Dan and Mr. Conner the sheriff showed up. She never trusted her aunt, worried she'd get bored with Edith, and out the door they would go.

Helen always pretended her job was fun, an adventure, for Edith's sake. She couldn't blame Edith for becoming so carefree. She hid the hardships. She lied about the aunt's meanness. The aunt did indeed eventually grow bored with the idea of a child. She became detached and unloving toward Edith as she grew older. Edith cried many nights, wondering what she did wrong to anger her new mother so. Helen would soothe her and tell her everything would be okay. She claimed that their aunt had become possessed by a dragon living in the cliffs down the road from their town. She'd flap her arms like big wings and crash into Edith's bed to make Edith laugh.

Helen made sure Edith was never without as a child and then again as a widower. She doesn't harbor resentment about her childhood. Her aunt was right that life isn't easy. She learned to be self-sufficient and quick thinking—two qualities she admires about herself. She can depend on herself. Important lessons learned. Lessons that have served her well throughout life. She was an outstanding teacher, all agreed at her retirement party. She never got fired but rather changed many aspects of the language-acquisition curriculum. She loved her students. And they loved her. She was as proud as any parent would be of the children who graduated and became successful in their careers.

Helen was cautious with her hard-earned money, squirreling away every penny she could in her teacher's pension fund. She would have had a nice nest egg for retirement if it hadn't been for that prime minister. How politicians can so easily cut this and that. They don't feel the pain. Her pension got cut in half. Sacrifice for the nation, the PM said. Boogers to that, Helen retorted. She already gave the country the best years of her life, morning to night, educating the next generations' minds. Good thing Helen is a survivor.

3

ALBERTO

Alberto Gonzalez weighed eleven pounds when he was born. They say it was his size that killed his mother. Normally, children in the jungle weigh no more than five to six pounds at birth. Alberto's mother had eight other children of normal weight. Five have survived to adulthood counting Alberto. Tall as a child and then sprouting to over six and a half feet by fifteen, he was considered by all to be a giant, especially in the Amazon. The kids in school called him *gigantor*, freak, and the Tower of Pisa—who knows where they got that one—to haunt him further. He already carried the weight of his mother's death in his heart.

Hearing other kids taunted for perceived physical defects, Alberto cowered in pain for himself and for the others even though they too wanted nothing to do with him. How cruel children can be. He was ostracized for something he had no control over. As he grew up, however, his attitude changed regarding the name calling. He found that he could come up with smart and funny comments to the names. And he liked the company. At least they were paying attention to him if only for a few minutes each day. What he despised was the loneliness his height brought. His only constant companion was his pet Alfie, a big, fuzzy black tarantula with bright pink toenails. He and Alfie spent long hours at home, studying, and Alberto discovered that he liked learning.

People repeat that money is power, but Alberto realized at an early age that knowledge was also a kind of power. He received lots of praise from his teachers; praise turned into opportunities which led to privileges. He stayed after school to help the teachers clean up the classrooms. He was allowed to join a reading club the principal started for interested teachers. Graduating at the top of his class, he wanted desperately to go to the university in Lima. If one wants to be taken seriously in his or her career in Peru, one must study in Lima. The best schools are always in the nation's capital no matter in which Latin American country one lives.

The money he needed for college proved too difficult to obtain in a part of the world where bartering and communal subsistence work are the norm. "No real jobs here," he would complain. In Iquitos, the only city in Loreto, the paltry cash earnings one receives are barely enough to cover basic necessities. He realized quickly that after graduation, he would never go to a university in Lima and probably not even the regional one at home. His father had died the previous year. Alberto's married siblings with children couldn't help. They all struggled.

His oldest brother Paco got him a job from a friend, driving a mototaxi the summer after high school graduation. Several years passed as Alberto worked day and night, saving every possible penny to pay the regional university's fees. Three days after his twenty-first birthday, he entered the Universidad Nacional de la Amazonia Peruana to study finance and administration. Finance because he thought that is where the money is and administration as a fallback, knowing Iquitos limited professional job market. The tourist sector continues to grow rapidly and remains most promising with new hotels, restaurants, and services needed. He drove his mototaxi in the mornings, took classes in the afternoon, and studied at night. Having been out of school for three years, he had to study to the wee morning hours to catch up. Fortunately, Alberto has a good memory. It also helped that he read almost every book in the tiny municipal library beside the main cathedral during those three years. The books spanned a variety of subjects: literature, geography, history, biology; so he was up to speed in no time.

The university was a different world, a better world Alberto thought. He met all kinds of people from Loreto. What you did mattered, not what you looked like or what name you have. It was refreshing. Gone the days when school meant taunting and loneliness. Now in the university, he found his height an advantage, especially with the young female classmates. At ease talking about class assignments and books because he loved learning so, women responded to him, drawn to him intellectually and physically.

Alberto thought the macho ideas of his father's generation and among many of his peers were old-fashioned. He saw himself as a modern, enlightened man ready to share a life with a woman as an equal. Machismo is backward. Respect is forward. He had his pick of the young women in the university and dated from time to time but always felt something was missing. The girls were smart, pretty, and agreeable. So agreeable, they became boring. He wanted a woman who would challenge him, debate the issues. In the start of his last semester, he met Ivonne in his Public Administration 389 class. She had transferred to the university when her father got a new political appointment in Iquitos and moved the entire family with him. The oldest of six children, Ivonne had a mind of her own. She spoke out in class, even debated with the professors. When she laughed, it was infectious and deep from her belly. She laughed so hard, she had to catch her breath afterward.

Alberto fell head over heels in love with her immediately. By the end of the second week, she agreed to go out with him. They met at the ice cream parlor next to the infamous Iron House. In the late nineteenth century, a bizarre set of circumstances led to the appearance of a house made entirely of iron in the town's main square. Eiffel, who built the Eiffel Tower in Paris, was commissioned to build a house out of iron for a wealthy merchant in Quitos, Ecuador. It was constructed in jigsaw-like pieces to be assembled upon arrival. A confusion along the way resulted in the crates arriving in Iquitos rather than Quitos during the rubber boom.

On their first date, Ivonne and Alberto discussed school work but quickly branched into politics, history, religion, and economic issues as they grew more comfortable with each other. She devoured books like he did since childhood. Their relationship grew intense as the semester passed. Alberto knew that she was the one with whom he wanted to spend the rest of his life and believed she wanted him as well.

Soon to graduate first in his class, Alberto planned to ask her father for her hand in marriage as custom still dictated. He considered himself a great catch as he had secured the top manager position at one of the new three-star hotels built to handle the ever increasing tourist trade. Alberto and Ivonne celebrated graduation with a bottle of Chilean wine along the Tarapaca promenade and even danced under the stars to the music he hummed. The next night, he put on his new suit he bought for his job interview and surprised Ivonne at her house. Rather than smiling that gorgeous smile, Ivonne's face showed concern, even a little fear. The evening was a disaster.

"Lousy *indio*. How dare you ask for my daughter?" the father responded. "Our family hails back to the original Spanish families."

"But, Daddy, you know everyone thinks that in Lima. We're not—"

Señor Torres cut her off. "You will speak when spoken to, young lady. I told your mother that you had too much freedom. Now look."

Ivonne burst into tears and ran into her mother's arms. Neither dared to say another word. When her father was mad, he can be dangerous.

"But, sir…" Alberto never got a chance to respond that his family also had European ancestry even though he thought those ideas were a thing of the past and didn't matter now that he graduated college. He was lucky to leave in one piece as the father grabbed a butcher's knife and chased him out the door. Ivonne vanished the next day. He heard from a neighbor that she had been sent to live with an aunt in Lima. When he tried to contact her there, she wouldn't or couldn't take his call.

Alberto was crushed. All the changes he underwent in the university, believing that one can make his or her life. Hard work and intelligence are what matter in this world. He realized he had been a fool. All his new beliefs were illusions in a place where the plague of racism remains intact. Brokenhearted, he vowed that he would put aside dating and women in general in order to focus all his energies on making money and rising to the top. Be promoted from the hotel's chain in Iquitos to one in Lima. Become a top executive. One day, he'd be so rich that Ivonne would run back into his arms. Her father would bow to him. One day.

* * *

To think of diamonds, South American is hardly the first place to pop into one's mind. South Africa, yes. Australia, yes. Places above stable continental plates. Yet diamonds are also found at sites of meteorite strikes. The famous Popigai crater in Russia which contains over a trillion carats was created by an asteroid striking the earth millions of years ago, similar to strikes full of carbonado diamond deposits found in Africa and South America. So when Peru Petrol cleared a large swath of jungle some thirty kilometers as the crow flies south of Iquitos and its oil-searching drills brought up diamonds instead of oil, geologists came from all over the world to discover indeed another lucrative, very lucrative ancient meteorite strike.

Covered by dense jungle until that moment, the land would never have been investigated for possible gem deposits. The area is located in what people call the lower jungle, land submerged under the ocean until several million years ago. It rose as the continent, drifted west, and an amazing diversity of fauna and flora species flourished to cover the new land.

Surveyors and geologists continue to clear large swaths of jungle near Iquitos in search of the tiny, clear stones. The hardest known natural material, diamonds are not just for adornment of the rich and famous but also for industrial purposes. In fact, over 80 percent of mined diamonds end up in industry, valued for both their hardness and thermal conductivity—ideal material for cutting and grinding, for use in microchips, and as a heat sink in electronics. However, most of the diamonds found thus far in the new Amazonian diamond mine will not be used in industry. As perfect as those found in New South Wales, Australia, the pure crystals will fetch top dollar in the global diamond market.

Not everyone shares in the glee of the discovery, however. The local people have already begun bearing the brunt of the mine's negative aspects since it opened. Run off of toxic materials into the river causes water pollution. The most upsetting result exposed recently is the substantial fish die-offs.

Alberto was hired as the mine's first onsite manager. He was extremely pleased because the pay was double his previous salary at a hotel. He never imagined the headaches that would accompany the job. One month after the mine opened, Alberto arrived at work early in the morning to find a dozen men with machetes in hand, threatening the mine's two front-gate security men. The previous day, the men from San Vicente, a village located between Iquitos and the mine, had set off in their canoes to fish for breakfast as they do every day. They had been having luck fishing on a tributary about two kilometers east of the Amazonian diamond mine. When they arrived, they were shocked by the number of fish floating dead on top of the small creek.

"You are killing all the fish," the men shouted, "and polluting our water. The rivers are our life. Where are we supposed to get water to drink? And water for our crops? We use this water on our *chakras*. You are killing us."

Alberto stepped off his boat and sought to pacify the men. "Please, let me investigate. I hear what you are saying, and I understand. I promise you, I will call the owners, and we will find way to stop the pollution. I'm from here. I know how much we all depend on the river. I promise you, I'll get to the bottom of this. Give me a few days, please."

The men grumbled and threatened Alberto, but they finally got back in their canoes, shouting that they will return with more men if something isn't done soon. Alberto called the mine owners as soon as he entered his office. Their response was not what Alberto wanted to hear.

The mine owners claimed the die-off to be the result of some natural phenomenon. After all, they stated, the tributary empties into the Amazon. Not vice versa. Alberto tried to explain that all the rivers big and small are interconnected. The pollution the mine discharges circulates into every river, creek and lake within who knows how many miles of the mine. He reiterated what the San Vicente men had said. The river is the source of life for local people. But Alberto had no luck convincing them that the problem will not simply disappear just because the men left that day. The owners ignored his warning.

Since then, people in the communities near the mine have tried legal means to stop the run-off, but lacking money and political clout, their pleas for help have had no impact. Scared for their lives, eight months later, they decided they had nothing to lose and organized a blockade across the river to stop anyone from reaching the mine boundaries. The press heard of the struggle and publicized what was happening, which saved them from being shot on the spot.

The negative publicity forced the owners of the mine to build a vat to store the contaminants. Then they were supposed to hull the toxic waste out of the Amazon region, so it could be buried somewhere "safe." What they really did was build the vat with an underground pipe to direct the run-off to the south side of the mine's boundary where less people live. A response not intended to solve the waste problem, only to hide it better. To dispose of the waste safely would cut into profits.

Scary as the pollution is, what really frightened Alberto and the local people was the night the entire community of San Felipe disappeared. San Felipe was a village of some three hundred people that had the misfortune to be located less than a kilometer east from where the first diamonds were discovered. The owners of the mine got a permit to explore the jungle further east. In order to do so, everything needed to be cleared. Overnight, houses were gone. People scattered to relatives in neighboring villages. The promises of compensation for the land appropriation have yet to be realized. If foreign lawyers hadn't taken their case, the payment for the town's land and resources would be lost forever. At least now, it is in the hands of the international court in Holland.

The plight of the San Felipians brought more attention to the mine and more problems for Alberto. Stuck in the middle, trying to help the local people who he feels have legitimate complaints while at the same time trying to keep his job, he constantly tells the bosses in Lima that they need to be more proactive and at least clean up the pollution. His bosses want Alberto to make the problems go away. "Handle it. They are just a bunch of Indians" is their response.

Ignoring the complaints resulted in twelve more lawsuits against the multinational company for failing to adhere to Peruvian environmental laws. Within six months, the bad publicity forced the owners to act. They decided to start a PR campaign to describe the positive benefits they assert the mine brings, benefits such as needed employment for local people. Unfortunately, it was not a strong argument for the mine since only five out of the fifty-eight employees are local, eight if you count the three people from Iquitos.

The company preferred to recruit miners from old mining towns in the Andes. Places where residents need employment after the closure of the now empty mines in the mountains. Places where toxic mining materials discharged into fields and rivers make farming impossible today. These men are willing to work one of the two twelve-hour daily shifts in hopes of sending money back home to their hungry families.

The owners also describe how the mine has increased regional revenue. Taxes paid to the state of Loreto. "Taxes or bribes?" the locals ask. The owners claim to have created new programs to help fight poverty. Yet no one knows what or where the programs are. They do purchase fish, fruits, yucca, rice, and drinks from the local communities at bargain rates. And other supplies are transported by boat from Iquitos.

The owners' assertions have yet to sway the press who they believe favor the local voices and accounts. In response, the company's top PR man came up with the idea to have site tours to provide the opportunity to tell their side of story. Alberto opposed the idea knowing that first impressions stick. To see the environmental destruction around the mine would not be favorable no matter what people are told on the tour or how many signs of happy locals they post. His objection was again ignored. The company now gives Amazon tour operators a cash incentive to add a visit to the mine as part of their customers' excursions. See the Incredible Mine: Making Life Better, announce the billboards around the Iquitos airport.

* * *

Alberto sits at his desk, fiddling with a bunch of papers. As the manager, he must stamp every report, marking his official approval. He wonders if anyone actually reads all these reports. In dealing with complaints and lawsuits, he knows that his opinion means little to nothing to his bosses. He grumbles at the excessive paperwork.

The mine is so security conscious, no one person, not even him, knows how the whole thing operates. Every movement of the personnel seems monitored. They even know how many times a person goes to the bathroom and how long it takes them. Only the big bosses in Lima who work for the Peruvian, American, and European owners have access to all the information. They visit once a month to do nothing in his mind, but just to harass all of the people here who do the actual work. Another inspection is around the corner, and Alberto must make sure that what happened last time doesn't happen again. Imagine finding two guys asleep in the mine, hugging their pickaxes. He almost got fired.

More importantly, Alberto realized in that moment how easily they would replace him. He always thought of himself as indispensable, having been the first hired. He has followed their instructions to the tee these last two years. He has put his life on the line with protestors. He has arrived daily at seven in the morning and has never clocked out before seven at night even though his contract states a nine to five work day. He has given them his life, working hard, never missing a day even when he got dengue fever, which almost killed him because he kept coming to work instead of sleeping like the doctor ordered. Hadn't he earned some respect? Some recognition? He realized last month that his dedication means nothing to them. He will always be just a rural jungle man with a degree from a provincial university. Only degrees from Catholic University or the National University of San Marcos count to Limeños, as the city people of Lima are called, just like Ivonne's father.

He slowly sips his black coffee, its bitter taste matching the bitter feeling in his heart. The upcoming inspection will go well. It has to. He cannot afford another screw-up even though under his supervision the mine is making the owners richer than Slim, the wealthiest man in all of Latin America. Never mind that. This job is a good one, he tells himself, especially in this region. Twice the salary he earned as manager of the Victoria Hotel although the hotel job was so serene compared to the problems he faces at the mine. Focus on the money. He knows that he can deal with any difficulty if the pay is good enough. Salaried jobs like his don't really exist elsewhere in the Amazon.

* * *

Alberto drifts into a daydream, remembering those wonderful nights walking with Ivonne along the Malecon Tarapaca, the promenade overlooking the river. He told her stories about Iquitos and his family. Never before had he shared so much with anyone.

"Everyone knows that Iquitos was founded in the 1750s as a Jesuit mission but what many don't know is the mission was almost lost several times over the next century. The natives weren't keen on abandoning everything they believed to be true. And Catholicism was strange to them. Just like the Jesuits viewed their beliefs. You know the story—same here as everywhere in the world. Cultures clashed causing conflict. So Iquitos never grew much. Only 1,500 people lived in this isolated town so far removed from the rest of the world at the end of the nineteenth century. But all that changed with the rubber boom," Alberto explained.

"Yes, one of my favorite teachers in high school taught us about the boom, a population explosion to a place that had basically no infrastructure. Tremendous wealth for a few produced by excessive cruelty and abject poverty for most. The indigenous and poor mestizo rubber tappers suffered virtual enslavement. On the other hand, I have to admit the rubber barons did use their money to hire people, who somehow managed to build these awesome houses and this promenade." Ivonne motions to the mansions along Raimondi Street and to the street in front of them. "I love handmade tiles. These are as fine as the ones made in Lisbon. Actually, they probably are from Lisbon."

Alberto stole his first kiss and many more while sitting on one of the tile benches in the cooler night air on the promenade. Wrapping his arm around her tiny waist or holding her soft hand while both gazed at the stars made his heart pound. He opened up and shared his true feelings. The story leading up to his mother's death was the most difficult.

"Uncle Pepe was a lifelong army sergeant. When he returned home for a visit from his station in Loreto, he convinced my father to go to Iquitos to get work. Dad's family is from Cajabamba in the northern Peruvian Andes, and Dad was the second to youngest of ten kids. My grandparents didn't have enough land for everyone to farm and survive, so most of my uncles had to go elsewhere to find work," Alberto recounted.

Oil brought Alberto's father, Josias, to Iquitos. Peru Petrol was hiring strong young men. What no one realized at the time was why Peru Petrol was always hiring. Yellow fever, malaria, and dengue fever eliminated the labor force as quickly as they could replace them, that is, expendable strong young men.

"Dad met Mom soon after he arrived. Mom's name was Cualli," Alberto pauses. He gets a little choked just saying her name. "She is, or was, Shipibo. My grandparents came to Belen a year earlier. They navigated their raft downstream from my family's native village on the Ucayali River for about a week or so."

A floating shantytown on the southeast side of Iquitos, Belen is home to hundreds of families who live in the rafts' makeshift huts on which they arrived. The homes rise and fall with the river's cycles. Called the Venice of the Amazon, Belen shares no similarities except for homes surrounded by water. Canoes carry food and other jungle supplies from house to house. The neighborhood is most famous for the Witches Market where fruits, dried fish and frogs, snake skins, black tobacco, piranha teeth, turtle shells, and a variety of soaking vines and other medicinal plants are found. Mainstays of the diet, sugar and yucca, are also sold.

"When Dad contracted yellow fever several months after he arrived, Mom used sacred plants she found in the Witches Market to nurse him back to health. Nine months later, she gave birth to my oldest brother. Dad worked on a supply boat, traveling back and forth from Iquitos to the drilling sites. The family joke is that every time he returned to Iquitos, a new son or daughter appeared in Mom's belly. Dad worked really hard and saved to buy a small lot on the end of Jose Galvez Street. Within a couple of years, they built our home, a small concrete block house with an outhouse in the rear yard. We didn't have much, just a few furnishings. Mom was really sharp with money. She knew well the art of bargaining for whatever we needed. She always managed to feed us even when Dad's earnings dwindled at the end of each month. But despite the financial struggles, people say they had never seen a couple so happy together. They say she filled everyone around her full of love and hope that is until I," Alberto stutters, "I, I killed her." He looks into Ivonne's eyes for her reaction.

"But how, Berto? I don't understand. You wouldn't hurt a fly." She takes Alberto's hands in hers.

"Well, no one has ever said that to me directly, but I know it is what people thought or, rather, think still today. She died giving birth to me. She struggled and struggled because I was too big."

"Oh, Berto. Women die giving birth even more so a generation ago. That's a fact of life. You cannot blame yourself, and I'm sure no one else blames you either." Ivonne strokes Alberto's left arm gently. "You get rid of that thought right now," she adds firmly.

Alberto smiles, remembering Ivonne's incredible kindness. She was the only person who helped relieve him of some of the guilt he carries in his heart. His mind, body, and soul still ache for her, her sweet words, her gentle touches. Her father would never approve of the small house he built on the same street as his parents. He doesn't use hammocks as most rural people do for furniture. He bought a sofa set, TV, stereo, and a real bed with a mattress. Still it is not enough for someone like Sr. Torres, so Alberto works sunrise to sunset. He barely allows himself enough time to eat and sleep. No distractions mean he can save most of his earnings. Only Sundays, his day off, does he enjoy a meal in a restaurant and drinks with old buddies. Sometimes one of his siblings invites him to eat and watch soccer games, which cost him nothing, so he can save more. He holds tight to his dream of finding Ivonne one day. Successful and rich, he will offer her the life her father judged that he never could. Many years have passed without any contact, but he chooses to believe that she is still waiting for him.

4

THE STUDENTS

During the last decade, Elizabeth and Bob have brought five groups of young American students to live San Jorge, a town of six hundred inhabitants, located on the edge of the Amazon River near the Pacaya Samiria National Reserve. The people are descendants of the Kukana Kukamiria tribe. Spoken only by elders in the village, the Kukana language is recently being taught simultaneously with Spanish in the local elementary schools, an important language recovery program. Some of the children have already learned songs in Kukana, a good way for them to train their face and throat muscles for the language's sounds.

The American students stay in an eco-lodge on the south side of the village. A young man from Lima, who attended university in the US, returned to his homeland with the goal of starting a business that would help preserve the Amazon rainforest. He followed an ecotourism model and built a lodge in coordination with the town's people. The basic idea is to generate income for the area's residents while preserving the land's beauty. Families in the village take turns providing the guests meals, housekeeping, and security from unwelcome animals at night. By having an opportunity to earn some cash income for the necessities they must purchase, the villagers can discontinue selling trees and making charcoal as the only cash options previously available to them.

The exchange with the foreigners has, for the most part, been positive. Their favorite experience by far though is the way the January Americans treat them, kind and respectful. The group seems genuinely interested in their lives. Who knows why, wonder most of the villagers? But as Alfonso said after the first time the students came, who cares why they picked us. The extra free hands during harvest season are a big plus.

At sunrise and sunset, life in the jungle is most active. Monkeys howl. Birds fly from branch to branch eating bugs. Frogs croak like a harmonious chorus singing. People rise before first light. The children scatter to collect fallen branches for the cooking fires. Men swiftly propel their canoes to good fishing spots while the women prepare the fire to cook the catch.

The visiting students wake up at five. By 5:30 a.m., they are ready to paddle quietly up a small creek in search of wildlife. A flock of macaws with bright blue-and-yellow feathers fly low over their heads from the bushes that spill onto the waters along the shoreline. Rey spots several men ahead fishing. Casting their nets from the front of their canoes, the men work quickly to catch something tasty for morning breakfast.

Rey stops canoeing to ask the men from San Jorge to show the students their nets and fish caught. Even though the group is interrupting the men's work and making noise that will surely scare away any remaining fish, the men happily comply with the request.

"Only smaller fish today, some *lisu* and *challa*. These are local names which have no English translations. The people will eat these fish whole, bones and all. The bones give us calcium," Rey explains.

One man grabs a round net about two meters in diameter and spins it out into the water. It slowly submerges. With a quick flick of his wrist, he snaps up the net. A fish struggles to get free.

"Cool catch. Is it easy to use that net?" Mike asks.

"Wanna try it?"

"Sure."

Rey asks the fishermen if they will show some of the students how to throw the nets. The men grin as two of the students get the net wrapped around their bodies instead of in the water. The volunteers try but, so far, are unsuccessful in catching any fish. Mike and Julie are the only two that keep at it, and soon they get the right spin so that net spreads evenly and sinks over a wider area. They pull hard together, and up come four fish.

"I guess we'll have breakfast after all," Elizabeth says proudly. Elizabeth instructs the group to say thank you to the men. They wave good-bye and slowly begin their return to the eco-lodge still looking at the beautiful birds and other wildlife out early in the morning. Elizabeth describes how the self-sufficient people gather necessities from the rich foliage of the jungle, such as plants for food, traditional medicines, and building materials for homes and canoes as they paddle along the quiet creek.

"Most groups in this area practice floodplain agriculture. As the river lowers in May and June, they plant yucca, rice, and watermelon. The last two crops to sell any extra in the market in Nauta. Remember the town where the ferryboat stopped before we got to San Jorge? That's Nauta, the largest town around here. It's where people purchase things they can't grow or forage such as cooking oil and salt. We think of salt as something bad because we have too much of it in our processed diet. But the folks here need it. It's an essential mineral and a scarce resource in the Amazon. Their only option is to buy it by the kilo in Nauta."

"The summer months, June to September, the crops mature quickly, aided by the rich nutrients the river lays on the land during high-water season." Elizabeth continues her lecture. "In October and November, they harvest the rice and melons. They wait longer for the yucca. They want the tubers to grow as large as possible since it is the most important survival crop. One can always eat yucca even when fish are dispersed and hard to catch during flood season."

"How do they know when to dig up the yucca?" Betty asks.

"Well, that's the risky part. They watch and try to figure how fast and how soon the waters will rise. The problem is that the river can be low, and then a week later, it has risen a couple of meters due to hard rains in the Andes. While the mighty Amazon has always been unpredictable to some degree, elders have used their experience to determine harvest times with a good deal of success. The past decade, however, predicting has become almost impossible, leaving many families hungry in the high-water season, a new phenomenon for jungle peoples."

"Oh, that's terrible," Sarah remarks. "Why has the river gotten more unpredictable?"

"Global warming, climate change, whatever you choose to call it. The Andes are losing their snow-capped mountains. I was hiking near Cuzco ten years ago and then again last year, and I saw first-hand that the snow, which had covered the top third of one of the mountains facing south, was completely gone. Gone. Then there's the El Niño phenomenon, which I will discuss later. We'll also talk with the people to learn more about these issues."

"As I was saying about the yucca harvest, the good news for us is that most families dig up the yucca in January, so we can help them. The children are on summer vacation from school, so they also will be working in the chakras or the agricultural fields."

"Summer vacation? But it is winter," asks Rachel.

"Remember we are south of the equator. Our winter is their summer and vice versa. Children get out of school the first of December and return the first of March."

"Will we have to wear these rubber boots all the time? They're hot and hard to walk in," inquiries Alison, who is having the most trouble adjusting to the heat thus far. Her pale milky-white skin is already beet red, and it is still relatively cool in the morning.

"Yes, I'm afraid that we must. You see, these thick rubber boots that you are wearing will protect us from snake bites in the jungle and the fields. Just be glad we can each afford a pair. Folks here often don't have enough money to buy boots for all the children. You'll get used to them soon, I promise. Anyway, the families work from early morning to late afternoon, returning home before the sun sets to have their second meal of fish and yucca, maybe some rice. You will learn about the ways they prepare yucca for storage, and we'll roast it too. We'll pick fruit and make juice. The jungle does provide a diversity of fruits that bloom throughout the year, providing many vitamins and minerals in a diet otherwise lacking in much diversity."

"One recent addition to their diet is powdered milk for the children from the national one-child, one-glass milk program started three years ago in an effort to battle malnutrition in Peru. The Amazon has been mostly forgotten by the powers-to-be in the nation's capital who view the area as environmentally hostile and culturally backward. Recently, political leaders have changed, however, and the Amazon territory and its people are now included in national plans. San Jorge has a milk committee, and its members travel to Nauta once a month to receive the town allotment of powdered milk and disperse it among the families. The milk is mixed with water carefully collected from a stream deeper in the jungle, cleaner than the Amazon, to help reduce stomach problems. We will talk with the members of the committee later this week." Elizabeth finishes her brief lecture as they arrive back to their new home. They scramble up the boardwalk and remove the rubber boats before entering the communal hut.

Mike hands the fish to Juanito. He likes practicing his rudimentary Spanish. "*Pescado fresco*, fresh fish." Juanito replies with that wonderful smile of his and tells Mike that he will cook them for lunch since everything is already prepared for breakfast. Mike just nods and says "*Si si*," understanding the words lunch and breakfast but not much in between.

* * *

The sweaty and tired students climb the steps of the boardwalk to wash up for supper. First full day harvesting crops with San Jorge families is done. They had planned to hike in the jungle with the town's *curandero* or healer to learn about medicinal plants, but the agenda changed when three mothers came to the lodge during breakfast to ask for help.

"The river has risen so quickly this year. We haven't harvested our corn," one of the mothers explains. "Now only the top halves of the stalks are above water. We're about to lose everything."

Elizabeth and Rey listen carefully. Bob asks how they can help.

"We need to pick the remaining ears today. By tomorrow, it will probably all be under water. The river is pouring in." The woman motions to the other side of the river where the land is lower. No one lives on that side for exactly that reason. Most families, however, do plant crops there. The soil is excellent for farming. Annual floods inundate the lower land, leaving it rich in nutrients. People sow corn, yucca, and sometimes rice, hoping for good yields.

As they talk, the students flow into the communal hut, ready for the hike.

"Listen up. Change of plans today. These folks need our help, so we are going to pick corn," Elizabeth informs them.

"Corn? I didn't know they grow corn here," Ed asks. He is writing his research paper on agricultural practices. "Does everyone grow it?"

"If they have chickens, they do. The corn is mainly for feed although I have eaten some delicious *humitas*, corn tamales, on special occasions. Chickens are the peoples' insurance. They fetch a good price in the market in Nauta. When a family has a medical emergency, such as a machete accident, people can sell a chicken or two afterward to pay the clinic. Most sickness is still cured using traditional medicine, but people can have illnesses or accidents that require urgent care from Western-trained doctors."

Claudine raises her hand.

"Yes?"

"All the chickens we see in the village, they roam freely everywhere. How do the people know which chickens belong to them when they are so mixed up? In the US, we keep chickens in buildings."

"I'm no chicken expert, but I do know that chickens are meant to roam so they can peck the ground to eat insects and worms, which should comprise most of their food. The people here only supplement the diet with a bit of corn. During the high-water season, they have to feed them more corn since the water invades much of their pecking grounds. As for ownership, chickens are different in colors and sizes. Families recognize them like you'd recognize your cat or dog even if he or she was on the street with lots of other cats and dogs of the same type. Plus at night, somehow, the chickens know where their nests are. You remember seeing those little wood boxes that sit about two meters off the ground behind the peoples' houses?" Elizabeth asks.

Claudine shakes her head yes.

"As the sun sets, the chickens return to their respective yards and scramble up the planks into the wood boxes on their own. It's amazing. Then someone in the family will lower the plank to the ground so no other animals can climb into the chicken coops and eat them. In their nests at night, they are protected."

The students follow the women down the bank to the boats. Children sit, waiting patiently in the mothers' canoes. Across the river, up a small stream, they arrive in an area that appears to be a lake with tall cornstalks poking out. The tassels on top gently sway in the breeze.

"All this land was dry two days ago," Rey tells the students. "The bank on this side is higher and protected the crops from the river until yesterday when the river burst through the spot we just paddled through. That stream," Rey points to his left rear side, "is new, and as you can see, the water is flooding this area."

The students look around unsure of how they will pick corn in the middle of a newly created lake.

"First, I want all of you to know that this is strictly on a volunteer basis. We will wade in waist-high water, pulling the remaining ears and toss them in their canoes. It's going to be tricky walking because you must keep your boots on. They will fill with water and be heavy, but since this area is recently flooded, there are all kinds of things on the bottom that you don't want to step on barefooted," Elizabeth instructs.

"What kind of things?" Charlene asks nervously.

"Roots, branches, tree stumps maybe. I'm not sure so take it slow and be careful."

Mike jumps into the water and wades over to the corn. He grabs the first ear and yanks. "Ow, ow, ow." He drops it in the water and flails his arm. "Ants, red ants. They're biting my arm." His arm is bright red and starts to swell.

Rey leaps into the water and grabs Mike's arm. He submerges it in the water which brings instant relief. Rey inspects the stalks and sees thousands of tiny red ants running up and down them. "The ants have found shelter on the cornstalks. They are covered with them." One of the mothers looks closer with Rey and murmurs something. "She says to grab the ear and dunk it quickly into the water. That way the ants will drown before they have time to bite you."

To test her theory and make sure the students don't get attacked by the painful little insects, Elizabeth grabs an ear of corn, rips it from the stalk, and submerges her arm into the water in one movement. No bites. Her students begin following her example. Soon everyone relaxes. They chatter and fill the canoes with the ears. The students move together in three groups, one per family. Suddenly a loud scream is heard. Everyone freezes while Rey moves swiftly to the student who screamed.

"I felt something swim around my legs. Something big," Jane says.

Rey laughs. "Probably a fish checking you out," he reassures her.

An hour later, the sound of soft sobs alerts Elizabeth. She follows the sobs to Charlene, who is trying to hide the fact that she is crying.

"What's wrong?" Elizabeth asks while patting Charlene's shoulder.

"I just can't. I can't."

"You can't what?"

"I can't take being in the water with creepy things. I keep thinking something is going to get me. I know it's crazy but," she sobs louder.

"Listen, Charlene. You've done a great job. We are just volunteers here. Why don't we walk over to the riverbank and you can take a break while the others finish up. I think we will be done soon. I can use a break too. Let's sit," Elizabeth motions for them to move to the riverbank.

Charlene shakes her head vigorously no.

"No? Really it's fine. Come. I'll sit with you. As I said, I can use a rest myself," Elizabeth says trying to calm Charlene.

"No. I want to help the families too. I know they need help. It's just, it's just…just…I just hate that I'm such a city girl!" Charlene wails.

Elizabeth can't help but to laugh. She hugs Charlene and guides her over to the bank where the boats are tied to the shore. After a few minutes, she has Charlene laughing at her own comment. An hour passes. The stalks are picked clean. Hungry, the students wade to the bank, empty the water-laden boots, and lift their legs into the boats. Jairo and Maclave grab the students' arms and hoist them in one at a time. The boatmen then paddle the boats through the small opening. As they head into the mighty river, they pull the cords on the 45 horsepower motors to travel against the swift current straight across the river to the eco-lodge.

Before the students left, the mothers had tears in their eyes as they told the students thank you a dozen times. The families' three canoes are brimming with corn. The children wiggle to sit on top of the yield without knocking one ear into the water. The mothers dig out a spot in front to sit and paddle upriver for about a kilometer, hugging the shoreline where the water is calmer. They then cross the river diagonally to the village, going with the flow. It is easier to row and, most importantly, less chance of spilling any corn. As the students climb out of the boats, they see the canoes crossing in the distance.

Always the optimist, Mike says, "This has been the best day of my life."

"Even with the ant bites?" Sarah asks.

"Especially with the bites."

"Oh yeah, looks like Mike is going native on us," Elizabeth remarks, laughing. She can see the smiles of satisfaction on her students' faces. Their hearts are full of the joy a person feels after help-ing someone in need. "This is what life is all about," she says to the group.

* * *

Life on the Amazon follows the cycles of the river and the sun. Hard work, love of family and neighbors, and the ability to think creatively to survive any surprises that spring from the river or the jungle defines the peoples' lives in this small village as it does most villages along the Amazon. And of course, a passion for the nation's favorite game, *futbol,* or what Americans call soccer. The evening hours are a time of relaxation, well deserved after a day of hard work. In the center of the village, a small L-shaped concrete school with six rooms, one for each grade, borders two sides of the concrete square used as a soccer field by teenagers each night. The parents sit along the benches that face the school, watching the game while keeping an eye on the younger children, who simply run around, playing tag or some other game.

After a hearty meal of fish, beet salad, rice, flan, and tropical fruits, the students have been invited to play soccer. The guys work-ing in the lodge asked if they could create a team. Soccer is taken seriously. Players bet on each game. Most of the students have little desire to play, but finally six of them agree to compete. The other students prefer to join in the games with the younger kids.

The students walk the path from the lodge to the center of town. Elizabeth and Bob plan to join them later. Last night rains caused the part of the path close to the shoreline to collapse, leaving a gaping hole to cross over. The hole is about six feet wide, too large to jump. The students guess that Julio and the Juans must have built the makeshift bridge out of two fallen trees in order to get to the lodge this morning. The students link hands, making a chain to pass steadily on the logs, which are not tightly secured. Once again, they feel an accomplishment since no one fell into the hole. It's the little things in life.

The students are greeted warmly by the town drunk who, by evening, is feeling pretty darn good. He bows. Sarah and John bow back. He mumbles something while putting his hand over his heart. Quickly, two men appear to politely usher him away. He is heard singing off in the distance.

"What is your name?" Julie asks a young girl sitting on the concrete sidewalk in front of the school. Julie's Spanish has a strong gringo accent but her kind eyes and big smile normally enchant the people she has met thus far in Peru. The little girl gets bashful and runs over to her mother. The mother continues her conversation with her friend seated next to her on the bench while her daughter climbs onto her lap. The girl's sister, Maria, who is three years older and much bolder, asks Julie for her sunglasses.

"These? You want these?"

Maria nods. She puts on the glasses, and the other girls who have gathered around all giggle hysterically. Another girl tries on the glasses also. Another fit of laughter. Soon the girls start fighting for the glasses.

"Whoa, one at a time." Julie motions to Claudine. "I have no idea what is so funny." Claudine smiles and shrugs. "Let me get my glasses out of my backpack." More laughter ensues.

The soccer game begins. The American students on this trip have only played the game occasionally in PE classes at school unlike the villagers who play every night. They have no chance of winning even with their sneakers. Sneakers are a luxury is the Amazon and the locals most often play barefooted or sometimes with one coveted shoe. The first game ends, villagers twelve goals, students one, an *autogol* (own goal). To make it more fair, they decide to share players. Each side wins several times, and the money from the bets ends up being split. It is a friendly game, quite different from the games in which the various river towns compete. San Jorge has won the regional championship seven times over the last decade, and the young men now count on it as an important source of income.

The younger children are chasing two of the students in tag. Colleen is teaching another group of kids duck, duck, goose, only she doesn't know how to say duck or goose in Spanish, so she calls it *gato, gato, perro* (cat, cat, dog). Most of the students have some Spanish training, and they are just beginning to have enough confidence to start using it. Who better than with children?

One of the San Jorge kids strolls by with what looks like a long, wiggly rope. Mike points to it and asks Rey what the boy is carrying. Rey whistles to the boy to join them. He hands Rey a harmless, two-foot, green snake. Rey motions to the group to see if anyone wants to hold it. He notices that John takes two steps back.

"It's harmless," he clarifies for John's benefit. Ed takes the snake while handing his camera to Anne for a picture. Cameras appear out of the backpacks. One by one the students pose with the snake. Some get silly and act like they are about to give it a big kiss.

Elizabeth and Bob arrived during the third soccer game. They met with Santos, the village mayor, to discuss the group's activities for the next few days. Elizabeth notices the snake photo op. She thanks Santos for his help and walks toward her students. She notices that John has kept his distance.

"Don't like snakes, eh?" she asks John.

"Ah, no. They give me the creeps. I kinda have a phobia about him," John replies.

"Maybe this is the perfect opportunity to conquer that phobia."

"Huh?"

"John, you trust Rey, right? You know he would never let any of you come in harm's way?"

"Yeah, sure. Rey is great," John responds. Like all the students, John has a deep respect for Rey.

"Then let him show you how to hold it. Or just touch it. You can do this. You'll be surprised how silky snakes are. I know I was." Elizabeth places her hand on John's back and gently pushes him toward Rey. She quickly tells Rey in Spanish about John's phobia. Rey understands and coaxes John to touch it. John's hand darts back one second after contact. Then he tries again.

"Lizzie," Bob calls to his wife to join him with Don Fernando, current president of the sacha inchi cooperative. As Elizabeth strolls toward them, she looks back over her shoulder. John is holding the snake. "Yes!" Elizabeth cries and pumps her arm in the air.

Darkness approaches. The group needs to return to the lodge before the light disappears. With only the stars as night lights, it becomes difficult to follow jungle paths after dark, even ones as well-worn as the path between the village and the lodge. Plus, now there is the added obstacle, the makeshift bridge to cross. The San Jorge families make their way into their homes where hammocks strung pole to pole serve as comfortable beds.

* * *

In rubber boots, long pants, long-sleeved shirts, the students grumble about the heat while boarding the two boats. Most are still tired from working and playing yesterday. They aren't used to so much physical exercise in one day. Once on the river where the wind serves as a natural air conditioner, their mood improves. They are off to work in the chakras as the fast rising waters make it imperative to harvest the yucca. The yucca fields are located on the opposite side of the river from the village near the corn fields they worked yesterday. The water is edging closer and closer toward the crops softening the ground to help release the tubers from the hard packed clay.

The students climb out of the boats and onto the shore where five families with machetes await. Even children as young as six know how to use a machete. It's the most important tool in the rainforest. Don Amelio swings his machete left and right, cutting off the tops of the yucca plants. The students working in groups of two or three to push the stalks back and forth to loosen the dirt that holds the tubers firmly in the ground.

Snap, snap, snap. The inexperienced students break off the stalks at ground level before any of the tubers peek out of the soil. Elizabeth stops the work to have them observe Dona Marta, a petite woman with the strength of a horse, gently rock the stalk as if luring their source of life to the surface. She tells the students to politely ask the life-giving food to merge—not so fast, not so rough. One must allow the plant to come to you. The students begin again with a little more success.

"Keep drinking water," Elizabeth instructs, seeing her students' clothing drenched in sweat. As the pile of tubers grow, so too their exhaustion. "Let's start taking turns scraping the sticky clay from the yucca so we can peel them," continues Elizabeth. "Betty, Julie, and Mike, grab some machetes and cut a thin line down the tuber like this." She delicately uses the tip of the machete to cut into the surface an inch or two. She slides her fingernails into the cut to lift a thick tough outer layer from the soft white flesh of the plant. The students begin but have a difficult time, so Dona Marta suggests that she do the cutting and the students can peel, wash, and place the yucca into the canoe. With her suggestion, all the students return to the village with their fingers intact.

The sun high in the sky makes the day hotter than they could imagine. Working since early morning, by noon, the students' attention to the tasks at hand dwindles. Several go to squat by the river, sticking their arms in the cool waters. Elizabeth figures it is time to retire from the fields before someone gets heatstroke. The canoe is filled to the top with peeled yucca. The families are grateful to have had help with this arduous task. Everyone is satisfied of the morning achievement. They push off, back to the bungalows where lunch and siesta are well deserved.

* * *

The students walk slowly on the afternoon hike to discover medicinal plants. Tired from harvesting yucca in the morning, they are quieter than usual. Elizabeth is glad. Her job of translating is easier when she doesn't have to tell the students to listen up every five minutes. The village of San Ramon is located on a tributary west of San Jorge. Although every town has a shaman, some are better at healing than others, which is why Elizabeth likes to visit San Ramon's shaman. He is known throughout the region as one of the best.

The fact that shamans possess a wealth of medicinal knowledge is not lost on Western pharmaceutical companies. Over the last decade, Elizabeth and Bob have been struck by the increasing number of pharmaceutical representatives in and around Iquitos each year, seeking shamans' wisdom for the next big medical miracle. They take their knowledge and synthesize Amazonian plants into pills Westerners can pop to heal their ills.

"Wow! It's like almost every plant can cure something. Awesome." Anne goes to pick a flower next to a bunch of tall ferns. Rey grabs her hand before she touches it.

"Those are poisonous, Anne. It will give you a rash so fierce that you will try to scratch your skin off. We have a saying that the prettier the flower, the more deadly it can be, just like women!" He laughs so heartily that it is contagious. Even the girls who don't think the saying is funny can't help but smile also.

"What about boys?" Jane asks.

"What?" Rey is confused.

"What about boys? You have a saying about beautiful women, so how about beautiful men?"

Rey ponders the question then shakes his head no. "Sorry. I guess we don't think of men as being beautiful. Tough, sturdy, yes. But beautiful? I'll have to think about that. Most women I know simply want husbands who are strong and hardworking." Rey notices that Elizabeth is motioning for them to be quiet so they can hear what the shaman is explaining.

After the shaman has gathered a large bag full of different leaves, root shavings, and vines, the group returns to his hut. His wife is brewing some plants in a large metal pot over an open fire.

"Is she making a cure for someone?" John asks.

"Nah," the shaman replies. "That's lunch." The wife scurries off to behind the hut, too shy to make eye contact with any of the foreigners. The shaman continues his lecture, showing the students how to prepare certain plants for stomach problems, headaches, and infections, the three most common ailments Amazon folks experience.

Loud thunder off in the distance captures Elizabeth's attention. It sounds like a large storm is brewing, and she wonders which way it is heading. The shaman finishes his talk and shakes the students' hands as they depart. The group meanders down a small trail to the river's edge. Elizabeth and Rey debate whether they should try to make it back to the lodge or wait it out in the village here. Since the lodge is only a twenty-five-minute boat ride back; they decide to risk it. Sometimes big storms will last all night, sometimes they blow over in an hour. Always unpredictable.

The students put their journals in the backpacks and remove rain ponchos. The rain has begun, and it is coming down hard. Jairo and Maclave start the motors with worried faces. Everyone knows not to be on the river in metal boats when there is thunder and lightning. They drive into the wind at full speed. They need to get back to the eco-lodge as fast as they can, yet they understand the increase danger of driving on any river too hastily.

At first Jairo's boat is ahead, but soon Maclave passes him. Then Jairo is in the lead again. The students laugh in delight, thinking that the two brothers are racing each other. They start shouting to go faster. The boats pound the river's waves. Some try to raise their arms in the air as if on a carnival ride but realize they better hold on tight if they don't want to end up in the river. The waves get bigger, yet the students still squeal as if the ride was a game. The boat drivers pay them no attention. They focus on the waves, the currents, and the bombarding rain. Jairo's boat strikes a massive log and almost flips. He slows down to try to watch for floating debris, but now the rain is driving straight into their faces and visibility is almost zero. Only lightning in the distance lights up the dark sky. Maclave sees Jairo slow, so he decelerates too, making sure Jairo is all right. Finally, they spot the eco-lodge's steps, and both brothers breathe a sigh of relief. The students disembark, still laughing. Another adventure they will write about in their journals. They never realized the danger they were in.

* * *

In the evening, everyone gathers in the communal hut. The rain continues to pound the thatched roof of the hut. Luckily, the rain held off until after the students hiked in the jungle, learning the names and uses of various plants. Elizabeth wished it could have waited a half hour more to show its tremendous force rather than on the ride back. Yesterday's puffy clouds are replaced by thicker, menacing ones. This is the kind of rain that will last through the night, its sound intensified by the lack of mechanical noises most humans are accustomed.

Rey clears his throat. The students sit in a circle, anxious to hear his scariest moments in the jungle. "About eight years ago, I was working at a different eco-lodge downriver from Iquitos. We had finished work that evening, only four tourists, and I knew that the neighboring village was celebrating their town's anniversary. Lots of dancing, and I love to dance. Lots of *masato*, and I love *masato*. You should try it."

"What is it?" asks Claudine.

"It's an alcoholic beverage made from yucca and women's spit," Rey replies.

"Spit? You're kidding, right?" asks Charlene.

"No, I'm serious. The women here chew the raw yucca, and their saliva ferments the yucca, making a delicious drink. So as I was saying, I really wanted to go to the fiesta. Most of my friends had already left, so I decided to walk through the dark jungle alone. I got my big flashlight and was walking on the path about halfway there when my flashlight died. I had a smaller one, not nearly as powerful but as a backup in my backpack, but when I turned it on, it didn't work either. I didn't know if I should turn back or keep going. I decided to keep going, hoping I'd hear the band's drums soon and I figured that I could follow the sound. I walked a little bit farther when I heard what I thought was another person. I called out, 'Over here, over here. My flashlights don't work.' I started walking toward the sound. I realized that I was off the path as the bushes got thicker and thicker. 'Hey, over here,' I yelled. 'Help me.' I knew that I was in big trouble. 'Hey. Hey, help,' I kept yelling. Finally, I heard, 'Rey? Rey, where are you? Rey?' 'Over here,' I replied. Two of my fellow workers who left after me to go to the fiesta suddenly appeared. They asked me why I was walking in the jungle off the path. They thought I had lost my mind. They kept saying that I must be crazy to go off a path in the dark. I found out that I was walking farther from both the village and the lodge. Someone or something had tried to lure me deeper into the jungle. If my friends hadn't heard me I wouldn't be here now," Rey concludes.

"But what was it?" Mike asks.

Rey shakes his head. "I don't know. Maybe a *chullachaki* or a *tunshi*."

"A what or a what?" The students crowd closer together.

"Chullachakis are creatures that live in the night. Some say they are spawn or agents of the devil. Or it could have been a tunshi, a ghost. I've never seen a chullachaki, but I have heard tunshis, ghosts or spirits of the dead who are stuck between worlds. And they are mad about it, which is why they try to trick you into getting lost in the jungle, so they have someone to torment because they are suffering. Many of them whistle like this." Rey places his hands together and presses them to his lips. Out comes a high pitch shrill. "If you hear that, don't go outside," Rey warns.

The students giggle nervously, not sure whether or not to believe Rey. Yet it seems anything is possible in the jungle. Slowly they stand, stretch, and decide to go to bed. Their muscles are screaming for deep sleep. Enough excitement for one day.

5

THE SISTERS

As the cruise ship motors up the Amazon, the guests return to the cabins to cool off their bodies, still unaccustomed to the heat and humidity. A long hike in the rainforest with only one short stop in a village has worn out most of the elderly white folk.

"Good Lord. I have sweated so much, I can wring my clothes out," Helen remarks while stripping off her blouse and culottes. "I must smell worse than a pile of dead fish. I need really hot water for a proper cleansing, but a miracle would have to happen to get some here. I thought you said that the brochures listed hot water under amenities?"

"It did, sister. Geez, can't you stop complaining for one second? The water is warm enough. It's refreshing even. Enjoy it. Besides, isn't all this sun and warmth a welcome change from dreary, chilly England? If we were home, you'd be complaining about the cold," snaps Edith. She can normally ignore her sister's cantankerous attitude but not right now. Edith is also hot and sweaty. Her underwear is sticking uncomfortably to her skin. She brushes her long silver hair and twists it into a knot to get it off her neck. Pouring cool, fresh water from the Victorian pitcher into the washbowl, Edith dips a clean towel in it. The wet cloth refreshes as she pats her face and chest.

"Hmph. At least in dreary, cold England, we have hot water. Plus, it needs to be hot to kill God knows what bacteria lurking around us in this place. We could get sick any moment."

"Really, sister? The people sure look healthy to me, and they live here all the time without hot water." Edith dips the towel again, rings it out, and lays it over her entire face. She wants to block out her sister or she might end up smacking her.

"Yes, well they have adapted to all the vermin crawling every-where. The point is, however, that they should provide what they advertise. Especially considering that they charge a pretty penny for a one week cruise," Helen retorts.

"But we won the trip. We didn't even pay an ugly penny." Edith laughs at her own joke while Helen ignores her.

"Well, if we had, they certainly would get an earful from me."

Edith sighs and says under her breath, "I'm sure they would."

The dining room is full of Victorian-era antiques and furniture. A romantic turn-of-the-century ambiance Pierre and Breton created for their boat. They print each meal's menu on small cards and place one on the passengers' plates. The cards and printing are similar in style to the ones former ocean liners used in the time of the *Titanic*. Fancy names are given for basically simply-prepared local foods.

The evening meal consists of fish, rice and yucca again with a wide assortment of tropical fruits sliced with native honey drizzled on top. Helen complains while Edith gobbles up the last piece of fried yucca on her plate.

"I don't see how you can eat the same thing we ate yesterday with such relish, sister."

"Because it's not the same. Last night the fish was *paiche*. Remember those huge fish we saw, the ones that can weigh four hundred pounds? I think Jose Antonio said that *paiche* are the largest freshwater fish in the world. Imagine that, and here we had the opportunity to try one. What a delicate taste. I love the way they grilled it with those delightful herbs we saw yesterday. What a treat to have seen their gardens behind their homes. You know, I think they may have used some of those same herbs tonight." Edith responds while looking to see what is on the dessert tray.

"Gardens? You mean those half-dead plants randomly growing alongside the huts? A garden has order, precision, balance in color and types." Helen snorts.

"Oh, sister, you just don't get it. People's ideas of what a garden should look like is different depending on climate, plants, culture, everything. I think their gardens are beautiful, especially now that I taste this typical catfish dish. What is it called? *Pata...pata...*something. Where did I put tonight's menu? Here it is. *Patarashca.* Taste the cilantro-like herb and the wonderful peppers—*aji* I believe they are called—along with this herb similar to the turmeric we have in our Indian curries at home. That's what gives it the yellow color. Simply delicious. Last night, the fish had a red sauce based on tomatoes, onions and herbs, not as spicy. You really need to try and enjoy these wonderful native flavors."

"Bread and tea will suffice until I see something I can recognize," Helen responds. "I'm not going to risk digestive problems, and you shouldn't either."

"Please, sister. Try to relax. We had a good day today, no? At least enjoy a glass of wine. It's French. That should be good enough for you." Edith reaches for the bottle, but before she can touch it, the waiter has it in hand, pouring her another glass. "What marvelous service."

The Wilson couple finally shows up for dinner. Normally, Mary Jo is the first to arrive, always famished. The look on her face says something has happened.

Alert for disaster, Helen asks, "Are you okay, dear? You don't look yourself."

"No, I'm not. Edward here thinks I'm so feebleminded that I don't know how much money I brought, how much I've exchanged, and how much I have left."

"Why would he think that, dear?"

"Because I know $500 is missing from my zippered pocket in my suitcase. The cabin boy must have stolen it." Mary Jo shakes her head. "You can't trust anyone these days. I know our things wouldn't be safe, but Edward confides in anyone and everyone. He told me just to leave everything on board. It will be fine. Well, it's not fine."

"Oh dear, that is dreadful. What else is missing?" asks Helen.

"Nothing."

"See, that is what I said," Edward finally speaks. "Our wallets, cash, credit cards, Mary Jo's jewelry, everything is exactly where we left them. Even a bunch of soles I put on top of the dresser in plain view are still there. Why would a thief leave all that?"

"I must agree with him, dear. That is odd," Edith remarks. "You know that the workers will be fired if anything goes missing, so I would think, if one was to steal, he would take everything because he will be kicked off the boat immediately and left on the side of the river. They don't tolerate thieves. It's not part of their culture. You know, many tribes in the Amazon don't have the word crime in their languages because there is no crime. And jobs on these cruise ships are coveted jobs. Maybe you are mistaken."

"Pay no attention to my sister, Mary Jo. She has gone bonkers here. In love with everything and everyone," states Helen.

"Well, I need to find the captain. He eats normally with us, but I don't see him. I'm going to report that we are missing some money because I know what I had," declares Mary Jo. She starts to walk toward the door.

"No, you are not. I'm sorry, but I cannot let you do that," Edward declares. "First, if the captain isn't here it's because he has import work to do, and I won't have you bothering him. Second, remember how you swore the maid stole your pink sweater with expensive pearl buttons from our hotel room in Rome only to go home and find it still in your closet?"

"Of course, I do. Everyone knows that story because you had to blab it last night. But this time, I know I'm right."

"Yes, honey." Edward pats his wife's hand. "But not now. I'm not going to have some poor Indian boy lose his job and be thrown off the ship in the middle of the jungle. I will not have that on my conscience, like the maid who was fired in Rome. You probably forgot to bring your emergency money as you call it."

"I didn't forget. And I did call that hotel in Rome and told them I found my sweater. Besides, you were only concerned because you thought the maid was a pretty thing, and she smiled at you in the hallway. Well, I am famished, so maybe I'll eat first and then speak to the captain. What is tonight's fare?"

"Fish, rice, and yucca. What else?" grumbles Helen.

"It's delicious," adds Edith.

The guests finish dinner while the boat nears a village. Mary Jo remains seated. Her husband's firm grip on her hand. The ship's motors slowly come to a stop. A group of teenagers in traditional clothing appear with a long stuffed boa, fresh flowers, drums and flutes made of bamboo. The waiters move one table and several chairs to the side of the dining area to clear a space. *Tap, tap, tap* starts one of the young men on a small wooden drum with a water buffalo skin top. Another player joins in on the flute. Two young men and two young women hold hands. They sway their hips and tap their feet to the rhythm of the music. Clearing their throats, they chant in key and begin slowly dancing. A soft, almost lullaby-like, song echoes in the stillness of the evening.

On the next song, they pick up the beat. The drummer stands with a bigger drum strapped around his neck and pounds it with the palms of his hands. Two young men play bamboo flutes. One of the young women grabs the stuffed boa to be her dancing partner. She makes it swim around the guests still seated at their tables.

"This is fantastic," Edith grins.

Ponytail man, as the sisters call him, comes through the door after having a smoke outside. He already has a reputation among the guests for being a bit annoying with his tall tales. Everyone is cordial though, and one of the widows often smiles at him. He walks to the side of the room where Helen and Edith are seated. He pulls out the empty chair at their table and sits facing the musicians. Helen rolls her eyes.

As the music plays, ponytail man turns to the sisters and begins wholeheartedly, "This music reminds me of 1976 when I went to live with the Yanamano, a fierce warrior tribe, north of here in the Amazon but Venezuela, not Peru. The only white men they ever had contact with before me was a few anthropologists, and that had been a decade before. I was shooting photographs for *National Geographic*. Of course, I was afraid, terrified. My heart totally full of fear."

Helen leans over to her sister. "That's not the only thing he is full of," she whispers softly. Edith giggles.

"All I could hear was drums like that one and flutes. I had fortunately arrived during a fiesta, a celebration for the chief. Otherwise they probably would have killed me for entering their compound unannounced. I knew I had to do it though because..."

Edith interrupts. "So sorry, dear, but could you be so kind and finish your story after the music ends? I do want to enjoy this moment so. Thank you." Edith pats ponytail man's hand. He closes his mouth and nods.

The group finishes the show by asking the guests to dance with them. Edith springs out of her chair and takes the hand of a beautiful young girl with long flowing black braids. She shows Edith the steps. The music plays, and a few more guests join in. Edith is happier than a dog with no fleas. She sees, out of the corner of her eye, ponytail man leaving with the smiling widow. She can't help but smile too. Sly fox.

* * *

At sunrise, Jose Antonio offers the passengers a chance to see the numerous colorful birds that are active early in the morning. Coffee and tea are served in the dining room, but breakfast will be upon their return. They only have a small window of opportunity to see the different parrots, macaws, parakeets, and other feathered friends, which is the primary reason many of the passengers come to the Amazon. Birdwatchers are Pierre and Breton's largest group of customers, their bread and butter.

Mary Jo and Edward are still arguing as they board the smaller motorboat. Helen had no desire to get up so early, but Edith said she was going, so Helen crawled out of bed also. She was afraid to leave her sister alone, even though Edith insisted that she would be fine. They leave the main river and head up a tributary for about fifteen minutes. The river narrows, and the tree branches are several feet away on either side, almost close enough to touch. The driver cuts the motor and pulls out two oars to quietly row deeper in the foliage.

"Squawk, squawk." Jose Antonio makes bird sounds and listens for a response. All of a sudden, two meters ahead in the low hanging branches, a dozen gorgeous red macaws fly out and over their heads. The birders in the boat press their fingers on their cameras' buttons, letting the cameras shoot one picture after another in rapid succession, hoping one photo will capture the resplendent birds. Everyone is now fully awake and thrilled to have seen so many macaws so close. The boat continues to snake along the little river. The birders witness more birds than they could imagine. They pat each other on the back in glee. After an hour with sun higher in the sky, most of the birds vanish. "Breakfast time is over for them now. They will rest deeper in the forest," Jose Antonio informs them. A group "aw" is heard for a moment, but then conversations pick up, discussing what they just had the privilege to witness. Several have bird books in which they check off the many species that they have just observed.

The driver uses the motor to return them to the ship faster. Jose Antonio operates his walkie-talkie to let the workers on board know that they will return in about twenty minutes, giving the cook time to get breakfast ready to serve. "Roger that," the voice confirms the message. The boat makes good time, winding through the water.

The voice calls again, and Jose Antonio listens carefully. "Yeah, we are almost to the turn off. Let me ask them. Okay, you are not going to believe it, but a harpy eagle has fallen to the ground in a small village about fifteen minutes from here. We can go see it if you want. Probably delay your breakfast for about an hour."

"Yes," Edith shouts out. The others agree.

Only Helen asks, "What's the big deal? All that way to see one bird?"

"Madam, you obviously know nothing about eagles. The harpy is the largest eagle, and one of the largest birds in the world. Makes the bald eagle look like a dwarf. Well, not quite but close. This is indeed an auspicious occasion," states Harold, the most fanatical of the bird watchers aboard. The eagle has brought a smile to his face again. He has been a sourpuss the past two days because he can't find his solid gold pocket watch. He worries that it fell out of his pocket while hiking in the jungle, in which case, he will never see it again. Helen doesn't reply to his remark about the harpy eagle. She doesn't really care about birds. She just readjusts her hat so the brim covers more of her face.

The boat lands where a small path clears the way to the village. Unlike most villages, this one is deeper in the forest. The passengers swat insects and tree branches, trip over roots, and arrive to a cleared area with six huts haphazardly built near one large open field. Only thirty-five people live here, but they still have cleared an open space to play soccer. A man approaches Jose Antonio. After some negotiating, Jose hands him some coins. The man whistles to his son. The boy struggles, carrying the enormous bird, which is about the same height as he is. The father grabs one wing and the boy the other. They stretch him open. The people gasp. The wingspan is over eight feet wide. The bird is awesome. No signs of any fights, wounds, or other indications as to how he died.

Edith inquires, "I don't understand. How could the bird just fall from the sky?"

Jose Antonio talks to the father to get more information of how they found him. "He says that the boys were playing soccer over in that field last evening, and in the middle of their game, one of them spotted the eagle circling. They looked up right when he was taking a nosedive straight to the ground. Dead. I guess he is very old and died of natural causes."

"Humph. I bet if you look closer, you find an arrow wound. One of the boys probably shot him."

Again Edith can't understand why her sister has to be so contrary.

For the first time on the trip, Jose Antonio gets angry. He looks at Helen and starts to say something, but thinks better not to. A minute passes. "Madam, just so you know, we do not shoot harpy eagles or any kind eagle for that matter. The people have great respect for these majestic birds. We only hunt animals for food, not for sport as people from your country do."

Edith gives Jose Antonio a thumbs up behind Helen's back. Maybe that will quiet her sister's haughtiness for a while. The birders snap dozens of photos. They take turns holding the wings for more pictures. As they walk back, they still can't believe their great fortune to see and touch a harpy eagle although it saddens them that the bird is dead, a reminder of the precious moments remaining in their lives now that they are in the sunset phase of life.

6

ALBERTO

The Amazon River starts rising every fall to reach its highest point sometime in March, a nature fact that Alberto paid little attention to, like the sun rising and setting, until last year. The flood waters rose over twelve meters, the highest flood in recorded history. Even village elders who recall past floods that carried entire villages away were surprised by the dramatic upsurge. Everyone in the state of Loreto was scrambling to save things threatened by the fast-moving water. People are starting to feel anxious now, wondering if this year will be a repeat of last. It is just January and already the river is high. Many villages have yet to recover from last year's inundation in which the power of the mighty river not only washed away homes along its shores but also shifted the earth. *Tierra firme*, ridges of tightly packed clay on which most villages rest, collapsed into the river, taking everything people had built and treasured with it. New creeks cut into the soil, creating new "roads" for the canoeing people to travel. Previously used routes were buried.

The floodwaters caused problems at the new navy station and the new diamond mine, both boasting high-tech infrastructure. Big problems. The water ripped away the new steel dock installed by the navy for the larger ships received from the United States in the fight against the drug cartels. Now the ships cannot dock. They sit in the middle of the river along with the new dock stuck, ending up in the mud. Last summer during low water season, the ships hogged the deep water channels, making it difficult for the ferry boats to navigate. The ferry boats are the local people's only transport for farther distances. *Piqué piques*, small motorboats, can only travel a few kilometers, about the same distance people can canoe, only faster, especially when heading against the current.

The broken steel dock is a new hazard. It looks like an abstract sculpture with its metal parts twisted into random shapes. For a while, it was such a phenomenon to see that some local businessmen thought about claiming it to turn it into a tourist site. But now that the waters have risen, that idea was abandoned. It soon became apparent that the mighty river is going to climb above it and drag it further downstream. Boat captains will have to keep a watchful eye, knowing its steel construction can rip their wooden ships apart in minutes.

Water and electricity are not a good combination as the owners of the new mine learned. The mine's entire security system depended on the string of new electrical poles built by the Loreto government to provide electricity to the mine from the city of Iquitos. The poles were built on tierra firme some twelve meters above the river. A section of them fell into the river as the flood waters carved its new patterns along its shores. The security system shorted. The bosses from Lima blamed Alberto since he is in charge. Alberto scrambled to quickly learn how and why the Amazon River rises and falls, so he could explain it to his bosses. The owners eventually calmed down, but Alberto could tell that they still remained somewhat skeptical. As if Alberto conspired with Mother Nature against them.

For the first time since its opening, the mine had only its employees to protect it from theft. The same employees that the owners don't trust, considering the security checks they go through each day, including Alberto. Alberto has always resented that he is subjected to the same checks as the other workers. He is their right-hand man, as the bosses call him when the mine has no problems and the money flows into the owners' pockets. But the moment something goes wrong.

In less than two days, an enormous generator was flown in by one of the Peruvian air force's helicopters to the mine. No one knows where they got one so large and how it could arrive so quickly. The mine has since never lacked electricity. The owners are comfortable now that all systems are running smoothly. They have stated publicly that all problems are solved. Armed with the latest in high-tech security, nothing can penetrate it. But one wonders if those people have underestimated the power of the Amazon River, which has a mind of her own.

Red lights are flashing all around the mine compound as Alberto arrives. He scrutinizes the dock and boats to make sure no intruders have arrived. 7:04 a.m. Definitely not a scheduled drill. He quickly runs quickly up the bank and enters the mine's front gate.

"It's in the mine," Javier tells him breathless. "The problem is water. Lots of water. Broke through the east wall. I've never seen anything like it."

Alberto thinks a minute. "Must be some type of underground stream or something that the engineers or geologists missed in their surveys." He doesn't want to say what he believes out loud, that any problem means somebody or a lot of bodies will probably get fired. It doesn't matter that it is not their fault. They fire people for any reason or no reason at all.

"Worse news," Javier adds. "One of the miners was knocked clear off his feet and hit his head. He's unconscious. They are bringing him up now. Look."

Alberto bends to see through the tree branches to the mine's entrance. Four men are carrying a young man with a bloody bandage wrapped around his head. He shouts, "Take him to the company's speedboat." Alberto fears the man may die. Everyone hustles to the dock. In the speedboat, it will only take thirty minutes to get to Nauta, the closest clinic. A piqué pique would take over two hours. Alberto climbs in the boat first and places his hands under the man's head. The others ease onto the vessel, placing the man in the middle of the floor. Alberto finds a blanket to cover him and a life vest to use as a pillow under his head. He's not sure whether it should be elevated or not but decides the pillow can absorb some of the shockwaves of the boat hitting the water. The man doesn't stir, but his pulse is strong.

The white concrete block clinic is far from having the personnel and supplies to help in many emergencies. Its four rooms are stifling hot. Light bulbs hang on a cord from the ceiling and give a dim light. Fortunately, sunlight enters the clear panels on the top of the walls. A sour body smell mixes with the smell of ammonia. Machete cuts, snake bites, stomach problems, the clinic's doctors can handle. An unconscious man, they can only watch in bed and pray he wakes up. Alberto is unsure whether to leave him or taxi him further to Iquitos where the Santa Ana clinic has a neurologist on staff. He hates to call his local boss, who Alberto still to that day cannot figure out what work he actually does for the mine except to harass them from time to time. After a moment, he dials the number of the Iquitos' office.

"Hello. Oh you already heard? They got you on the short wave. Yeah. We've had a serious accident...Yes, water...No...No. The good news is that it didn't flood the mine. Just about a half meter of water on the floor. The bad news is it hurt one of the miners pretty bad.

He's unconscious. Hit his head on the ground. We're at the clinic in Nauta. All they can do is observe. I think we should take him to Santa Ana to have the neurologist examine him…What? No. He's vitals are stable…What? Are you sure? Okay. We'll leave him here for a day and see what happens…Yes, I'll return to the mine and make sure everyone is back to work…No. We don't want to make things worse by falling behind in production. What about the hole? Good. Good. Glad to hear the engineers are on the way. I'll meet them as soon as they arrive." Alberto hangs up. At least for now the problem is in the hands of someone else. But he does worry. It's January. The river will keep rising for another two months. Everything is connected in the jungle. That's what city people don't understand. More water will come when the river stretches deeper in the forest. The engineers better find a solution, and they better find it quick.

The river is calmer on the return trip. A breeze created by the speed of the boat refreshes Alberto, awakening his senses. For a moment, he allows himself to take in the simple beauty all around him. He breathes deeply. The quiet hum of the motor becomes like meditative music. He shivers when he realizes that he just left a man to chance rather than taking him to a real hospital. What am I doing in that place? He pauses. Then the crackle, crackle of the boat's radio jogs him out of his trance. He is getting close to the mine. There are people to deal with, production issues. Alberto shakes his head vehemently to refocus on work. That is all there is. We are just cogs in a wheel, he tells himself.

The engineers come and go. Alberto follows them as they survey the area above ground where the water flowed below. He hates walking in the mucky grey clay with chopped-up jungle. After a few hours, they declare the flood an anomaly. No worries. Alberto figures it's easy for them to say. They'll get paid and be on their merry way. But what if it happens again? Or worse, the whole mine collapses? Water is the most powerful force on the planet. Alberto has seen it move mountains. The bosses in Lima are reassured, so everything is to continue as planned. Alberto certainly is not going to rock the boat. He needs to focus on the preparations for the upcoming inspection. Thank goodness the mine is dry; the water seeped quickly through the floor. The workers hauled fresh clay to patch the hole in the east wall.

Alberto receives the best news. The worker has regained consciousness with no apparent damage. A splitting headache, but with a shot of morphine, he rests peacefully. Alberto is relieved. By the evening, it was as if nothing ever happened. No more gossiping, just work as usual. The paperwork for the accident and damage has been written and is ready to send to the bureaucrat in Iquitos. Tomorrow is just another day.

* * *

The bright, clear sunny day after the accident makes Alberto contemplate the qualities the mine's diamonds possess—colorless, flawless. He's searched the Internet to learn as much as he can. The best have no blemishes or inclusions of any type. Crystal clear makes them more valuable since colorless diamonds are rarer. Carat weight is the most important attribute. Out of five million diamonds mined, only one will weigh two carats or more. Unbelievably they have already found several two carat sizes, and two days ago, another that weighs a little over three carats!

The grading report completed by the American Gem Society was met with skepticism, even though they are an independent gemological laboratory. "Just too good to be true," remarked many geologists. So now the Gemological Institute of America (GIA) scientists will visit to verify the first report, which means more work for Alberto without more pay. The bosses will arrive and find new "necessary" tasks, change the way we run the mine even though everything runs smoothly. He hates change because change means more paperwork for him, more reports to fill out. Already working a twelve-hour day, Alberto realizes that he is never going to get ahead or get any of the credit he deserves.

He pushes back his chair, grabs his clipboard, and with indignant reserve, proceeds to do his morning inspection. The workers know to keep their heads down and focus on their shovels whenever they hear a person enter the mine. No greetings as custom would dictate. They don't exist, just extensions of the shovels. The dirtier they are, the better. Blend in with the walls of the mine means less chance of being yelled at.

Alberto never stays longer than a few minutes in the actual mine. Although the air in the mine is cool, outside it is hot and humid. He prefers the comfort of the air-conditioning in the building. He nods to the guard to open the gate. Following the path to hall A, he opens the door to head to the vault on the other end where all the diamonds are kept. A slot on the side of the vault door allows Raoul, the head of security sent from Lima, to deposit the daily find inside in the presence of Alberto and three armed guards. The slot only pens outward and is so thin, no hand can fit in it. The diamonds slide down the chute several feet long into a bin at the bottom. No one on the site knows the vault combination. Once every two weeks, one of the big bosses arrives to carry the new shipment of diamonds to Lima handcuffed to his wrist. Where they go after that, Alberto has no idea.

Alberto hears a faint rumble and feels his body sway for a moment. What in the heck was that, he wonders? Please not another problem in the mine. There are no red lights flashing. All is quiet. He resumes walking in the hallway when a rumble twice as loud and strong shakes and knocks him to his knees. He grabs the vault's door to pull himself up. The lights flicker. *Zap, zap*. The lights are out. The sunlight beaming in from high windows on the right side provide the only source of light. He hears several strange clicking noises and slowly realizes that they are coming from the vault's door. As Alberto regains his balance, he pushes down on the handle, and it opens. What the hell? He's so surprised that his body freezes. Confusion clouds his mind. How is this possible? he asks himself. Finally, in what seems like an eon, he looks around and sees no one in the darkened hallway. No one should be in this hall he remembers. All the offices are on hall B.

Alberto's dread, fear, and frustration surface. He slows opens the door, waiting for the alarm to sound or at least for a guard to appear. Nothing. He quickly slides into the vault and runs down the five stairs. He sees the bin full of diamonds. Without pause he grabs a big handful of diamonds and shoves them into his pants pocket. He jumps up the steps, slips out the door, and pushes it closed. One of the diamonds stabs him in his thigh; he realizes that it must be pretty large. He moves the door handle back in an upright position. It clicks. He tries to pull the handle down again, but it doesn't budge. Secure once again. The lights buzz and flicker on. The generator has restored power. He checks the hall and sees the only door opening. Two security guards walk quickly toward him.

This is it, he thinks. Jail. I'm going to jail for the rest of my life. He fingers the stones on his pocket.

"Everything okay, señor?" asks one of the guards.

"Ah ah, yes. Ah, I was doing my inspection, and I felt…felt… ah, what was that?" Alberto responds, trying to look authoritative, but his voice squeaks out of fear.

"An earthquake. Or at least that's what they think it was. No breaches in security though. Everyone appears to be okay."

"We don't have earthquakes here." Alberto's voice regains confidence. "The generator is supplying power now?"

"Yes, we lost power for just four minutes," replies the guard.

Four minutes. Alberto can't believe it. Just four minutes to change my life forever. He shakes his head, trying to brush away those thoughts and focus on the situation at hand. "The vault is secure. I checked it. Come with me to the mine," he orders. Stern faced, the three walk to the other end of the hall. What the guards failed to notice was Alberto's little jig of joy.

* * *

Diamonds in my pocket. Isn't that a song title? It should be if it isn't. Alberto cannot stop touching them. For the last two hours, he has walked the entire compound, checking that all is secure. Secure everywhere except in my pants. How ironic, he muses.

He returns to his desk to start writing another incident report. The bosses are really going to be unhappy. Two reports in two days. They never want to hear any bad news, just stability. Albert wonders why, all of a sudden, after two years, there were two significant events back to back. Mother Earth is speaking. Is she upset with the mining? With the destruction? She has a right to be. It looks bleak as far as the eye can see. A lifeless grey mud surrounds them. A month ago, none of these thoughts would have ever passed through Alberto's mind. But everything is different now. He has been given a way out, a chance to live a different life, and he is taking it. What's a handful of diamonds to them anyway? They have unearthed bucketful.

He sips his cup of coffee. First, he will get a big house in San Isidro where the who's who of Peru lives. Maybe restore a vast colonial house with beautiful handmade tiles from Lisbon on every floor, wall, and bathroom. He'll buy more tiles than those covering the buildings on the promenade in Iquitos. How Ivonne loved looking at them. And imagine a house with more than one bathroom. A brand new BMW to top it off—classier, he thinks, than a Mercedes. Great parties with top-quality champagne and a chef to make sinfully good food. He has never drunk champagne, but it must be delicious since all the rich people on soap operas drink it daily.

Paco's children will go to the best schools. Paco is his favorite brother. He has always been there when Alberto needed something. Now he can return the favors. He knows that he was the cause of many arguments between Paco and Lupita, his wife, when he needed money to finish his last year at the university. He overheard his brother saying, "But, Lupe, he's almost done. Imagine someone in our family a university graduate. We can't let him come this far and not finish. He'll pay us back one day, you'll see." His sister-in-law agreed but not without her doubts. Alberto has been uncomfortable in her presence ever since, even though he did finally pay back his brother all the money last year. He discovered recently that Lupita thought he owed them interest too. Well, now she'll get the interest a million times over.

Can it be possible that all his dreams will now come true? Dreams. He pictures Ivonne in a white lace wedding gown with a veil that trails for the length of the church. A huge bouquet of white roses, her favorite flower, tied together with silk ribbons. My god, she is beautiful. He will purchase a tailored Italian tuxedo, maybe two, white and black tails. An extra one to use to propose to her again. Their children will never want for anything, filling their magnificent home with laughter as they chase each other from room to room. They will have exotic vacations, eat at the best restaurants, and own a swimming pool with crystal clear water.

"Berto. Berto," Javier gives Alberto's shoulder a good shake. "You okay? I've been talking to you. What's wrong?"

Flying back through a lighted tunnel Alberto realizes that he is sitting in his office, not swimming with Ivonne and their nonexistent kids. "Oh, Javier. Ah, sorry. I was in deep thought about our security, making sure we didn't miss anything in our review of the compound today. What did you say?"

"That everything seems to be in tiptop working order. Raoul wants to see you in the security computer room. He wants to consult with you about something they caught on camera. Says you need to see it. He seems quite agitated."

Alberto's heart races. Obviously, they got him on tape, entering the vault during the earthquake. His dream is just a dream.

"Ah, thanks, Javier. Listen, can you finish the daily activity report and send it to the office in Iquitos? Gomez may have more information on the quake to add before it goes to Lima.

"Sure thing."

Alberto hands the papers to Javier, who takes them to his desk and begins writing. Alberto stays at his desk. He reaches into his desk drawer and pulls out a padded envelope. He stands and walks to the other side of the file cabinet, out of Javier's view. Very carefully he slips the stones from his pocket into the envelope and seals it. Opening the middle cabinet drawer, he puts the envelope all the way in the back, under some files. A temporary hiding place. He cannot very well walk into the security office with the stones on him. Maybe he can escape when they come to search his office. With his head hung low, he goes to see Raoul.

Raoul shakes Alberto's hand upon entering the main security office. Ten file cabinets in a neat row span the back wall. A desk sits to one side with piles of folders heaped in columns like mini towers. Scores of electronics fill the wall to the right. Two dozen computers are stacked in the center. Three rows of eight are assembled on top of one another. Before flat plasma screens a security guard sits, watching the different areas that comprise the mine's complex.

"I was reviewing yesterday's tapes. We have a problem behind Hall A. Look." Raoul instructs Alberto and points to camera five.

On the screen, Alberto sees a troupe of howler monkeys running across the top of south wall. It takes him a minute to realize that the problem has nothing to do with the earthquake in the morning. "Monkeys. So what? There are lots of monkeys around here, no?" Alberto asks.

Raoul frowns. "They are walking freely." He pauses. "Do you not see that? The electrical lines across the top are obviously not working. Those monkeys should be dead. The current is supposed to be two thousand volts."

"Ah, yeah, sure. Yes yes. Have you checked to see if there is a break in the lines?"

"Of course. I inspected them myself early this morning. I was on my way to talk to you about it when the earthquake hit. Now everything seems to be working after the generator kicked on. We can't afford to depend on the electricity from Iquitos. My guess is that sometimes the power isn't strong enough to maintain the voltage we need. Or worst, frequently it isn't. We are lucky no one else has realized this before."

Alberto stares at the screens. He focuses on the one with the clear image of the vault door. He doesn't want to think about the problem now. He has his own priorities. He feels a tightening in his chest. His heart swells and he gasps for air. Raoul does not notice, still staring intently at the image of the south wall. Regaining his breath, Alberto suggests, "Listen why don't we wait a few days until the bosses come, and we can talk about this security problem. If I send a third report today, we'll all be fired. You know that. In the meantime, have your men pay close attention to all the walls via the cameras and do some extra physical inspections daily. Most importantly, make sure no one else knows about this. You see anything come directly to me."

Raoul nods that he understands. The security guard watching the computer screens does not say a word. It is as if he isn't there at all. Alberto exits. As he walks back to his office, he is shocked by how many problems are suddenly appearing. The place is going to hell, Alberto worries. He stops dead in his tracks and realizes that maybe, just maybe, this is another lucky break. More confusion may help.

* * *

Alberto knows the clock is ticking. The GIA inspectors come Friday; the Lima bosses, who knows how many, will arrive on Wednesday. He reaches under the top drawer of his desk to feel the envelope holding the diamonds still firmly taped to the bottom of the drawer. A better hiding place than the filing cabinet. He figures security is too tight for any employee to carry out the diamonds, but maybe a visitor on one of the new tours can. They leave their stuff at the Welcome Center. Employees, including Alberto, the *jefe*, is subjected to a full-body search and that brain thing. Visitors however are only required to go through the NLDS, the neuron linguistic detection sensor. And since the unassuming tourist would not know that he or she has diamonds, the machine cannot detect a lie. Perfect. But how to get a visitor to carry them through security and afterward how will he retrieve them? There is no logical reason for him to inter-act with visitors on the tour. Although as the compound's manager he can go where and when he wants. He reasons that this will take some careful plotting so no one gets suspicious, especially that Raoul, who is like a hound dog.

As Alberto sits at his desk, pretending to look at some papers, he focuses on his problem. Maybe Anita who works in the welcome area. She goes to the cafeteria for her break and back out through the emergency exit. Only when she leaves for the day does she pass through security. Can't be the other older woman, Reina, who works the other shift because she would like nothing more than to turn him in ever since he slept with her daughter. Maybe Anita. No no. He realizes that even though she likes him, she's a woman, and he knows that you can't trust a woman. They often go and get all righteous, afraid not to do what is right. What they are told. He sighs. Although Anita is young and innocent and she always laughs at his jokes, no, she's not the right person. She's bound to tell someone. He needs someone desperate or greedy, someone who hates his life. A man.

The intercom buzzes. "Yes, I'll be right there," replies Alberto. He scuffs his chair back from his desk and shuffles to the door. As he reaches for the handle, the door springs open. Juan, the janitor, starts to push his cart through.

"Oh, pardon," whimpers Juan, afraid the boss will yell at him. Normally, Alberto would; he likes using his authority. Forget the team concept. He is the boss, and he wants people to act like they remember that fact. Today, however, he is too wrapped up in his thoughts; he just pushes Juan aside and grumbles under his breath.

Juan slowly closes the door. He begins emptying wastebaskets like he has done a thousand times these past two years. "Crap job," he says to himself. His mind wanders back to the best day in his life, the day his soccer team won the state championship. Best in Loreto. He was the star, center midfield, the most important position. He had the rare ability to be equally agile with both feet. He scored the highest number of assists and goals recorded in the state, again unusual for the midfielder to score more than the striker of the team. The team was invited to Lima to play in the national tournament. His family was so proud. They just knew that he was the ticket out of their poor, hard life. And the girls, *las muchachas*, all wanted to date him. Even Ana Maria the prettiest girl in school. How great.

Alberto slams the door and jolts Juan out of his daydream. "You still here? Hurry up. I have important work to do," says Alberto with a scowl. Then it hits him like a bolt of lightning. He can't believe that he hadn't discovered this security breech before. It's perfect. "Ah, wait a minute, my friend."

* * *

The cart squeaks as Juan pushes it down the hallway. Two of the wheels are about to fall off, making it harder to push. But Juan isn't thinking about the cart today. He can't believe what he just heard. Juan realizes that it must be a test and he just failed. What an idiot I am. What will I do without this job? He chides himself for being so stupid. A permanent job with doctor benefits is rare in the Amazon. Yes, the work is tedious, hard, and really stinky in the bathrooms, but he gets paid on time every two weeks.

His family now lives in a concrete block house in Iquitos, a vast improvement over the shack they erected on the wooden raft tied to other rafts in Belen, the floating city. Thousands of families have left their lives in the jungle and floated down the Amazon in search of a better life in the only big city, only to find little or no work and land so expensive that rafts become permanent homes. But not Juan's family, thanks to Juan. Juan bought his parents a real toilet for their new home. They have relatively clean water from a spigot, not the dirty river water which gave them all chronic diarrhea as kids. Oh well. He figures that he has really messed up this time. Nothing he can do about it now but wait for the end.

Juan wanders through the empty hallway to the next room and sighs knowing that at any moment, security guards will come and escort him away. He knocks over his bucket of water with his mop in it he is so distracted. Yet the hours pass and no one comes for him. He can't believe it. What if Alberto really wants his help? What if he was being truthful?

The clock rings three in the afternoon. Realizing he has only finished half of what he is supposed to have completed, he decides to drive their conversation out of his mind. Just finish up. Focus on work. Tonight, at home, he'll figure things out with a stiff glass of *aguardiente*, the local sugar cane rum to calm the nerves.

Raoul appears around the corner. Juan has never spoken to him, but he knows who he is. Juan stops his cart, leans against the wall, and closes his eyes. "You there," Raoul shouts. "No napping on the job. Get to work." His head stuck in a folder, Raoul walks past Juan to enter the room at the end of the hall. It takes a minute or two for Juan to move.

The next two hours of his shift feel like a hundred. Still anxious at any moment they will tell him that indeed it was a test, a test of loyalty. Saying yes lickety-split meant he wasn't very loyal to the company. But who would be? They are making tons of money, amounts that Juan can't even fathom. He makes a wage so low, he can barely meet his immediate needs. It took six months to save enough for a toilet. Still he is better off than most people, especially his friends. Stop this, he tells himself. Work now. Think later.

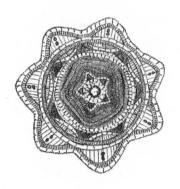

7

THE ARTISANS

The cruise boat pulls alongside the little village of palm huts. Kids splashing in the river run along the water's edge to meet the boat. San Jorge, or Saint George, the town is named. St. George the dragon slayer is a popular saint across the world, revered as a protector against dangerous animals. The crew pushes the long wooden planks from the boat to the shore for the passengers to disembark. They must climb a steep hill to visit the artisans' workshop, the Pua Kamatawara (Working Hands) Artisan Cooperative. Helen questions her sister's ability to maneuver the handmade steps cut carefully into the clay wall. Edith insists. She wants to see this more than all the birds, monkeys, sloths, and iguanas they have seen so far combined. Native women making crafts by hand. 'What a joy!' Edith exclaims. She used to make lots of things by hand—her precious Sally's clothes, some of her toys, and her favorite stuffed bear. She stuffed it with old pantyhose, so it would be soft and cuddly. But that was decades ago.

She sighs. Just thinking about her daughter brings a tear to Edith's eye.

Helen, still worried, says sharply to her sister, "You could have a heart attack. And what would I do here in the middle of nowhere? Call a voodoo doctor?"

"Voodoo is a religion in West Africa, sister dear. In the Amazon, you should call a shaman. He or she will fix me right up."

"Make fun of me, but you'll see when you are taking your last breath." Helen frowns.

"Oh, don't be so dramatic. I'll be fine. It's just a few steps."

The view from the top is breathtaking. The sky's midmorning sun hovers over the bend in the river, reflecting colors on the water's surface and making the river shimmer. Patting the sweat from their foreheads, the sisters walk toward the sounds emanating from behind two rows of broad palms planted alongside a brand-new concrete sidewalk. They see the group of native women as they expected but are taken by surprise to find a bunch of American or European-looking young people sitting on the floor of the open-air building, pulling apart long strips of fibers.

Jose Antonio gathers his group together to explain. "This plant is called *chambira*, or its full scientific name is *Astrocaryum chambira*. It comes from one of the two thousand types of palm trees we have here in this part of the jungle. People use its strong, yet flexible, fibers to make baskets, hammocks, string or rope, and bags. It is so useful that the women need to search farther and farther into the jungle to find it because all the trees next to the village are gone. However, here in San Jorge, two years ago, the artisans received some training to improve the quality of their crafts and, most importantly, to learn how to use their most valuable resource in a way so that their children and grandchildren will have it. They have planted many *chambira* shoots in the forest over there." Jose Antonio motions toward the south side of the artisans' hut to the plants growing outside.

"They also grow all the plants they need to make the different natural dyes. This color comes from *guisador* or Indian saffron. It's also used in cooking. These over here, the brown are from coffee leaves, and the yellow from mango leaves. The bright pinks to dark wine colors are from mahogany tree roots. They don't hurt the tree by shaving slivers off the roots."

The students sit on the floor in a circle, separating chambira fibers. Juanita takes a handful and places them in a pot with lime juice to bleach them. Anita, the current president of the artisan cooperative, shows everyone in the hut the *huingo* fruit. Mashing it so its juices flow, she adds a few drops of baby oil to the water and juice to make the dye colorfast. With their new two-burner stove fueled by propane gas in a small tank brought from Nauta, they can dye the fibers much quicker and more consistently than when they had no option but to boil them over an open wood fire.

After watching the fibers absorb the dye, Anita hangs the long strips over a clothesline to dry. The students are instructed to start making their own baskets. Each of the artisan women work with two students, using fibers that the Kukana women cleaned, bleached, and dyed yesterday. John and Jane are having a difficult time pushing the needles through the group of twisted, flat fibers to make the base of their baskets. Nanci, an experienced basket maker, helps them while Edith bends down to see better.

"Hello, young ones. You know, I used to be pretty good at basket weaving. If you use your thumb to push the needle like this, it slides through easier. Let me show you." Edith motions to John, who hands her his fibers, and she whips the threads together to make a tight U that will start the base of the basket.

"Thank you. That does help." Jane smiles at the elderly lady.

"So I'm guessing by your accent that you are American students?" Edith pushes back the floppy brim of her hat.

"Yes, we are from York University, the one in Pennsylvania, not England, on a study-abroad trip. Our professor is an anthropologist. She and her husband have worked here, helping this village for many years now. We are learning how the people live and are supposed to figure out some solutions to problems the people face," explains Julie, a student seated next to Jane.

"My, that sounds difficult. How long are you staying?" Edith inquires.

"A month." Julie continues. "But we first spent five days in Lima. Then we flew to Iquitos and jumped on this really cool ferry boat where we slept in hammocks overnight. It took twelve hours to arrive at San Jorge. We've been here a couple of weeks, and unfortunately, we'll be leaving in a few days to go back to Iquitos to visit some other tribes before we go home. But I don't want to go. This place is so special, especially the people and their kids."

Edith is distracted by Jose Antonio's voice and tries to straighten up. John jumps up to help her, and she pats his back in gratitude. Jose Antonio is telling them that the artisan group is rather new. It was founded two years ago with the help of a Spanish NGO and an American fair trade company with the Peruvian minister of Environmental Affairs stamp of approval. The women erected a small cooperative building to host tourists, who hopefully will buy their crafts. The Spanish NGO paid for the building materials: concrete, wood, and metal. The women and their families provided the labor. Besides the town's church, it is the only building in the town to have a metal roof. Metal and concrete are too expensive for people to buy, so the roof and concrete floor are a source of great pride. Built to last, they say.

The crafts' origins stem from utilitarian goods women have made all their lives. Gourds, which serve as handy containers, are carved with bird and flower designs. Plain string bags used to collect seeds, fruits, medicines, and other necessities from the jungle are woven with brightly dyed fibers for the tourists. "The materials and designs highlight the magnificent biodiversity here in the Amazon, don't you agree?" Jose Antonio asks his group.

One of the students, Betty, who is researching the impact of the cooperative on the women's lives, approaches Edith, who seems the friendliest of the elderly folks, to ask who they are and why they decided to visit the artisans. "My sister and I and the others are on an Amazon cruise, dear. The guide basically plans our days for us although he has asked if we have any special interests. I used to fashion many things by hand. We have been in the reserve, seeing wildlife. Lots of birders on the cruise, you know, but I became excited to hear that we could visit an artisan group. After all, we've seen lots of interesting animals, but I like to meet new people when I travel, especially the local people."

Betty diligently writes everything Edith says in her field journal. "You are all from England?"

"Yes, dear, but from different parts. My sister and I are from London. All retirees in the sunset phase of life. It's good to travel while young when you are still strong and don't have so many aches and pains to worry about." Edith laughs. "Although my sister will tell you that I don't worry enough, especially about my health."

"I want to travel everywhere. That's why I'm studying to be an anthropologist," Betty states.

"I thought anthropologists dug up dinosaurs. Or is that archaeology?"

"Paleontology. Anthropologists study humans. Archaeologists dig up past human civilizations. My professor has been all over the world. She and her husband help a lot of artisans by finding markets for their stuff. They do fair trade."

"Fair what, dear?"

"Fair trade. It's a global movement of businesspeople who believe people come first, and we shouldn't exploit poor people just because we can. We should pay them fairly for their work and treat everybody with dignity and respect. You know, like we want people to treat us. We also have to take better care of the environment. We only have one planet."

"I couldn't agree more, dear. And I must admit that my generation certainly hasn't taken very good care of our one planet as you say. Oh no. My group is going to leave soon. Sorry to leave you, dear, but I do want to look around. I hope we can talk again sometime." Edith makes her way around the artisans' tables. The works are striking, so creative. She picks up a basket with deep blue fibers woven across a natural background. Little seeds sewn into the sides create open spaces. Just beautiful, she sighs. Her mind wanders back decades ago when she used to craft handmade clothes, baskets, and even ceramics to make a living. She would tell storeowners on the West Side that she was from Arkansas and that she made genuine Southern artifacts, unique in the British market. It was a good selling strategy since, at the time, Londoners were quite enamored with all things American.

"It's quite spectacular, no? It looks simple but, boy, is it hard," remarks Julie who has stood up to stretch a minute.

"Yes, I agree. The amount of work, the time it takes…," Edith murmurs her mind still in the past.

"Excuse me, but I thought you all are British, but now you sound Southern?" Julie asks.

Helen, who has been not so patiently waiting for her sister, butts in, "Oh, that's just Edith imitating American film stars. She just loves American films. Hollywood and all that. She spends more time watching movies than anything else. I believe sister was doing her Scarlet O'Hara. Did you recognize it, dear?"

Puzzled by the bizarre response, Julie replies, "Ah, kinda. I have to get back to work. See ya." She walks over to her open spot on the floor, snatches another long piece of chambira fiber and starts twisting it for her basket. Helen watches her as she pretends to look at some masks carved out of coconut shells. Julie giggles with the student beside her, and they help each other twist the fibers.

Helen gives her sister a dirty look and heads to the sidewalk outside the workshop. Edith pays for her basket and joins her sister. "What was that all about? I never watch movies."

"Come on, sister. Let's get back on the boat before you mindlessly do something else," Helen grunts as they head for the steep, slippery stairs studded down the clay wall to the riverbank. Unfortunately, money ran out before the group could make concrete steps.

* * *

Anita and Nanci stand beside the tables on which their artisan work is displayed for sale. The Pua Kamatawara cooperative has sixteen members, but Anita and Nanci are, by far, the most talented basket makers, making perfectly executed palm baskets with vibrant colors and finished with rows of seeds sewn tightly in the designs. The two women discuss the exchange they just had with the visitors. Brilliant, just brilliant craftsmanship, the Brits said about their work. The older white cruise passengers were generous with their compliments yet stingy with their purses.

One of the couples put a one sole coin in Nanci's hand and walked off with a large seven-point star basket that took Nanci three days to make. She didn't know what to say or how to stop them. Luckily, Elizabeth stopped the couple dead in their tracks.

"Really? You think this basket is worth thirty-three cents? Seriously?" Elizabeth's face was beet red, not from the sun, but from the anger brewing up inside her. She struggled to remain calm and polite.

"I, ah, we, I…," stammered the wife.

"These kinda people don't need money. They're naturals. Everything they need is free. They hardly wear any clothes for goodness sake," replied the husband. "Plus, goods are cheap here. I got this rain jacket for less than a pound in Iquitos. I'm sure that coin will go a long way for them." He started to move forward. Elizabeth stretched out her arm.

"Not so fast. I don't think so. Here is your coin back. That basket costs forty soles, not a penny less," Elizabeth said firmly.

"But that is like seven pounds!" exclaimed the wife.

"You betcha. It took Nanci three days to create this gorgeous basket. The workmanship is exquisite and unique in the world market. There are no other baskets like these anywhere on the planet. Back home, it would sell for well over two hundred dollars."

"Don't be ridiculous." The husband got more aggressive. "What would an Indian do with that kind of money? These are simple-minded folks." He laughed mockingly.

"They would do the same thing as you would do, buy necessities, school supplies, medicine, cooking oil, and other household items. You don't understand about different currencies. Things seem cheap to you because you exchanged British pounds for soles. But when you earn in the local currencies, such as in this case soles in Peru, goods aren't so cheap." Elizabeth took a deep breath. She continued in a more gentle tone, "Listen, I am not trying to give you a hard time. I'm just hoping that you can be more reasonable with your purchases. Giving someone a coin and walking off with whatever pleases you is unacceptable. You don't do that at home, so why here? You know you can certainly bargain for what both parties involved consider to be a fair price. Just be a little more respectful is all I am saying."

The couple looked at each other. The wife said to her husband, "It really is beautiful, Harvey. And it will look beautiful in the grandchildren's room. Okay?" The husband shook his head begrudgingly and opened his wallet to hand Elizabeth forty soles.

"No, not me," Elizabeth responds and then points to Nanci. Nanci thanks the couple when they hand her the money. She reaches for one of her seed necklaces and places it around the wife's neck.

"Oh, no," the wife remarked. Her husband is about to say something, but before he can utter a word, Elizabeth translates what Nanci said to the couple.

"She says that it is a gift. She hopes that it will bring you good health and happiness."

"Oh my. Thank you." Nanci bows respectfully to her. The wife does the same. The husband tugs his wife's arm. "Come on." The couple descends the deep steps to board the boat where the other passengers are waiting for them.

Anita and Nanci have no idea exactly what Elizabeth said to the couple, but they are grateful. Anita gives her a big hug. She says in Spanish, "Thank you. We know that we need to learn how to communicate with visitors now that we have our artisan market. The guides sometimes help us, but they don't want to get involved when money is exchanged. They worry the visitors may think that they are taking our side. And their tips will suffer if they make any tourist annoyed, or worse, angry. And we understand. They have families to support also."

"How about if I write some phrases on a piece of paper in English with Spanish on the back so you know which one to use," suggested Elizabeth. "Let's think about how to describe your work, the time it takes, the meanings the different seeds have, and anything else you think can help."

"Yes, that would be very good. But still we don't know how to pronounce the English words. It is very hard."

"You can hand them the words written. Like if you couldn't speak and you had to communicate by the writing. Also maybe next year we can do a workshop and learn a few phrases. The students can tutor you guys."

"We would really appreciate that." The two women laugh and punch each other in the arm as if a great joke had just been told. Elizabeth doesn't understand why, but she guesses just the thought of speaking foreign words is funny to them.

The other artisans continue working with the students but haven't missed a word of Elizabeth's conversation with Anita and Nanci. The group only has one year of experience selling products, and as novices, they know they still have much to learn especially in dealing with non-Amazonian people. The dozen or so tourists that have visited them thus far have, for the most part, been kind and willing to bargain in a way that each side felt they received a fair price.

Anita describes to Elizabeth the one bad experience Esperanza had with a woman who picked up a coconut mask and then tossed it back on the table haphazardly. It knocked over and broke three of her chullachaki wood carvings that fell like dominos. The woman walked away as if nothing happened. She didn't say a word or offer any compensation. Anita concludes, "Esperanza cried. So much work ruined and not even an apology. She really didn't want any money, only a simple 'I'm sorry' or some acknowledgement. It was as if Esperanza didn't matter."

"I understand. You know, I'd like to think that the woman probably didn't know what to do or say, so that's why she said and did nothing. She doesn't speak any Spanish and felt embarrassed. On the other hand, there are a lot of people in the world, especially from my culture, who unfortunately only think about his or herself." Nanci gives Elizabeth a confused look. "Yes, I know. Sounds crazy. But not everyone in the world looks out for one another the way you do here. You will meet all kinds of people who live and think differently now with your market," Elizabeth tries to explain but knows that it is difficult for them to understand this. Organizing an artisan cooperative was easy to do in San Jorge because Kukana people already live and work cooperatively. They can't believe that others don't do the same. The Pua members share resources, knowledge, and skills. Nanci has spent numerous hours, days, or weeks, helping different members of the group improve their basket-making skills. "If only people could learn to share, the world wouldn't be such a tough place," Elizabeth laments.

* * *

Monica exits the river taxi that serves the Napo River. She had run out of the black and gray clays to paint cloth and returns from her native village with several large bags of the assorted muds. In the old days, her ancestors made bark cloth, gently slicing the bark from the trunks of trees, careful not to cut too deep as to hurt them. Insects attack any fresh flesh, be it tree or human in the rainforest. She's glad that now they can buy bolts of white muslin fabric on which they paint their intricate geometric designs. The designs appear abstract to foreigners, but for the Shipibo, each drawing conveys their relationship to the gods above or to the land and rivers which give them life.

For the past six years, Monica and her aunt have lived permanently in Iquitos, selling their wares to tourists. She loves seeing her family but is more than happy to be in the city rather than her ancestral village. Bathing in the river, doing one's business in the forest, and no contact with the outside world is not how she wants to live her life. She is a modern woman. Yes, that's what she is now. She's on Facebook. Her traditional dress stays folded in the room she shares with Shala, her aunt. Shala, her mother's younger sister, is only two years older than her. Her other aunts and uncles, parents, and three siblings hate Iquitos where people make fun of them, or worst, try to cheat them in any business transaction because they think indios are stupid, backward. Monica cut her hair short and wears clothes made in factories to blend in.

When she arrived in Iquitos, her Spanish was understandable, but she spoke with a heavy accent. That accent is gone. A good listener, she'd repeat softly conversations that she heard from others in the San Juan de Dios artisan market, making the Spanish words come easier when she needed them. Unmarried at twenty-four years old means she has no role in her culture. Not a child yet still not a woman since women have husbands and children. To care well for the family is a Shipibo woman's badge of honor. Monica's choices puzzle her family, but her decision to live where she can make money for them is one they appreciate. They see her only a couple times a year, like now when she needs the raw materials to make their artisan goods.

Monica checks her Facebook account as soon as she arrives in Iquitos in a small Internet café located close to the port. Her friends from the north have arrived several weeks ago. Darn, they will only be here a few more days. She met Elizabeth and Bob six years ago after living in Iquitos a few months. Interested in how the native women make ceramic pots, tablecloths, table runners, and clothes using only mud dyes, Elizabeth always brings a group of young people to visit them in the open-air artisan market where Monica and her aunt rent two spaces. It's an event they look forward to since the market rarely has such a large group visit.

The bigger tour companies sometimes bring groups, but they breeze by the Shipibo work and are guided to Don Julio's stall where he sells caiman heads, anaconda skins, piranha jaws, dried tarantulas, poison dart frogs, stuffed bats, boar heads, and other scary things from the jungle. The uninformed tourists buy them, only to have them confiscated at customs. Monica knows that many of the guides don't tell them it is illegal to transport such items because Don Julio gives them a cut of the sales. In the past few years, most vendors in the market have also started paying the tip required to get the guides to favor their stalls. Times have changed since she first came, and people seemed more willing to help one another. She and her aunt still refuse to pay mainly because they can't. They make so little from the items they sell.

Labor-intensive work rarely has the luxury of being highly profitable. Tourists want a bargain. Life is a daily struggle to pay their living expenses and send money home. If no one comes to the market during the day, they have to carry loads of painted cloths to hawk in the main square where tourists roam in the evening, looking at the Iron House and the main cathedral. They approach tourists drinking cold beer in the Jungle Bar or eating ice cream in the Natural Fruits Ice Cream Parlor, the two busiest businesses that border the east side of the main square.

Monica sends Señor Roberto a message that she is in town and wants to meet with him as soon as possible. Sales of their craft have dropped precipitously since Sr. Wang stole their designs and had cheap imitation copies made in China last year. Mr. Wang has cornered the dry goods market in Iquitos with five large stores. Monica almost had a heart attack last summer when she turned a corner and first saw "Shipibo" sheets, pillow covers, and tablecloths hanging outside one of his shops. He sells them for pennies because, basically, they are cheap, mass-produced by machines. But businesses that depend on tourists started purchasing them to make their hotels or restaurants look more exotic, more fake authenticity. Those tourists interested enough to purchase one can now choose to spend more money to buy an original handcrafted mud cloth from Monica or Shala or pay less for a cheap copy at Mr. Wang's. Just a souvenir to show friends and family, they end up buying at Wang's, completely unaware that they are knock-offs.

San Juan de Dios market is a cooperative, and all must pay dues to have a stall. The dues pay for the land rent and the use of water from a spigot in the middle of the complex. For the past two months, Monica and Shala have not earned enough to pay for the two stalls they occupy. The current president is threatening to throw them out. Señor Roberto and Doctora Elizabeth will help them. Last time, they bought them a new sewing machine to replace their former one that had died. Sr. Roberto sent a message two weeks ago to set a time to visit the market and have Shala teach the students how to make mud dyes. Monica left just before the message came and hasn't been able to answer him until today.

Monica secretly hopes one of the young Americans may take a personal interest in her. She dreams of leaving Iquitos and living in *gringolandia*. So far that hasn't happened because, unfortunately, it seems Doctora Elizabeth teaches mainly females, never more than a few young men on the trip and lots of girls. At least the girls spend lots of money, buying Shipibo products. Monica and Shala now cut and sew many of the mud cloths into apparel. Their attempt to diversify the traditional products has resulted in increased sales. The young foreigners buy more pants, shirts, and skirts than the large, tablecloth-size hangings.

The income Monica and Shala earn from Doctora Elizabeth's groups in just a single day pay all their expenses for the month with some leftover. It's the only time Monica has a little extra cash to buy something for herself like makeup. Her aunt Shala also appreciates the sales, and moreover, she loves the attention that she receives when teaching the students. Normally, Shala is too shy to interact with the tourists, letting Monica do that. But Doctora Elizabeth asks questions clearly and simply so that Shala now feels comfortable, even excited, to speak to her groups.

* * *

In the evening after dinner, the students beg Rey to tell them another jungle story. Not caring if myth or reality, anything seems possible in this alien land. He tells them with such gusto, maybe he has actually experienced them all.

"Well, all right, one more. This last one sounds funny now, but it wasn't at the time," Rey begins. "Two Australian families came to another eco-lodge I worked at."

"The one with the ghost?" Mike asks.

"No another one." Rey is a member of the Jibaro tribe. Jibaros live along the headwaters of the Maranon River and its tributaries in northern Peru and eastern Ecuador. The name, corrupted from the name Shuar, was used by the Spanish to signify savage, uncivilized folk. A good student from day one, Rey had the exceptional ability to learn other languages. His tribe spoke Jibaroan. He learned the basics in Shipibo from a neighboring tribe as a child. Spanish in school was no problem. When he turned fifteen, he worked with some America biologists, carrying their things in an expedition to record flora and fauna. The biologists stayed for eighteen months. Enough time listening to them talk day after day, Rey discovered he could understand most of their conversations. Maybe not word for word, but the general gist of the discussions. He learned the scientific names of the plants and animals the biologists studied. One biologist took a particular shine to Rey, and at night, he would teach him the same names in English while they sat around the fire at the campsite. After that expedition, he decided to leave his home village, move to his aunt's home in Iquitos to study for a nature guide certificate at the university. It was hard financially since his parents had no money, but the pay he received from the expedition paid his school fees. Twelve years later, he is one of the most respected guides in the region.

"I took the Aussie families on nature hikes. We saw lots of animals, even heard a large troupe of howler monkeys howling for a good hour. I remember that well because I had never heard so many at one time, never in my village growing up. We always returned to the lodge at sunset since everyone knows, the later you stay out, the more likely you are to run into something dangerous. Somehow that fact didn't seem to bother these guests because, after dinner each night, they would mention how cool it must be to hike in the jungle at night. The teenaged kids whined to their parents about wanting more adventure, like in the movies I guess. On the fifth night, the parents kind of ordered me to take them on a hike that night. I didn't think it safe, so I convinced them to take the long boat out for a ride. Go up some of the creeks figuring less harm could come to us in a boat. Maybe we could spot some caimans who, if you don't mess with them, they won't mess with you."

"What's a long boat?" Jane asks.

"The long boat is basically an elongated dugout canoe with a small motor on the back end. Because of its length, it's too heavy for a person to paddle it alone, especially when you have a few people on board. With the combined weight of the two families, me and the motorist, the boat's motor was straining that night. We headed up a creek from the Maranon River when we ran into what looked like a large tree fallen into the creek. The motorist revved the engine again and again. Finally, we pushed over the tree. Only the tree wasn't a tree. It was an anaconda about a foot thick and long, really long. We heard a big splash, and the next thing I see is its head out of the water, trying to slither into the boat. One of the younger boys was sitting on the side of the canoe right where the snake wanted to crawl in. I could say he freaked when he saw it, but that really doesn't describe the panic and fear racing through his body. Panic and fear which spread to everyone else."

"In an instant, the families all pushed to go to the other side while I'm screaming for them not to move or we'll tip over. It was crazy. Fernando, my friend driving the boat, grabs his paddle and starts hitting the anaconda's head over and over again to get it to go back into the water. Everyone is screaming. Aaay! Aaay! The boat is rocking, totally unstable. It was like a horror film. But that darn snake kept pushing against the paddle to get in the boat. And Fernando kept smacking it with all his strength. Thump, thump, thump. He's cursing at the snake and praying to the Virgin Mary at the same time. Finally, the anaconda took the hint and splashed back into the water. As it started to swim away, it struck its tail against the boat almost capsizing us. I guess it didn't like us running over it." Rey laughs.

"The families, you can imagine, were in shock. Then the parents grew really pissed, blaming me for taking them to a dangerous place. I wanted to defend myself and say I told you so. The most dangerous animals in the Amazon are nocturnal, which is why we don't hike at night. But I figured they had the adventure they wanted, and by morning, the anaconda became their best story of the trip. Their last night, however, no one said a word about going out." Rey finishes his tale laughing again.

"Wow, that was amazing." Mike loves Rey's stories more than anyone. "I hope we get to see an anaconda."

"I rarely see them in the wild anymore." Rey adds, "Sadly. But I know a couple people that have them as pets. We'll see if we can hook up with them before you guys leave."

"Pets?"

"Sure. Boas make great pets. They keep vermin out of your house." Rey yawns and calls it a night.

Most of the students rise also to get some sleep. The lights in the kerosene lamps flicker along the boardwalk to the bungalows. Anne asks Julie as she opens the door to their room, "Do you think Rey made it up?"

"Made what up?" Julie responds.

"That anaconda story. Dr. Long says anacondas do not attack humans except in Hollywood movies. Boas are constrictors and will only constrict what they can fit in their mouths and swallow."

Julie thinks about this and replies, "I guess any animal will attack if it feels threatened. Rey said they ran the boat motor over it. I bet the blades cut the snake's skin. That would make it attack. Are you worried, Anne? Because remember the big rainbow boa we held at the zoo? I thought it seemed happy when we petted it. And when we put it on our shoulders to take its picture, it didn't constrict anyone."

"Oh, I know. No, I'm not worried. I just wonder if Rey is pulling our leg sometimes." Anne slams the door shut and double checks to make sure it is secure.

8

JUAN

The sun lowers close to the horizon. Streaks of red, orange, and purple hues are created by the wispy clouds above. The river becomes a mirror reflecting the jungle in its gentle waves this evening. Juan slips into his canoe and paddles, closely hugging the shoreline. The current is against him, which makes his half-hour trip turn into an hour to get home, just as darkness falls.

Juan's mother offers him some rice and fish as he walks through their kitchen area. His desire to be alone in a small house of seven people overtakes his hunger. To answer his mother, Juan mumbles, "No thanks. Already ate leftovers from a boss meeting at the mine." He opens one of the two bedroom doors, hoping his brothers and sisters are out. Sitting on the bed, chatting on her cell phone, his older sister yells something at him, and he closes the door. "Please, I need quiet," he whispers and carefully opens the other bedroom door. Finally, an empty room. He shuts the door and drops onto the only bed. He takes his little bottle of aguardiente that he bought in the corner store and takes a big gulp.

Juan thinks about the task Alberto asks him to do. To take the diamonds and hide them in a visitor's bag. He reflects on the times he had to move visitors' bags, so he could clean underneath them. No one even looks at me or talks to me. I'm invisible. But maybe somehow they can watch me. They say the walls have eyes, and someone is always watching. But Alberto would know this, wouldn't he? And isn't it Anita's job to ensure that the visitors' bags are not disturbed? Although Alberto did say that he will distract her. If I get caught with the diamonds, I'll go jail for life. Or worse, they will probably just shoot me on the spot and dump my body into the river. Actually, that would be better than going to jail, starving to death little by little, getting beaten every day.

He pauses, lost in his dream of becoming rich. What am I thinking? This is crazy. Why would I trust Alberto? He is always rude, condescending, and pretentious. But he has told me his plan and admits he already has the diamonds hidden somewhere in the building. Must be in his office. What if I can find them and just run? Who would I sell them to? Ridiculous. Still if he told me his plan, then he must trust me. I shouldn't even be in this situation. If it hadn't been for this damn ankle.

* * *

Five years ago, the plane left Iquitos for Lima early in the morning just as it does today. Juan and his high school buddies, bursting with excitement, kept punching each other on the arms.

"We are going to win the national tournament for sure," squealed one of his buddies.

"Yeah, and become rich and famous," giggled another.

"I can see me on all the billboards with a beer in one hand and a blonde girl in the other."

"Hah. No one's gonna put your ugly face on a billboard," Juan teases.

The coach smiles listening to his players' dreams but knows he needs to keep control. Seventeen-year-old boys are a handful. "Boys, settle down and get serious. We are about to land."

Walking into the National Stadium of Peru in their brand-new uniforms donated by an Iquitos merchant, the team thought they were ready. Teams from all over the country are warming up, teams with bigger players and nicer equipment. A unified gulp sound could be heard as the team crosses the field to their spot. They drop their bags and run through some drills to warm up. First game is against one of the best teams from Lima. The coach wishes that they had an easier draw; he knows it will be next to impossible to beat the Lima Pumas. At least, the boys will have had an opportunity to play in the National Stadium of Peru. A memory they can boast to their grandchildren one day.

"The Pumas are a good team, but we are better. Nothing around here matters, only the ball. Control the game, we will win!" the coach shouts. "Huddle up. One, two, three, Jaguars! Jaguars! Jaguars!" The boys lift their arms in the air and run to take the field.

The game begins at 4:00 p.m. Two minutes later, the Pumas score. It was a bad start. Half-time passes. The score is still 1 to 0. The coach gives directions and points out the Pumas weak spots. "The game is wide open. Let's get out there and win. Take it, it's yours!" he shouts, hoping to inspire. They return to the field. It is all or nothing. Juan and his buddies gain their rhythm. *Bam.* Goal! The Jaguars on the sideline cheer. One minute left in the game. A long pass from Juan to the striker, who went past two defenders and scored a goal! The underdogs win their first game. The Lima crowd can't believe it. The Pumas favored to win the tournament have lost. The Iquito boys are ecstatic.

The next morning, the second game was against Ica, a team from the southern coast of Peru. Forty-five minutes into the game, the score was zero to zero. No one has scored although Juan sent a great pass to his teammate who missed the top corner of the goal by an inch. On the attack again, Juan dribbles pass a defender. He has a clear shot at the goal. He goes to shoot and *wham*! From behind, another defender slams into him. Both tumble to the ground with the goalie falling on top. Pain. Intense pain. Juan has never in his life felt anything like it. He screams. The referee, still blowing his whistle, pulls out a red card. The next few minutes become a blur until Juan hears the word that would shock him back to his senses. The word that would kill his dreams forever—broken. Left ankle, broken. They carry him off the field and place him into the ambulance.

Two days later, a quiet, somber team of boys board the plane to return home. And that was that. His ankle healed, but it would never be the same. Life would never be the same. They won one game. They didn't win the national title. They wouldn't be famous, have their pictures on billboards with beer and girls, or become professional soccer players. They know life will be as difficult for them as it is for their parents, struggling to earn enough to survive. No extras.

Juan's mother's voice arouses him back to today. "What?" he asks. "No, I'm fine. Just tired. What? No, I'm not sick, okay?" He hears her move from the door. She yells at his little brother for a mess he just made. Juan returns to examine Alberto's proposition. He realizes that if he is going to do this, he's got to be smart. Think every step through and figure out how Alberto will try to cheat him out of his share of the money. Because that is the one thing he is sure of. Alberto will try to get rid of him as soon as he has the diamonds. That partner stuff he talked about is malarkey. Alberto told him that Juan's share is a million soles, over three hundred thousand US dollars, more than anyone earns here in a lifetime or two lifetimes, even three. Juan smiles at the thought of ending his "career" as a janitor.

No more stinky toilets to clean. No more Mr. Invisible. He could be somebody, start a business. Electronics, that's where they money is and turn his share into millions more!

Juan could finally ask Claudia to marry him. She has been by his side since the accident. When others stopped calling because it became apparent he would never play again, she never deserted him. She deserves a good life, no, the best life. When he thinks of Claudia crying, worried to death about her father who went missing last month, it makes his stomach turn.

His girlfriend's father went fishing early one morning when a violent storm brewed suddenly. Lightning bolts struck the river for most of the day. Her father didn't return home that night. Fearing the worse, relatives and friends searched the closest rivers and found the family's boat turned over and beached. It took three more days to find her father in a gully near the river's edge. He fell in it while he was scrambling to get home with a broken arm. Juan winces at the pain he remembers on Claudia's face during those awful days.

He could give Claudia the best life with that money. Otherwise, nothing will change. He'll end up an old drunk like his father, always promising a better life and never making it happen. Think, Juan, think. How can he make sure Alberto pays and he doesn't end up taking the blame? A set up. He could snitch on Alberto. There may be a reward, but who would believe him? Ummmm, he must write everything down, the whole plan as Alberto laid it out today, give it to Claudia in sealed, notarized envelope. Yeah, he won't take the fall alone. He can use it to blackmail Alberto if he tries anything. He'll have proof it was Alberto's idea. He's the one who stole them. He's the one responsible. All Juan did was put them in a bag. With a deep breath, he decides that he'll do it. He knows that this is his last chance to be somebody.

* * *

Alberto gets up before sunrise. He looks at his calendar and realizes that the celebration of *Carnaval* begins that day. In Iquitos, like elsewhere in Latin America, people go wild dancing in the streets, drinking and parading in costumes for a week before Ash Wednesday strikes and the season of Lent begins. What were the best days full of fun and craziness in his youth, he has come to detest. People throw water on everyone in the streets. One never knows from which window a bucket of water may fly. Alberto hates that. Last year, he didn't duck in time and got his new suit soaking wet. He only has three suits. He worked hard to purchase them. As the only employee at mine required to wear a suit and tie, Alberto takes pride in looking his best as the onsite manager.

He leaves early before Carnaval revelers rise. Anxious to hear Juan's decision, his mind races, and he stumbles on a broken part of the sidewalk, falling into the arms of an acquaintance from university days. "Oscar. What good luck. Thanks for catching me. I could have torn my pants. How are you? Still at Hotel Victoria?"

"Yes, still night manager. It used to be so quiet. I almost felt guilty taking money to basically sleep through my shift. Lately, however, things have been busy, lots of tour groups. No more siestas!" Oscar laughs. "You know how younger kids are, partying late at night. Not anything bad, just talking and horsing around, making enough noise for the other guests to complain. The other week, we had a large group of teenagers from Canada. Really beautiful young girls. I don't think they slept at all. Bought some rum and started dancing by the pool. I had to wake up their teachers to get them quiet. Another group of American students arrive in a few days for a couple nights. Hopefully, they won't be so rowdy."

Alberto looks at this watch and remembers that Oscar can talk and talk. "Well, my friend, again thanks. I've got to get to work. We should go have a drink together sometime." He doesn't wait for a response and heads to the river.

"Yeah, right," Oscar replies.

Alberto turns to see Oscar walk in the opposite direction. He slows his pace a little so as not to sweat. He wants to get to the mine early in case Juan has also. As he drives on the river, he tries to think of another way to get the diamonds out in case Juan says no. Alberto doubts Juan's abilities. After all, he's a janitor. Juan probably never finished grade school. If Alberto could figure out another way, he would not rely on someone uneducated. A janitor, for goodness sake. Alberto knows that he may be unfair in his assumptions, but he believes them all the same.

If Juan won't play, Alberto is sure that he'll have to pay him a bribe to keep his mouth shut. Hopefully, it won't come to that. He's pretty sure Juan's answer will be yes. He saw his eyes light up at the thought of having a different life. Alberto parks his boat in his normal spot, below the mine's only entrance, and says his good mornings to the security guys upon arrival.

He punches the time card and checks the mail box. Just a few routine notices. He goes to the cafeteria. No one there. He walks both halls and again sees no one. Alberto realizes Juan is not at work yet, so he decides to finish up the paperwork from yesterday first and then perform his morning inspection. Surely, he will catch Juan in an hour. No luck. Alberto doesn't understand why on days that he has no interest to talk to Juan, he sees him everywhere. Today when he is going nuts to speak with him, he can't find him anywhere.

No knock, just a push opening his door. Alberto prepares to yell at the person. A stranger in a nice gray pin-striped suit asks, "Are you Alberto?" Alberto nods yes. "Mario Fernandez. I'm the new regional manager from Iquitos, replacing Gomez. I thought it a good idea for me to see personally how things are running. And I brought some of your reports we can go over."

Alberto stands, shakes his hand, and motions for him to sit in the chair beside his desk. "What happened to Gomez?" Mario just shrugs his shoulders. Alberto thinks, great just what he needs, some-one noising around his office. He's probably here to replace him too. He wants to get rid of him as quickly as possible, so he focuses on the task at hand. Mario opens a folder thick with papers, and the two men discuss the entries.

Juan pushes the heavy, wobbly cart into Alberto's office, grin-ning ear to ear. Alberto looks up as the door opens, and he shakes his head with a frown. What the heck, Juan starts to think but then sees another man in a fancy suit reading something in a folder on the other side of the room. He lowers his head and grabs a wastebasket to empty. Alberto speaks sharply. "We don't need the floor mopped today. Just finish what you are doing and leave." Juan nods. He won-ders who the man is and what his business is here. He shuffles out of the room. Closing the door tightly behind him, he heads for the men's toilet, the worst part of his day.

A few minutes later, Alberto pops in the restroom and turns on the faucet as if to wash his hands. Alberto knows what's on Juan's mind. He checks to make sure they are alone before he speaks. "Mario Fernandez from Iquitos. He's the new guy there. He came to do a pre-inspection today to prepare for the big bosses and the GIA inspectors on Friday. The Iquitos office decided because of the flood, the tremors, and last month's incident, they better check things out and make sure all is well. At least the place hasn't caught fire. If we are going to do this, it has to be today or tomorrow. By Friday, they'll know some of the diamonds are missing. Are you in?"

"Who's coming? And I thought you said no one would ever know any are missing?" Juan meekly asks now not so sure about helping him.

"The GIA. They certify the quality of the diamonds. Don't worry about it. I got it all covered. They may figure what's in this week's bin isn't as much as it should be. But by then, they'll be gone."

"They'll be gone? Who?"

"Not who. What. The diamonds. I told you. We'll put them in a visitor's bag and get them later."

"How are we going to do that?" Juan is still unsure.

"Let me worry about that. I'll find out where the visitors are staying. There are only three lodges on this part of the river. Each place only has a few visitors at a time. It won't be too hard to find them. Now are you in or are you out? I have to know right now," Alberto barks.

Juan stutters, "I-I-I guess so."

"I guess so?" Alberto's face reddens. "We're talking rich, and you guess so. You got to be sure and clear headed and confident. We'll only have one chance, and we'll have to act quickly."

Juan nods yes. "Yes, I'm sure. I can do this. Just don't try anything funny. And I want my money."

"Of course," Alberto smiles like the Cheshire cat. "We are partners now."

9

THE MINE

The *Grand Amazone* rides upstream helped by a crosscurrent caused by a sudden bend in the river. It pulls up to the dock, one of the few constructed docks along the Amazon. The river rises and falls at least nine meters each year, so no one bothers to build docks. They just get swept away in high-water season. They have already replaced the mine's dock twice.

Not all the passengers want to see the mine. The last few kilometers as they neared the mine, the scenery changed dramatically. An ugly contrast to the rich, green tropical forest they normally cruise by. A real jolt to the eyes. Edith wants to see everything, so Helen helps with her boots, and together, they carefully walk across the plank to the dock as the boat rocks.

"My, my. Just think of the value of all these diamonds right beneath our feet," Helen whispers to her sister as they walk toward the welcome center.

"Don't even think about it, sister dear. We are doing just fine on this trip," remarks Edith while grabbing onto the makeshift bamboo hand railings. It is a slippery place without any vegetation.

"I'm fine, sister. Don't worry. Doesn't hurt to dream now, does it? Besides I'm just window shopping," she teases. A rare mood for Helen.

A typical thatched roof hut with concrete floors is the welcome center. Pictures of indigenous kids playing with big smiles, teachers in schools, and mothers holding bags of rice hang on the center's walls. A huge sign reads, Amazon Diamond Mine. Below the name, the attached tagline says, A Community Partnership. Working for a Better Life for All.

"Yeah, I bet," hisses Helen.

"Shhh, sister. Be good."

Arms stretched wide, Manuel, the mine's official tour guide welcomes everyone. "Come. Come this way. I want to share with you all the great things we are doing here. On this tour, you can witness firsthand the operation of a diamond mine. To begin, it is necessary to leave all bags, hats, cameras, and umbrellas here with Anita. Everything will be very safe, I promise you. We have the world's best security. In fact, when you leave, you will see the world's most advanced machine to prevent theft," Manuel proclaims proudly.

The older folks reluctantly leave their things after first threatening Manuel that if anything is missing, there will be hell to pay. Manuel just nods. He has probably heard that before.

"Si si si. Yes yes yes. Very safe for sure. Now follow me."

Alberto walks in the corridor to the cafeteria when he notices the visitors approaching the mine's front gate. He pours himself a cup of coffee and asks Maria Ester, a coworker, if she knows who the tourists are.

"Off one of those luxury cruise ships. Gringos from America or England. Manuel was practicing his English earlier. I guess they don't have enough diamonds of their own, so they have to come see ours. Or maybe they are already theirs or their rich friends, no?" Maria Ester shakes the front of her shirt to get rid of the yucca cookie crumbs that have fallen from her mouth. She grabs her coffee cup and leaves.

Alberto doesn't really notice, saying, "Ah yeah...," after she has left. He catches sight of Juan out of the corner of his eye, sitting at a table in the corner, sipping on a glass of water during his five-minute break. He motions with his eyebrows toward the door. As Juan leaves the cafeteria, he sees Alberto heading into the men's toilet.

"This group won't work," he tells Juan after checking under the stalls to ensure no one else is there. "These cruise ship people typically go straight from the boat to the airport. Only occasionally do they stay an extra day or two in Iquitos. We can't risk not having enough time to retrieve the diamonds. I hear that there is another group coming later. So keep on the lookout and I'll try to find out who they are."

"What do I do when I see them?" Juan asks.

"You come tell me of course," instructs Alberto, annoyed by what he perceives as a stupid question. He worries again about getting Juan to help him. It may be a huge mistake, one that will cost him everything if the kid blows it.

"But how do I do that? I have already cleaned your office."

"Just walk down the hall. No one pays any attention to you. Don't worry. If someone asks, say that I spilled something in my office and instructed you to come clean it up. Carry one of your rags in your hand. I have to get back to my office before Mario notices something." Alberto briskly walks out of the men's toilet.

Juan takes a deep breath. Okay, you can do this, he tells himself. Keep a lookout.

* * *

The one-hour tour drags on as if it were four days. The bored cruise visitors chat among themselves, wondering about news back home. They haven't read a newspaper or seen a television for a week. Some did not realize how isolated or cut off from mainstream forms of communication they would be.

"I thought we would at least have Internet. I assumed it is everywhere in the world by now," one of the passengers complains. The man standing beside her nods in agreement.

Helen grumbles at her fellow passengers' ignorance but is more annoyed with the tour's propaganda. "I don't see everyone living better. The kids here are thin as straws. It's a wonder that they can concentrate on their studies. Food for the poor. The only big guy wears a tie, so I think he must be eating their share."

"Hush, dear sister. The children aren't thin as straws. And we don't know what they do and don't do really," Edith responds, always giving people the benefit of the doubt.

Overhearing the sisters, ponytail man loves to butt in and give his opinion, his correct opinion, of course, on any topic with delight. "We need more diamonds to continue our technological advancement." He likes using big words to impress others. "In semi-thermal conductors only diamonds can take the heat and cut with absolute precision."

Helen can't resist debating the know-it-all her view of him. "Technology smuckology. We already have too much technology. Kids today can't have a conversation without using some gadget. Our social skills are eroding along with patience and manners. No one asks the ethical questions. We can do this and that, but the question remains whether we should do this or that. Look at the field of medicine. Keeping people alive by machines, one to pump the blood, one to pump the air, one to pump the food. Meanwhile, the poor soul is dead as a doorknob. And the family has to keep visiting the doorknob and pay to keep the doorknob's machines going. It's terrible.

Now a million gadgets to stay connected, yet never in our history have we been so disconnected. Facebook friends instead of real ones. I wonder what will become of our society. I'm sure—"

"Sister," Edith cuts her off, knowing Helen will not stop. For all her complaints of ponytail man, she can be quite similar. "They want us to keep moving. We finally get to see the amazing diamonds that we've read about."

The group saw only one real diamond the entire tour, and that was the reason most came. What a disappointment. They expected to see pails full of diamonds that news reporters had expounded on week after week in newspapers back home. One small shimmering gem. The guests are anxious to leave and relax on the lavish cruise boat.

To exit the building, the visitors must pass through a small room marked security check out. Manuel opens the door and notions them to follow. In the room sits a small machine next to a chair with an armed security guard. The group waits for instructions.

"Each one of you will be asked two questions in the chair with that machine connected. And make sure to tell the truth because that machine is the new NLDS. So sensitive, it can detect even the tiniest of white lies. No one can fool it," Manuel informs them.

"NLDS?" inquires one of the cruise passengers.

"Neuron linguistic detector sensor," replies Manuel. "It's the most advanced lie detector test approved by the national association of polygraph examiners."

"I'm not putting that thing on my head. Not with the shoddy electricity around here. I'm likely to get electrocuted," Helen states firmly.

"Well, if you want to leave and not live here forever, you will," Manuel tries to joke, but Helen isn't buying it. "Everyone signed an agreement to go through security."

"Why not just search us? We have no bags, nothing, no way to take anything. Besides we only saw one diamond, and you still have it."

"We do the same screening with all our visitors and our employees each day. People are becoming cleverer, finding new ways to hide diamonds, so we have to use new technology, advanced technology. Don't worry. No one has been electrocuted yet!" Manuel's joke falls flat again. "Who wants to go first?" Manuel asks without looking in Helen's direction.

"My feet hurt with these heavy boots," complains Edith. "Gimme that contraption and ask away. I need a cup of tea."

The guard puts the device on her head and asks the two questions. "Next," he says. The door automatically opens. Edith sees the guide from the boat waiting outside. After twenty minutes, everyone is cleared and moves toward the welcome center to collect their belongings. Everything was safe, and all are happy to have their stuff returned. One of the men fumbles with his iPhone. "Lordy, lordy. I've got three bars!" he shouts in glee. Immediately, other passengers who have iPhones search their bags to connect. "Why didn't they tell us they have a cell tower? This is the best news of the day. The guide certainly yakked about everything else."

"I agree. This is fantastic. Makes my day." Hazel quickly strolls down, checking her e-mails.

Some of the cruisers descend slowly back to the boat while the phone folks are frozen in space, fingers and eyes scanning the gadgets as if a new life rained down upon them from above. Jose Antonio calls and motions to them to board. No one moves. While physically still in the Amazon, their minds are back home again in England, engaged in family and friends' gossip. In an instant, the gadgets eliminate the thousands of miles between here and there.

Helen and Edith, who don't have iPhones, iPods, iPads, or any device that begins with an *i*, watch their fellow passengers. "Why pay all that money to come to this magical place and then be jubilant about getting bars…whatever they are. I don't mean to be judgmental, but I think traveling is to experience life away from home. You know, sister, Joy, the young yoga teacher in our apartment building says this is why people are so dissatisfied with their lives. Never living in the moment. Not appreciating what is right in front of you."

Helen sighs. Normally, she and Edith see the world from different perspectives, but this time, she is in complete agreement with her sister. "Come along, dear. We certainly don't want to be left at this dreary place. I'm sure there's a great meal awaiting us," she adds sarcastically.

Down the hill by the dock, two more boats have arrived filled with the university students they met at the artisan cooperative.

"Look, Helen. It's those nice kids we met the other day. Remember they were making baskets with the Indian women. Yoo-hoo! Hello!" yells Edith, waving her arm vigorously. She loses her balance and falls, sliding a few feet on the muddy slope.

Two students run to help her.

"My goodness! I'm okay. Just grab my arms so I can stand up. There. That's better. My, what lovely students you have," Edith remarks to Elizabeth, who also ran over to make sure the elderly woman didn't break a bone.

"Yes, they are. Thank you. Are you sure you didn't hurt yourself?" asks Elizabeth.

"Oh, just my pride, honey. You go on now and enjoy yourselves. As you can see, I need to freshen up. Although I have to say the tour is quite dull. Monotonous, really. And they only showed us one diamond the entire time."

As the students approach the welcome hut, Manuel appears, arms stretch wide again and gives the same welcome speech as before. The students and professor leave their bags and turn to listen attentively to the guide.

* * *

Juan finishes the last room on hall B. He goes outside the building to empty the trash when he hears strange noises at the welcome center. He can see through the fence that the second group has arrived. White people. Probably from the US or France. No wonder he can't understand any of their chatter. He throws the trash bag into the big container and closes the lid. With a rag in hand, he tries to walk casually into the building and along the corridor to alert Alberto. Casually becomes, quickly, a semi trot. He's so nervous. He knocks. He opens the door and slides in. Alberto is alone.

"They are here. A large group of white, young people, lots of pretty girls with an older woman. They just began the tour," Juan tells Alberto without taking a breath.

"Calm down." Alberto glances at the clock. 2:30 p.m. Good! Most of the employees will be in the cafeteria, having lunch. The cafeteria is located on the opposite side of the welcome center. "The tour begins on the cafeteria side, and if anyone is wandering around, they'll probably be trying to get a look at the girls. This will work." He reaches under his desk top drawer and careful removes the taped envelope.

"Okay, Juan. Here we go. Put this envelope in your pocket and go get your cart. Put the envelope deep in the trash bin and push it to the welcome center like you normally do."

"But I normally clean the hut's floors later in the afternoon, after the last tour leaves."

"Well, you have to go now. It's now or never. We have less than a half hour to get the diamonds in one of the bags. If anyone asks, say someone reported that the welcome center needs cleaning because the gringos think it's dirty. Everyone will believe that."

"Yeah," Juan agrees.

"Start cleaning the way you normally do and look for a bag with deep outside pockets. Like we talked about, remember? Deep, so the diamonds will settle to the bottom of the bag and the person won't notice them. It's great that they are young. Kids don't pay attention to anything. I'll be there in fifteen minutes to distract Anita, so you don't have much time to find the right bag. After you find one, hold it up to me, and I'll touch my nose if I think it's a good one. Then pour them out of the envelope, slip them into the bag and go back to cleaning. I'll order you back inside, and you hurry off to where you would normally be."

"What will you do then?" Juan asks fingering the stones in the envelope.

"I'm going to follow them, of course. That's why I need fifteen minutes to clock out and get searched. Man, you are sweating like a pig. Are you sure you can do this?" Alberto asks concerned.

"Yeah." Juan wipes his face with the rag he brought. "And I'll meet you tonight or what is the plan?"

"No, not tonight. We'll need time to retrieve the diamonds. I'll see you tomorrow here at work like usual. Now get going. And stop sweating."

Juan doesn't like the idea of Alberto retrieving the diamonds without him, but he guesses that he has no choice. He tries his best to walk calmly to his cart. Just focus on the floor. One step in front of another becomes his mantra. He reaches his cart and places the envelope deep inside the trash. He wipes his face again. As he heads to the welcome center, he is amazed that no one ever looks his way. He repeats the mantra. The guard opens the emergency exit door, so he can push the cart through and gazes at the sky outside. Juan keeps his eyes focused on the sidewalk. He feels better once he is inside the center lifting his mop out of the pail to start swabbing.

"You're early today," Anita comments without looking up from her *Star Magazine*.

"Ah, yeah. Ah…dirty. They sent me." Oh, shut up, he tells himself. He stares intently at the mop.

Anita still doesn't look his way and turns the page of her magazine. After a minute or two, Juan realizes that she is not paying any attention to him. He begins assessing the backpacks as he moves his mop back and forth, back and forth. A bigger bag is better, more room to hide. He remembers Alberto said to look for one with lots of outside pockets. Hmmm. He moves slowly and watches the clock's big hand count off the minutes. Just as he moves close to the bags, in strides Alberto.

"Hello, beautiful. What are we reading today?" He smiles at Anita, teeth gleaming. Alberto spent good money last year to have his teeth fixed. He loves his perfectly straight, bright white teeth.

Anita coyly looks over her magazine but doesn't respond.

"I'm off early today. What time do you finish? Maybe I could buy you some more magazines?"

Anita laughs, enjoying any break in her dull routine. She has heard that Alberto has a bad reputation when it comes to women. She has no intention of letting him buy her anything although the offer is tempting. No. She rather just have him flirt with her. A good way to kill part of the last hour of her shift.

"Aay, Berto, I thought you and Rosalee had a thing going on."

"Rosalee is pretty, but not as pretty as you." He smiles again, flashing his pearly whites.

Ugh, she thinks. What a stupid thing to say. Does he really believe that works on a girl? He must think she is so stupid. But she smiles anyway because he is the manager and maybe he can help her get a better-paying job in the one of the offices.

Juan is practically doing jumping jacks to get Alberto's attention. Alberto finally wakes up from his I'm-so-cool daze and checks out the tan bag Juan holds up. He touches his nose. Big, roomy, lots of outside pockets. Maybe Juan won't screw this up. All he has to do is sneak them inside. Under his breath Alberto coaches Juan, "Open the zipper. Yes, good. Open the envelope and pour them in. Yes, now zip it close. Great."

"Hey, Berto, I asked you about the office clerk job they are advertising. What do you think?" smiles Anita.

"Sorry, love. Just realized the time. I need to go to an important meeting in Iquitos this afternoon. I must run, but we can talk about the job tomorrow. And I'll give you another chance to go out with me," he says while winking. "You there, *mozo*. Get back to hall B. Someone has tracked a bunch of mud all over the floor," Alberto barks.

Under her breath, she whispers, "Yuck. What a pompous jerk." A squeak makes her jump in her chair. She turns and sees Juan, who she completely forgot was in the room. Juan is pushing his old cart out the door. "And I think my job is crappy.

10

NAUTA

"How weird was that?" asks Sarah.

"Yeah, like anyone would say, yes, I have stolen some diamonds, and yes, I have them here in my back pocket," adds Mike.

"Nah, it is new technology. They know you can't fake it, so no one would even try to steal. Not even one little diamond. That machine is super sensitive. It reads brainwaves. How cool is that?" replies John, who studies engineering and is fascinated by any new tech gadget.

"Too bad we couldn't take pictures of us in that helmet thing," Claudine laments. "No one will believe us."

The students head for their boats, disappointed by the tour and what they learned. The opposite effect that the mine owners desire. The group splits into the two boats. They grab their water bottles and take a long drink. Jairo and his brother start the boats' motors and ease into the river. A family in a small dugout canoe paddles alongside them, closer to the shoreline. Boat drivers always move slowly to minimize the wake, careful not to tip any canoes. Jairo looks at the sky ahead. Dark rain clouds loom above the river.

"They never answered my question. I wanted to know who exactly owns the mine. And where they are from? Everyone is a partner? Who is everyone? I rather doubt the money is shared. Everyone is treated as a family? I wish he would have talked honestly instead of in PR sound bites." Julie begins the conversation about the mine and its impacts. "I understand that a big company owns it, and probably, there are investors and stockholders from many countries. If there is nothing wrong with that, why hide it? It made the place seems more sinister."

"What bothers me is the environmental destruction. It is so obvious. Look how gray it is around here. Like death itself has come to roost." Colleen is an environmental science major and wants to save the rainforest. "I guess that's why they only talk about the economic benefits. Once here, you can't hide all this." She gestures a panoramic view. "On both sides of the river, not a living tree to be seen. Just burnt-out stumps. I hope it is true what the guy said that the mine won't expand and that they will replant all the trees when they finish."

"Do you know which villages receive food and where they built the new schools, Professor Long?" Anne asks.

Lost in thought, Elizabeth realizes she was asked a question. "Sorry. What was that?"

"During the tour, Manuel said the mine provides food and education. And Sarah asked what kind of education, and he said that they build new schools but didn't say where."

"I'm afraid that I haven't heard of or seen any new schools in this area. Let's ask Santos when we get back to the village. He's well connected to everyone in this region. As the community's *apu*, he visits other villages frequently. We have much to digest. This mine touches on many of your research topics either directly or indirectly.

Obviously, for you, John, you got a lot of information today. You may want to check with your classmates to look at their notes and make sure you got all the details in your field notes."

As they head onto the river, a rainstorm breaks, causing the boat to bounce harder on the tumultuous water. Three to four foot waves are created by the stronger winds. The students put on their ponchos and hold tighter to the sides of the boats. Visibility is rapidly disappearing. Rain falls in torrents like a massive waterfall covering the river and jungle. Its impact produces a thick mist, obscuring the line between the surface of the river and the rain.

"How do they know where to go?" Mike looks back at Jairo, who holds the motor's handle steadily with one hand gripping tight as the rain smacks his face. Waves smack dangerously close to the top of the sides as the boat pushes forward. Everyone is quiet and huddles close together. Anxious. This is the biggest storm the students have experienced on the Amazon. Only one time previously was the rain and wind almost as strong. No one speaks for the first time in weeks.

Everyone shivers from the cold rain. It is hard to imagine being cold so close to the equator. Hard to imagine three to four foot waves on a river. Elizabeth and Bob glance at each other, knowing that they shouldn't be on the river in a storm like this one. Hunker down, ride it out. There is nothing else they can do. Its times like this, they pray for Jairo and Maclave to get them to safety.

They finally arrive home intact and scramble out of the rocking boats. "Go get dry and let's meet in an hour to talk about today's tour," Elizabeth instructs. Quietly, she says to Rey, "I heard about the mine, but I never imagined the destruction it could cause. I don't believe that they are going to stop. Looks like they will clear cut the jungle all the way to the reserve."

"I've heard rumors that people in Lima want to clear-cut the entire rainforest to see if they can find any more ancient asteroid strikes. And the president ordered permits to be given to geologists from all over the world. They'll need guides so that's good for us, but it's going to be bad, real bad for everyone else. Worse than the rubber boom for the people here. At least with the rubber boom, they needed the trees for the rubber. Unfortunately, these people don't understand anything about the jungle." Rey lowers his head and shakes it side to side, dismayed. It was the first time he had taken the tour, and it made him sick to his stomach.

* * *

Alberto strides swiftly from the welcome center. He walks down the riverbank to his small aluminum boat equipped with a 25 horsepower motor. A half year to save enough to buy the boat, small but much better than using the water taxis or paddling each day. Although he has to admit he was in much better shape before when he only had a canoe and had to paddle everywhere. He taps his finger on his forehead, grinning ear to ear. Now the only muscle he needs to exercise is this one here. He can't believe his plan worked. He keeps looking over his shoulder to see if anyone is after him. It was too simple. Now he imagines the faces of all the people who had ever belittled him or treated him less because of his height or ethnicity or for whatever crazy reason. He will show them. He can already feel the money in his hands. He pictures how he'll look in a brand new shiny BMW just off the boat from Germany.

A noise jolts him out of his daydream. Pedro yells and waves to Alberto. "Alberto wait, wait. Carlos needs to see you. Right away. He says it's urgent." Samuel walks across the front lawn and finds Pedro with Alberto. "Oh good. You found him. I'm going back inside."

Alberto's heart begins beating faster and faster. His mind races. Why in the world did I think I could get away with this? How could they have found out so quickly? That kid. That stupid kid probably found the diamonds in his backpack. I'm ruined. I'll be fired for sure even though I can put the blame on Juan. Those bosses in Lima will congratulate me on finding a security breach and then they'll fire me, just because they can. They'll get someone from Lima to be manager because they think themselves so special. Maybe it is better this way. I'm killing myself working and will never get ahead. I should just give myself up, tell them everything. How I discovered the breach. Not as stupid as they always assume we are. Or maybe I should run. He feels a hand on his shoulder.

"Alberto, come on. What's wrong with you? Carlos needs you to come immediately."

"I'm coming."

They head straight to the security door. The guard opens it. Pedro heads back to his office while Alberto walks to where Carlos stands in his office doorway in the middle of the corridor.

"Alberto. Sorry to have to call you back, but this report got ruined when I spilled coffee on it. We need it for the meeting, and with the inspectors coming, I thought you'd want to redo it right away. I'm so sorry. It will never happen again. I swear on the Virgin Mary."

"What?" Alberto realizes his hands are shaking so hard, he can't take the report from Carlos. He clasps them over his head. It takes him a minute or two to understand the situation. He is not under arrest. "No problem. We can redo it in the morning. There is time." He clears his throat and tries to resume his more authoritative speech he uses with the office employees. "Now I have to get to an important meeting, and you've made me late. I can't believe you couldn't handle this. Use that brain of yours, or do I have to do all the thinking? *Pinche cabron.*" He practically runs through the hall and is out the door while Carlos is still saying sorry, then mumbles, "*Jefes*, go figure. If I tell him, he's mad. If I had waited, he'd be mad."

Alberto enters the security exit room and sees it crowded with the students. He whispers to the guard so he can cut in line and goes next. He needs to get his boat up river into the little opening by the big kapok tree and out of sight when the students pass. Got to find out where they are staying. Maybe he can somehow pinch the diamonds tonight. Out the door, he flies down the riverbank. Three hard pulls, the motor spits and sputters to life.

About a half hour passes. Just as Alberto's heart resumed its normal beat, it begins racing as Alberto starts to panic again. How could he have missed their boats? They should have left fifteen minutes ago. They can't be downriver. There are no eco-lodges between the mine and the reserve. A bad rainstorm began with large, fat raindrops, and he has only his office jacket. In all the excitement, he left his raincoat at work. With a driving rain, it is next to impossible to follow anyone. And the sky is threatening worst. He thinks he better get to town. Better safe than sorry, especially now that his life can truly begin. Just need to be smart, he reminds himself. Alberto starts the boat to head to Nauta to ride out the storm. Maybe someone there knows where the students are staying. Hard not to notice a bunch of gringos running around here. Full speed to Nauta he goes.

He arrives soaked. The sky let loose. A torrential downpour. A cousin of his friend Jose has a small cantina close to the main dock. He runs for cover. Slowly, his eyes adjust to the dim light inside, light that peaks through the clapboards, the door opening, and the few holes in the palm roof although, today, more rain than light falls inside from the roof. Five strategically placed buckets catch most of the raindrops. A couple of men sit on the two wooden chairs available. The "bar" is a table with a few half full bottles stacked on one end. The bottles contain sugarcane rum or aguardiente as the locals call it and the various fermented root concoctions known by their number—7 roots, 13 roots, and the mind-blowing 21 roots. Who knows what proofs these homemade brews are? Enough to take the chill off a drenched fellow, that's for sure.

Alberto sees Gordito, Jose's cousin, and greets him with a wet embrace. "Gordito, how have you been?"

"Alberto, good man. I haven't seen you since Jose sold his moto-taxi. A year ago, no? Come. Let me pour you some of the good stuff."

Alberto thinks, Good stuff? Yeah right. Probably made two weeks ago. But instead of answering him with something sarcastic, he just smiles and nods yes. He raises his glass. "*Salut.*" He gulps the shot. The rum burns all the way to the stomach but isn't as bad as he expected. Another? Of course. Men here are serious drinkers. Another shot. Gordito pours a third, and this one Alberto sips from the brim. He must keep his mind clear and focused. "So we had a big group of gringos visiting the mine today. I should say gringas. Almost all girls. And what beautiful muchachas." Alberto speaks loudly for the other men to hear as well. "I wouldn't mind having some stay with me. Hah! You know what I mean, real beauties" He sips on the third shot again.

Gordito just nods, not sure what Alberto means or what he's supposed to say.

"Have you seen any beautiful muchachas?" Alberto asks, trying to be more direct. The other men sit with their backs to Alberto and mumble to each other. One of the men starts to slide out of his chair. His friend grabs him and sets him upright in the chair again. They pay no attention to the man in a jacket and tie.

"Ah ha." Gordito realizes what Alberto means. "Listen, friend, I know exactly what you want. My wife's cousin, Paulette, is a real beauty. Doesn't charge much either. She lives just up the street from my house. I can take you there."

"No no no." Alberto tries to laugh it off. He finishes the shot and listens to the rain pound harder. Gordito continues to talk about other girls he knows. Alberto ignores him. He realizes that this is a dead end. Bunch of drunks. Who should he ask? Maybe someone in a store. Gringos always need lots of supplies. They carry packs full of stuff wherever they go. Nauta is the main distribution center on this part of the river. He gives Gordito a couple soles. "Thanks, old man. Good to see you."

Gordito puts the money in his pocket. "Why so fast? It's still raining. Have another. On me."

Alberto pats him on his shoulders. "Tomorrow. Tomorrow." Gordito grabs his hand and Alberto shakes it while moving to the door yanking him along. "I have to meet someone."

"Oh. You dog. Fire in the pants. Can't wait. I get ya." Gordito waves his glass to him.

The rain lessens and the sun breaks through some clouds to the west. Let's see, which general store? he wonders. Alberto notices that over the last year, the town has changed, grown significantly. There are more buildings along the shorelines. He heads toward a new building made with concrete blocks, rare in that part of the Amazon. Two light bulbs dangle on their cords from the roof and illuminate each side of the entrance. ABARROTES in capital letters is freshly painted on the front wall next to the door.

He slips in, shaking his jacket at the door, and gazes at the variety of products. In one corner women's notions—threads, ribbons, pins, buttons, and other needlepoint supplies. Different dry goods—canned food, Jell-O, yucca flour, tiny packets of spices, and larger bags of salt—along with cooking oil, plastic buckets and cups fill the handmade shelves nailed into the east wall. Candles, matches, rubber boots, machetes, aspirin, cigarettes, nails, rope, knives are on the opposite wall. Five-liter bottles of water stacked in the shape of a pyramid sit on the floor next to the end of the counter. Beside them are a rack of locally made banana and yucca chips. Near the box that serves as the cash register, someone had just arrived with three large *dorado* or catfish. The fish can grow to forty or fifty pounds, and with no bones in the filets, they are especially prized in this region. The three look to weigh about twenty-five or thirty pounds each and have banana leaves wrapped around them. A middle-aged woman appears from the backroom through a sheet used as a curtain. "Can I help you?"

"Ah yes. Just a minute." Think, Alberto. Buy something so she doesn't get suspicious. "I need a rain poncho."

"Yes, it looks like you do." She laughs then climbs on her chair to reach several ponchos and sets them on the counter.

Good. Relax. He also laughs at her joke and shines his pearly whites in her direction. "Nice store you have here. Pretty new?"

"About a year. You must not come this way much."

"Not in Nauta. I pass by it though on my way to the mine." As soon as he said the word mine, he regretted it. You idiot. Do not mention the mine. You don't want her associating you with that place. Alberto grins at her again.

"You want a thicker poncho? Last a lot longer. Only four soles more."

"No, this one is fine. How's business? Probably good with the increase in numbers of tourists. They all come through here on the way to the reserve, don't they?"

"Don't know anything about that. Business is okay. Anything else? How about some boots? Those shoes are too fancy for the muddy streets here."

Alberto politely declines and pays. Strike two. Maybe this isn't a good idea. He throws the poncho over his head and exits. There is only a trickle of rain now with the sky clearing. Maybe he should cruise to the lodges he knows about on this part of the river. But he is unsure of how to snoop around the lodges without being noticed. They are built on higher ground, a couple meters higher than the riverbanks. The vegetation along the shore obscures most of the buildings except the roofs. Plus, it will soon be dark.

"Piss, piss. Hey, buddy."

Alberto turns to see one of the men from Gordito's bar, the one who could hardly sit in his chair. He is having trouble standing now, swaying from side to side. "Come here, buddy." He flaps his right hand, motioning Alberto to get closer. The combined smells of alcohol, sweat, and urine make Alberto step back, not closer. "No, buddy, here. Come down here. I got top secret information you want. Sshh." Alberto bends down to look the fellow in his eyes. "You want gringas, no? Babes from America. Make them your slaves, no? I know what you said. I pay attention. People think I don't, but I do."

"No. I don't want any slaves. I think you need to rest. You live around here?"

"That's the point, buddy. You guessed it. I live upstream in 25 de Noviembre. I see."

The village of 25 of November is about fifteen to twenty minutes by piqué pique from Nauta. Alberto knows that he shouldn't encourage the drunken fellow who has had enough shots to be hallucinating, but curiosity has taken hold. "You see. You see what?"

"The muchachas, the babes. Las gringas. Lots of them. All beautiful. They came to my village, stayed all morning, cooking with our women."

"When?"

"When what?" he staggers off to the left and trips over a branch. Alberto helps him to his feet.

"When were the babes there, I mean, the gringas?"

"Yesterday or a few days ago. Some time. Now how about a little tip, fancy pants?"

Alberto reaches in his pocket for a twenty-five centavo coin he got as change in the store. This guy is bad news, attracts too much attention. He gives him the coin, pats him on the back, and turns to walk quickly to his boat.

"Hey, buddy. Thanks. Just let me know if you want to see them."

"What?" Alberto stops dead in his tracks.

"You know, see them. They're staying just pass Pedro's family's farm. I can see them from the path to my chakra."

"So you're saying that they are staying in the eco-lodge next to San Jorge?"

"Yeah. Haven't you been listening? That's what I've been telling you, buddy. Give me a ride home, and I'll show you the path."

"Thanks, but I'm going the other way." Alberto hears the guy yelling but is too excited to care. He jumps in his boat and drives toward Iquitos, watching for the drunken guy to wander off. When he does, he sharply turns the boat around, making a beeline to San Jorge.

* * *

The sun is getting close to set. Alberto knows he hasn't much time. Although he has passed the San Jorge eco-lodge many times on his way to and from work, he's never actually visited there. No reason to. He has just seen the steps on the riverbank. He arrives as the sun sets. There will be enough light for at least another half hour; enough time to snoop around and get the layout of the place, so he can figure out a plan tonight at home. He cuts the motor, passing north of the entrance and drifts back to the shore beside the steps. Two boats are tied to some tree trunks, but fortunately, no one is with them.

In his haste to arrive, Alberto realizes that he hasn't thought of a cover story in case he runs into someone. What is most logical? Pretend to be looking for a tourist. Yes, that is perfect. Now what name he asks himself? Maybe Smith. Yes, Mr. Smith. In American movies, there is always a Smith. But what if that is the name of one of the students or worse the older couple with them? He knows that he needs to add an unusual first name, better in another language like French or something. What's the name of that famous French actor they used to watch when he took Ivonne to the movies? Ouch. Just thinking her name still hurts his heart. Jean-Marc. That's it. Okay, Jean-Marc Smith. Stupid, but at least it's something.

Alberto crawls off the end of his boat onto the steps, careful not to muddy his pants. He quickly scrambles the steps to a small hut that is basically empty except for a few benches along the walls. From there, he can see most of the buildings. The boardwalk goes straight to a large hut. Must be where the group eats. Behind it the boardwalk runs across the back of the cleared area next to higher hill thick with untamed jungle. A bunch of small wooden bungalows with pointy thatched roofs are spaced evenly along the walk. Each has an entrance off the boardwalk and another on the back through a porch with a hammock strung across it. He hears the students chatter punctuated with bursts of laughter coming out of the large hut.

He ponders his next move, realizing that if everyone is in the large hut, he could have time to search the bungalows without anyone noticing. The front doors face the higher hill, impossible to see from the large hut. What luck. He crawls beneath the boardwalk to walk in its shadows. With the sunset, dark shadows envelop the land around the buildings. Suddenly, he hears two people walking behind him on top of the boards from the direction of the river. He wanders if they saw his boat. How could they not. He thinks about returning but hesitates. Listening carefully to their conversation to see if he should flee, Alberto discovers that they are two villagers there to pick up the kitchen staff who have finished serving dinner and are ready to go home. They make no mention of his boat.

Alberto continues moving along the poles of the boardwalk to the end. He starts at the farthest bungalow, less chance of being seen, and hopes that he will get lucky. He jumps up and slowly opens the door. The room has three single wood beds with mosquito coverings hung from the ceiling. A small table is buried in clothes, empty water bottles and an array of toiletries. More clothes are scattered on the floor and two chairs. Some shirts hang on nails near the back door.

He sees several suitcases open but no backpacks. He peeks in the bathroom. None there either. He goes to the front door, pauses, hears no one and opens the door. He moves to the next hut. Same layout inside, only two beds rather than three. There are more clothes though. Again, strewn around the room. He picks up several shirts to discover bags full of handmade crafts and wool sweaters under them. Stuff must be from folks in the Andes. Like the shop in Iquitos that sells similar items to tourists since no one in his or her right mind would buy wool anything here in the jungle. A string bag hung on the wall has seed necklaces and piranha teeth mounted on a stick. Again he glances in the bathroom. No backpacks. They must be with them in the large hut.

Darkness falls, and Alberto knows time is running out. He hears someone walking outside the door. Panicking, he turns to the backdoor but then stops. The steps are moving away. He returns to the front door and cracks it open. One of the caretakers has placed kerosene lanterns along the boardwalk's railing to light the now darkened walkway. Alberto slips out and under the boards. Some of the students are returning to their rooms with flashlights in hand. The caretaker rushes to give them lamps for the rooms.

Alberto squats under the second to last hut, unsure what to do. He crawls to one dark corner where he has a pretty good view of which students enter which huts. All are girls so far. He remembers only a few boys at the mine. If the backpack belongs to one of the boys, it will be easier. The two rooms he entered are definitely housing girls. An eerie wind chills his spine, a sign he needs to get out of there. He starts to creep quickly to the next hut when he hears something. He focuses on the sound. A hiss. Yes, a hissing sound. *Ay, Dios,* a hissing sound! He reaches in his back pocket for a small flashlight he always carries in case of an emergency. He shines the light on the ground to his right where he believes the sound was. Nothing. More students' feet pound on the boardwalk above. He turns off his flashlight and waits until the three girls go into the last bungalow.

When they settle and the quiet returns, he hears a sound in the leaves behind him. Slowly, very slowly, he turns the flashlight on in that direction. Something slithers on the leaves. Suddenly a head pops up, a triangular-shaped head. Viper. This is it, he thinks. I am a dead man. Only a miracle can save him. Alberto feels a warm wet flow on his left leg. Must be from a bite. The poisonous venom is now surging up his veins in the leg. But wait. The warm feeling is traveling down his leg, not up. Alberto realizes that he has just urinated on himself. Fear. Total fear. He turns the flashlight to the same spot and sees the body of the snake, thick and long. It is a tree boa whose color and head shape are similar to the fer-de-lance viper. He lets out a huge sigh of relief. Boas are harmless, so he is safe. He looks at his wet pants in disgust. All he wants is to get home. He needs a drink and some peace and quiet to figure out a safe plan to retrieve the tan backpack.

Only the lanterns now glow in the dark. No moon tonight. A few stars in the dark sky twinkle as if someone punched pinholes in a piece of paper with a shining light from behind. They provide enough light for him to run across the clearing in a straight line, directly to the steps that lead to the river. He jumps in his boat, pushes off with the paddle, and drifts with the current downriver about a half kilometer before starting the motor. Sounds carry far across the jungle, especially at night. Better make sure no one at the lodge hears his getaway.

11

RIVER CREATURES

Thousands of leafcutter ants live in a colony for ten to fifteen years. Divided into castes—gardeners, foragers, riders, soldiers and queens—they mirror the way most humans in the world are born into their stations. Everyone works for the queens. The soldiers patrol the gardens. They have evolved with large, scary mandibles to defend the colony from attacking army ants. Rey explains, "Ants dig huge deep nests in the ground. The foragers bring leaves and spread them around the opening of the nest. The gardeners compost the leaves, so the ants can eat the mulch. Inside the mulch is the nutritious fungus they need to grow."

"They are so cool looking," Claudine remarks. "The way they carry leaves bigger than their bodies on top of their heads like umbrellas."

"Yeah. And look how long the trail is, each one following behind the other." John jumps off the boardwalk and walks approximately twenty meters on top of the riverbank, following the trail of the leafcutter ants. The ants walk single file at a quick pace. "The trail keeps going," John motions further upriver.

Rey continues to give more information on the hundreds of species of ants in this region and their important role in the ecosystem. It's early in the morning. The rising sun over calm waters and wisps of clouds cast an earthy glow. The students descend the steps to the boats to visit Santa Clara. A friend of Rey's father built a fish and caiman farm. In the quiet, motionless morning, the sound of a piqué pique motor in the river behind them catches some of the students' attention.

Julie is the first to notice. "How odd. Look over there." She nudges Mike's arm. "Never seen a man so dressed up in a piqué pique before."

"Yeah, I didn't know they have ties here." They laugh together.

The boats' motors start and the students chat. This has been one of Elizabeth's most talkative groups that she has brought to the Amazon.

The ride is only ten minutes or so. Santa Clara is a small village up a tributary near San Jorge. One of the residents served in the Peruvian army for thirty years, earning enough necessary capital to start a new enterprise. He grows paiche, the world's largest freshwater fish, in one manmade pond and caiman in the other. While it is illegal to sell wild caiman meat, farmed caiman is allowed. Local people love caiman meat. And poachers love their skins. So much that they are on the verge of becoming an endangered species. On the other hand, conservation programs for the paiche have been successful, and their population is steadily rising after years of being endangered. Farmed paiche is encouraged as a way to meet the growing demand of this fish for tourists. Restaurants prefer the large steaks its size provides.

The students walk a windy path that follows the curves of the riverbank to arrive at Don Maleche's farm. A large round circle of jungle has been cleared, providing space for the two ponds, the large grassy borders around them, and a small concrete house. An outdoor cooking patio topped with a thatched roof for shade from the hot sun and for protection from the hard rains sits a few meters from the house. A red macaw greets the students with several screeches as they enter the farm. Instantly, cameras appear. Each student takes turns standing beside the beautiful bird for a photo op.

Don Maleche, a short, muscular man, shakes Elizabeth's hand. For Rey, a hug is custom. They chat in Spanish for a few minutes as the students finish shooting the bird.

The group walks on the path to the caiman pond first to watch Don Maleche feed the prehistoric creatures. The caimans eat twice daily, after sunset and just before sunrise, being nocturnal by nature. That day, Don Maleche waited to give them breakfast until the students' arrival. He laughs. "They're sure to be ornery this morning, being real hungry." Don Maleche grows the more docile of the two types of caiman in the Amazon but still both types command respect.

At first the students do not see any caimans in the pond. Elizabeth tells them to look closer at the water. Pairs of little beady eyes hover just above the waterline. Don Maleche grabs a large chunk of fish and throws it over the fence to the edge of the pond. Loud splashes ensue as several three- to four-feet caiman go for breakfast. More chunks are thrown, more caiman surface. About a dozen in all. They snap their large, ferocious jaws at each other competing for the food. One of Maleche's sons arrives, carrying two buckets full of big gray patties.

"It takes a lot of food to grow caiman. I use some of my paiche mixed with these patties made of ground-up fish parts," the farmer explains.

After eating, the caiman rest in the sun for their morning nap. The group crosses over a little bridge to the other path. It ends in a small kiosk built on the pond. Another son arrives again with two more buckets. Don Maleche grabs a bamboo pole left on the floor of the kiosk and stirs the top of the water in a circle. He throws a piece of fish in the middle of the swirl. A wide mouth gobbles it as soon as it hits the surface. The water begins to stir around the entire kiosk, making it sway. Don Maleche motions to the students to feed the fish. The more fish and patties that are thrown, the closer and more aggressive the paiche are. Enormous heads with giant mouths and thick long bodies.

"For sure, that is the biggest fish I've ever seen," says Ed. "And I've caught some big boys back home."

Rachel squeals when a paiche jumps at her hand she inattentively dangled over the water.

"Careful," Elizabeth warns.

Each student throws a couple chunks of fish but only a few of them stay interested and continue feeding. The others pose for pictures. The farm is beautiful. Flowering bushes border the property. Large camu camu and other fruit trees give shade to the paiche pond.

"Most people assume fish don't eat fruit," Rey explains. "But dozens of Amazon fish do. Fruit is the mainstay of their diets. During the high-water season, the Amazon floods over a one hundred thousand square kilometers of riverside jungle. The fish swim in the forests, eating fallen fruit and snatching fresh ones from low hanging branches. I bet you didn't know that we even have vegetarian piranhas!"

The students laugh. One asks, "Do these big fish eat fruit?" She points to the trees.

"Yes, paiche are fruit eaters. It is an important part of their diet, which is why Don Maleche planted all those trees around the pond. You know when we talked about problems villagers face today like declining fish yields due to logging? I forgot to mention this connection. Loggers cut indiscriminately, taking trees of all types to open large swaths of land to extract the big mahogany and teak trees. The result, less and less fruit. No fruit, no more fish. Many of the communities are now planting fruit trees along the river and in flood areas. Folks from Pro-Naturaleza promoted this idea. Most people agree it is a good idea. Women bury fruit seeds, pits along with peelings, fish bones and other organic waste from meals just under the ground's surface to grow more trees. So far, we have a lot of young saplings sprouting all over this region."

While the students learn more about life in the Amazon, there is some commotion on the other side of the village. Upon arrival at Santa Clara, some of the students left their backpacks on the boat, knowing that the boat drivers always watch their things. Theft is rare, almost nonexistent, in Amazon villages, but as more tourists arrive with all their clever devices, the locals fear someone may get tempted. The boat drivers secured the boats after the students departed to visit the farm then walked over to a small hut on the right, closest to the river's edge. The brothers' cousin, Pepe, lives in the house. Most folks in Santa Clara have a few relatives from San Jorge. They catch Pepe before he leaves to tend to his fields.

Pepe pours some fresh *masato* his wife made yesterday from freshly harvested yucca. Jairo's brother lies in a hammock and quickly nods off. Soft snores radiate from the swaying hammock. Pepe and Jairo exchange local news, make a few jokes. They notice a man in a suit and tie approaching slowly toward the village, but as he putts past, they pay him no more attention.

Alberto knows that anybody still in the village can easily see him motoring up the stream, but he desperate to get that tan backpack. He assumed it would be easy. He assumed wrong. He spots the two boats from the San Jorge lodge and decides to motor past them and the village. He cuts the motor, reaches for a paddle to guide the drifting boat back to the other boats. At least it is quiet. He sees no villagers and figures that everyone is off, working in the yucca and banana fields. He glides his boat next to one of the lodge's boats and grasps its side. No one is in it or the other one. Good. He can barely see some backpacks tucked under the seats. Even better. Without making a sound he crawls into the first boat. On his hands and knees in his good suit no less, a thought that infuriates him, he starts searching for the tan bag. Damn. Not here. He pauses to listen for voices before he lifts his head. No one in sight. He rises and grabs the side of the second boat and pulls it closer. The boats clink on contact.

"Jairo, what's that guy doing in your boat?" Pepe asks.

Without answering, Jairo jumps up, flies out the door, down the steps, over some logs on the riverbank and leaps into his boat. He seizes the fancy dressed man as he turns in surprise.

"Put down that bag," shouts Jairo. By now, Jairo's brother is running out of the hut to be by his side. Alberto stutters. Holding the tan backpack, Ed's backpack, in his hand he believes that he can smell the diamonds. They are so close. Alberto tries to speak. No words come out of his wide open mouth. Jairo's brother jumps into the boat, grabs the bag, and starts to growl in Alberto's face.

"Calm. Calm. *Tranquilo, hermano.*" Jairo stares deeply into his brother's eyes. The brother releases Alberto's shirt. "Now tell me why you are here and why you're trying to steal from us."

At first Alberto begins rattling off nonsense: "Visitors…the mine…Found something, no, lost something. Security." He stops. Taking a deep breath to quickly come up with an excuse, Alberto explains that he was to meet a tour group, and he thought this was their boat. He wanted to make sure by checking one of the visitors' bags.

Jairo looks at him puzzled. The man is dressed well but something about him makes Jairo doubt him. A compassionate person at heart, Jairo decides to let him go. "Go on. Get out of here. Don't let me find you sneaking around here again."

Alberto doesn't need to be told twice. He jumps to the first boat but one leg falls short and is drenched, the water soaking his pants and shoe. He stumbles across the boat and more carefully gets in his piqué pique. As he motors to the big river, he can't believe how close he was to the diamonds. So close, so close, he moans. This can't be happening. He turns right to go upstream to the mine. He is late for work. Time is running out. He thought that he could grab the diamonds and flee today. Leave Juan in the dust. He didn't care if he squealed. He realizes now how imprudent and stupid he was this morning. Greed possessed him. He knows that the students will be here for a few more days. He found that out from Manuel, the guide at the mine after the students' tour. His head feels like it will explode. He needs quiet. Just get to the office. He'll explain that he had an accident which is why he is late. The wet pants and shoe will help. Quiet. Quiet. He needs to figure out a smart plan and make sure Juan doesn't say or do something stupid. "You can do this, Alberto."

* * *

After lunch, the students have free time to work on their research papers. They sit in the big room in the communal hut talking, writing, listening to music, and staring outside. Rey shows Alison a book on the region's aquatic creatures. Glossy photos of the Amazon manatee, pink and gray dolphins, two types of caimans, the giant South American river turtle, dragonfish, and a variety of other reptiles and amphibians grace the pages. Alison wants to be a vet and has decided to raise funds for Monkey Island as her project for the Applied Anthropology course.

Seven days ago, the students visited Monkey Island. Elizabeth explained that a Peruvian of Italian descent started the refuge for recaptured monkeys destined for the black market. Inspectors find the poor animals in Iquitos ports and at the airport. Most are pre-adults, so releasing them into the jungle alone without a family is the same as killing them. Now they can go to Monkey Island where they integrate into troupes.

As the boat approached the island, a couple of monkeys amazed the group by running down the riverbank to greet them. As soon as the boats got close enough, the monkeys jumped onboard and welcomed everyone. They leaped from one lap to another. Squeals of delight were heard all around.

Two huts sat side by side with a boardwalk connecting them. One is home to Paolo and his family; the other a welcome center for visitors. The smell of cooking fish wafted from the kitchen. Monkeys swung in trees and scooted on the ground as curious of the students as they were of them. The students climbed up the stairs into the center and sat on one of three long wooden benches. They faced a map of the region of Loreto, posters defining species of monkeys, and a chalkboard. Donations from a Swedish NGO allowed Paolo to build a modern restroom for tourists last year. Paolo explained the plight of the monkeys, ending the talk with words of encouragement of how we can make a difference. How to change the dreaded scenario of death and extinction.

Alison decided right then, she needed to help in some way. And if the inspired speech wasn't enough, what followed, playing with the monkeys, sealed it. Spider, capuchin, tamarin, woolly monkeys and titi monkeys ran among the students, grabbing hands and climbing up their legs and into their arms. Pascua, a little spider monkey, nestled on Alison's shoulders, wrapping her tail around Alison's neck to settle in for a nap. She felt her little heart beat and heard her soft breath purr. Alison had never felt so much joy. "Miracles, these creatures," she whispered. The entire group grinned ear to ear on the boat ride back to the lodge that day.

Rey promised to bring Alison his mammal book, which has a large section on monkeys, after they finish discussing the aquatic species. They turn the page to see photos of the famous pink dolphins jumping out of the mighty Amazon River. Rey explains, "One wouldn't expect to find dolphins, a saltwater creature, in a freshwater river. Yet both the gray and the pink dolphins were trapped inland as the continent rose and they adapted to the changing environment. The pink dolphins first grabbed the attention of modern biologists because of their unusual color. Rrreally, rrreally pink," Rey exaggerates the rolling Spanish *r* as all Amazon guides do to the delight of their tourists. Explaining studies of their evolution fascinates even the most aloof visitor.

After dinner, Rey agreed to share more Amazon legends, although he dislikes calling them that. He tells the students that they are real, truer than what the word legend implies. He begins with an example that seems like fantasy but has happened too many times to not be true. "Almost everyone knows of women who are seduced by pink dolphins and disappear." Rey stops.

"But let me start at the beginning. Pink dolphins are respected by people for the highly intelligent creatures they are and for their ability to transform into human when they touch land in shallow waters. They look totally human except for their blowhole on the top of the head, so they always wear a cap or hat. Beautiful beings. Very seductive. They come on land to find a human mate and prefer visiting when a village hosts a fiesta, so they can see all the young women at once and decide."

"Wait a minute," interrupts Ed. "What do you mean a human mate? Two different species can't mate."

"I'll get to that detail in a minute." Rey continues, "So the poor young girl who captures the dolphin's attention has no chance to escape, so skilled the dolphin is in charming her into a trance and luring her to the river. Once in the river, the dolphin changes back and makes her a dolphin too" Rey nods to Ed as if that solves the interspecies mating problem. "Some say that they've run to the river when hearing a woman's scream, but all they find are two pink dolphins swimming side by side. In the morning, the townspeople will realize one of their women is missing, never to come home again."

"So what is this supposed to mean?" Ed smirks. "It cannot be literal. People just don't turn into dolphins here or anywhere."

"Why not? How do you know this doesn't happen?" Sarah snaps back.

Elizabeth interrupts. "Listen. I think we can look at this story from several perspectives. It does contain important safety messages: Don't walk near the river at night. Don't go off with some stranger. Both of which can be dangerous for many reasons. And I also accept that the story is a part of their oral history and as such real whether one chooses to believe it or not. Why not ask some of the people from the village or Juanito or Flores and learn what they think? How about another story, Rey?"

Rey sits quietly for a moment. He is a very jolly fellow, so it is rare to see him so still and contemplative. "Well, I could share what happened to my grandmother's cousin if you want."

"Yes," shout Julie, Anne and Sarah in unison.

"Okay. So my grandma's cousin, Elecio, is quite old now, maybe over a hundred. He lives alone deep in the jungle. Most people say he lost his mind because of losing his true love, Carmelita. He met her when he was in his late twenties. He started fishing in a new black water lake that was created from the previous high-water season. The first day Elecio fished when he drew in his net, he saw the most beautiful face with long golden brown hair just below the surface of the water. He thought that he must be hallucinating from too much sun. But the next day, he went back to the same spot, and she was there again. And the next day again. And the next again."

"The fourth night, Elecio dreamed of the same woman who told him to have no fear of her just because she was a mermaid. From that night forth they spoke in dreams at night and stared at each other during the days. A year passed. They fell deeply in love.

Wanting to be together desperately, Carmelita decided to live with him on dry land in human form but on one condition. Her beauty was so overwhelming to humans that he must first leave his village and build them a home deep in the jungle away from everyone. If another man was to see her, that man would kill Elecio to steal her for his own. And she could not bear to have that happen. Elecio agreed. The couple lived happily for many, many years. Elecio would farm yucca. Carmelita would fish. When she entered the river, she would become a mermaid again so they always had lots of fish to eat."

"One day, Carmelita spotted a group of hunters. She hid but not before one of the men saw her. She knew that he would return to kill her beloved Elecio. She decided to prevent that. She held Elecio in her arms and whispered in his ear that she will always be with him in their dreams but she must now return to the river so he can live. She could not let her soul mate die, you see, so powerful was their love. Elecio argued no, but Carmelita jumped in the river. Elecio jumped in after her, calling her name, 'Carmelita. Carmelita. *Te quiero. Te quiero.* I love you. I love you.' But it was no use. She was gone physically forever. Yet they still reunite each night in their dreams. And while most people say that he is crazy, my grandmother says he lives in the night world rather than the day one."

"What? I don't understand," asks Julie.

"Well, shamans say that we have two worlds. The one we are experiencing right now, the day world, and the other we call dreams. Only dreams aren't dreams. They are our real life, one that is connecting us to all lives through our cellular memories to the beginning of time. The day world is superficial. We live both but choose to prioritize one over the other," Rey answers.

The students are quiet once again, trying to grasp Rey's words to write the stories in their journals.

12

OSCAR

Alberto's afternoon at the mine is uneventful. He does his routine, hoping to clear his mind. He knows that the students will leave soon, returning to Iquitos where they have reservations in the Victoria Hotel for two nights. Glad he ran into his friend Oscar who gave him this information a couple evenings ago. He can't risk returning to the lodge again. The two brothers who drive the lodge's boats would recognize him. He needs to be inconspicuous. No trouble. He'll have to retrieve the bag in Iquitos. Maybe he could cut Oscar in. Surely he would open the students' rooms one evening for a chance to make a ton of money. He wonders how to approach him.

Alberto stands from his desk to take some reports to the security office and passes Juan in the hallway. Juan gives him a "what's up" look. Alberto pauses but thinks better not to stop with the cameras recording their every move. He motions with his eyes toward the cameras. Both continue walking in opposite directions. At least Juan has sense enough to be quiet, Alberto realizes. But what about

Oscar? Would he turn him in? The mine's owners will certainly offer a reward for information once they discover missing diamonds.

Alberto's original plan to recover the diamonds right away and keep working at the mine until he could contact the Lizard, a man whose reputation with black market dealings is unsurpassed, is looking impossible now. He must recoup the diamonds in Iquitos and plan to leave for good. The easiest way would be to break in the American students' hotel rooms. He'll pay his friend Oscar a visit tonight. Feel him out to see if he will help. If a no-go, then he'll have to think of something. Surely Oscar will play.

The afternoon bell sounds. It's five o'clock. Change of shift. His contract says he is to work until five but rarely does he leave work until a few hours later. Not tonight. He needs to catch Oscar before he goes to work at the hotel at eight o'clock. He puts the last reports in a folder, places them in his top drawer, and locks it. He snatches his raincoat and cotton tote bag, he never has bought a briefcase like a manager should have, and heads to security. He passes Raoul near the exit.

"Everything okay on the back wall?" he asks quietly.

"Yeah. Power is fine so far." Raoul is about to say something else, but Alberto takes long strides and arrives at the exit room. He passes through security and, finally, is outside. Hopefully, he can get to his boat without any interruptions. Once on the riverbank, he scans a spacious view around the mighty river. The sun creates warm colors across the sky. A soft breeze creates a few ripples on the river. There is no one in sight. As he tosses his bag into the boat, Alberto is startled by a voice.

"Where are you going so early?"

Alberto turns to see Juan tucked between two boats seated on a log.

"What are you doing here?" growls Alberto.

"Hey, my shift is over. I thought I'd ride home with you. Give us time alone. Time for you to tell me what the heck is going on. And when do I get my money? How?" Juan blusters.

"Ssshhh. Come on. Quickly, before someone sees us. Let's get out of here."

Juan pushes the boat off from the shore while Alberto starts the motor. Soon they are putting some distance between them and the mine. Shouting over the noise of the motor, Alberto begins his attempt to reassure Juan.

"Listen. Yesterday at sunset, I tried to get the backpack. I found out which lodge they are staying at." He tells Juan the whole story and then what happened this morning.

Juan doesn't say anything for a while. To Alberto's surprise, he asks the most logical question next.

"So what is our next move?"

"Well, I can't go back to the lodge," Alberto replies.

"I can."

"Nah, everything is so open, and those kids running all over, very unpredictable. If I couldn't do it, there's no way you can. You have to think on your feet. As I was going to say, I have a contact in Iquitos at the hotel where they will stay two more nights. I'm going to see him tonight."

Juan wants to reply to Alberto's latest insult but decides to say instead, "I'll come with you to see this friend."

"No, not a good idea. I need to hint around to see how open he is to committing a crime."

"Jesus, did you have to say crime? I thought this was justice under the radar as you said. A few little stones that no one will even notice are missing."

"Whatever. Listen, we both have to show up at work and be cool. Act normal. Do our work. I'll see you in the cafeteria tomorrow and will let you know how it goes tonight."

"All right. Just know that I'm keeping my eyes on you." Juan looks sternly into Alberto's eyes. Alberto is taken by surprise how brazen the meek janitor has become. He's taken to the dark side like a bee on nectar.

The sun falls low in the sky. The air cools as they approach Iquitos. They disembark and head in the direction of their respective homes.

* * *

Known for his warmth and humor, Oscar is actually native-born unlike most people in the city. Iquitos population has quadrupled in the twenty-first century. Oscar has never spent time in the jungle nor does he plan to. About ten years older than Alberto, Oscar struggled to get through the university, having to support his family at the same time. He remembers how Alberto was so at ease in school, chatting with the professors, always the right answers. You can't begrudge a man for being smart, but still, there is something about Alberto that doesn't seem quite right to Oscar.

Ana Maria fixes her family's dinner and gathers the children to the table so her husband won't be late for work. They hold hands and give thanks for the food, a ritual every evening. Oscar and Ana Maria may live modestly, but they feel blessed to have come so far. And all four children healthy. Nothing is more important than that. Oscar asks the children if they have done their homework. He was answered by a united, "Aw, Dad."

"First thing after supper." Oscar hears Ana Maria clear her throat. "That is after you help your mom with the dishes."

His youngest son whines, "But that's for girls."

"We will have none of that in this household, young man. Your mother works hard at the Wang store all day on her feet. Then comes home and makes this wonderful meal for us." He grabs the piranha jaw from his plate and snaps it at his son. They all giggle. "Everyone pitches in no matter what the task."

Oscar glances at the clock. He has plenty of time to get to the hotel before eight o'clock. A nice walk rather than the bouncing, loud mototaxi ride. He kisses his kids' heads, his wife's lips, and throws his jacket over his shoulder.

The streets of Iquitos were once smoothly paved with unbroken sidewalks bordering them. Now one must watch every step as the roots of the trees lining the streets have uplifted large chunks of concrete. Potholes cut the avenues like a tic-tac-toe board, making the mototaxi drivers swerve and dodge. It feels like a challenging videogame just crossing corner to corner.

A couple blocks from the hotel, Oscar sees Alberto standing on the corner. Alberto is one person you can't miss. He's the only guy in Iquitos that tall except for some of the foreign white-skinned tourists.

"Hey, Oscar. Can't believe I've seen you twice in one week." Alberto smiles.

"Yeah, kind of odd since before now it has been months since we have spoken." Oscar doesn't have a good feeling. He checks his watch. A quarter till.

"Well, I'm glad to see you now. Wish we could have a drink. But I guess you are on your way to work."

"Yes, guess I am."

"Those gringas coming tomorrow night. Busy, I bet."

Oscar now understands. Alberto probably wants him to hook him up with one of them. They are much too young. Oscar blames himself for mentioning the hotel's guests the other night. Unprofessional. He learned that in his business ethics course. He needs to get to work. He stammers, "Gotta go" and tries to continue walking, but Alberto grabs his arm. Alberto starts to ask a question as Oscar blurts, "Listen. I am not going to get you a date or introduce you or anything. You are way older than them. Besides, you know that a hotel manager can't and shouldn't do that. It's wrong."

Oh, that word. "Wrong." It reverberates in Alberto's head, Wrong, wrong, wrong. Alberto realizes that there is no chance of Oscar helping him. If he thinks helping a guy get with a young girl is wrong, there is no way in hell he will cooperate in grand larceny. But he has four kids. They won't starve on a night manager's salary, but they certainly won't have any extras in life, not like the kind one hundred thousand soles can buy. About $30,000 is what Alberto had planned to offer, but now he is unsure of his next move. He sees that Oscar has walked halfway to the hotel while he was thinking. Another blunder. At least he didn't ask him outright and let him know about the diamonds. Alberto strolls across the street to the Jaguar Bar. Lights flash around a large wooden jaguar mask by the door. Its huge canines' white paint is chipped. Someone has drawn a Charlie Chaplin moustache where the whiskers once were.

"A Cristal." Alberto orders his favorite Peruvian beer.

The bartender opens a bottle, "Lousy day?"

"Does it show that much?" Alberto replies, chugging half the liquid in the bottle in one swallow. Now what he asks. A new plan. Seems like every hour calls for a new plan. He finishes the beer and drops some soles on the bar. Maybe some sleep will help. He heads home.

13

LOCAL ENTERPRISES

Amazonian peoples are known for their ability to overcome all types of disasters, mainly environmental ones but problems in economic realm as well. However, lacking basic modern infrastructure and capital, small enterprises tend to come and go as quickly as the ideas and people to create them. The last few decades have encompassed a new dimension to the initiatives—the overseas connection. Whether for profit, not-for-profit, or nonprofit ventures, many more foreigners are working in the Amazon. The new endeavors coupled with eco-tourism may make Iquitos an international hub again soon, similar to rubber boom times.

The students take a final outing to a small town up the creek further west of Santa Clara on their last full day in the Peruvian Amazon. A year ago, one of the guests at the San Jorge lodge, a Frenchman named Maurice Beaumont went berserk when he saw the size of the snails women of San Rafael village harvested along the creek's mud beaches. "The size of a baseball," he exclaimed! A joint venture began three months ago upon his return from France. The women in the village collect fresh snails, remove the shells and pack them in airtight containers to send to France where they are transformed from big ugly snail to tantalizing, lip-smacking escargot. It's all in the packaging and marketing. Beaumont is paying a decent price for the snails, and the villagers are grateful to have the income.

The students listen to the leader of the San Rafael snail business. Previously, the women never gathered many snails at one time because, quite frankly, the river creatures are not one of their favorite foods. If you have the right spices and oil, they'll do in a pinch. Beaumont had a hard time explaining to the villagers that, in France, they are a delicacy. People pay a great deal of money to eat them in restaurants. Only one man in the town had ever eaten in a restaurant, so the cultural difference remained not understood. In the end, the women cared little why the French people wanted them, just that they did indeed desire them. The San Rafael women have some cash income for the first time in their lives. The leader smiled as she told the students this last fact.

Two other women pull in one of the large nets in which they keep the collected snails until they have a sufficient quantity to send. A snail is plucked out of the net and passed around, so all the students can touch it. Collen asks about the supply. "How do you know how many to collect and how many to leave so that you'll have more next year?"

The group leader doesn't grasp the question. "The snails always come when the river rises in the winter," she answers.

"No, that's not what I mean. How many do you have to leave so they can reproduce? You know, make baby snails?" Colleen is trying to find out if they believe that there is an endless supply. Again a blank look on the woman's face. Elizabeth nudges Colleen to rephrase the question. She does and gets her answer. Basically, no one has ever thought about the issue of sustainability. The project is new. Snails are plentiful. Colleen is disheartened. Elizabeth tells her not to worry. She doubts they'll go extinct with the current size of the enterprise. She not even sure if it is yet profitable for Beaumont due to shipping costs or how long he will keep it going. Most foreign buyers stay for a few years and then are never seen again.

Lunch is on the river as the students requested, floating serenely along the small tributary, watching an occasional bird fly or a fish jump. They eat the leftover yucca empanadas they made yesterday. They prepared lots of yucca dough, so they ended up with a hundred and twenty-six empanadas, more than this hungry group and the staff at the lodge could eat in one meal. Fresh fruit is passed around—bananas, guavas, oranges, granadilla or passionfruit, and jungle grapes. They have one more stop before they return to the lodge to do the unthinkable. Pack. Pack to go home.

The last village is named 15 de Enero, the 15 of January, the official date of the town's founding. Many communities are named like this in the Amazon. Only a dozen families live in the Cruzista community, People of the Cross. They belong to a Christian faith founded and prophesized by Jose Francisco da Cruz in the 1940s in Brazil. The religion spread into the Peruvian Amazon by the 1960s. Da Cruz opposed much of the Catholic Church's preaching and the fees charged to perform important religious rites. He believed priests should execute baptisms, confirmations, and other services for free. All people should have direct access to God. The Cruzista church has no priests or ministers, only lay leaders. Everyone is invited to speak and share the Word each morning at service. It is similar to Quaker meetings. The men dress in white shirts and black pants, and the women ankle-length blue skirts and yellow blouses. All followers wear a large wooden cross around their necks. Instead of the houses circling a soccer field or school as in most villages, here they flank a small church with an enormous cross at its entrance.

Bob goes to meet Elisa, one of the lay leaders. She is also the women who invented the recipe for *sacha inchi* brittle. Previously, people simply roasted the nut and ate it with a touch of salt. Elisa added sugarcane juice and some spices then cooked it a special way to make it into brittle. Bob paid her to teach the San Jorge cooperative members her method several years ago. Still today, no one can make better brittle than Elisa. She stretches out her arm to shake Bob's hand.

"How are you?" Bob asks. "Your family?"

"Same as last year. Blessed to be alive and hear his Word," Elisa replies. She greets Elizabeth and the students as they arrive up the little hill. In a makeshift shelter to the left sit several young men and women with small objects in front of them.

The students had learned about this unique faith in the Amazon while visiting a more populous Cruzista community earlier in the trip. While Elisa sees the young people as an opportunity to convert, Bob asked her if they could visit to talk about the crafts they make instead of their religion. Not so direct as that, but she got his drift. Elisa reluctantly agreed because, being a practical woman, she knew this is also an opportunity to make some cash for her church.

Elizabeth begins explaining about the craft they see before them. "To support the mission of the church, the women and men in the town make things out the *tagua* nut. The nut grows throughout the region and in Ecuador also." She picks up an original nut that is about the size of an apricot. Then she grabs one that has part of the brown skin carved off and hands them both to the students. "This brown skin once removed, which is quite difficult, reveals the pure white nut inside. People call it Amazon ivory so similar its texture and color is to elephant tusks. Only no animal has to die. The Cruzista women carve miniature animals—dolphins, fish, cats, turtles, frogs—out of the nut, often using the brown skin as a contrast on the figurines. In other areas here in Peru and in Ecuador, people make beautiful jewelry—necklaces, bracelets, earrings, and rings, and beads from the tagua—but in this community, the people only adorn themselves with a cross. Jewelry is considered embellishments of the devil. The figurines are amazing pieces of art."

The students divide up and surround the young people slicing. "They don' have any patterns or anything?" asks Anne. "How do they know what to do? They just carve from memory?"

Elizabeth translates the question, and Elisa replies, "We live with God's creations. They are a part of us like he is. They are in our hearts and souls. Our spirits guide our hands." The young people avoid eye contact with the students, but every now and again, Elizabeth sees one of them lifting his or her curious eyes to get a better look at the American students. They are more sheltered here than kids in other communities.

Elisa nods to her daughter, who hands a nut and the razor sharp knife to Sarah. Sarah pushes the knife along the outer coating, but it slides over rather than cuts into the brown skin. "It's super tough. I can't get it," Sarah moans and hands the knife to John. John is very athletic with strong arms, and he proceeds to cut deeply into his finger rather than the nut.

Elizabeth takes a bandage from her pack and wraps John finger while she instructs the students to watch. "I tried a couple years ago with another group of students to carve tagua nuts, but everyone ended up like John. I think it is better just to watch them." The students stay for an hour, enjoy some of Elisa sacha inchi brittle, and buy one of the tagua figurines. Elisa offered them at too low a price. Elizabeth suggested to the students that they pay a little more, knowing the amount of time every piece takes to make. The students agreed. Mutual thanks and hearty hands shakes are given for the demonstrations and the purchases. As the group departs, Elizabeth looks back and sees Elisa smiling happily. They sold almost every sculpture they had prepared for the visit.

On the boat, they head back to the lodge. The gloom on the students' faces is more than Elizabeth can bear, so she has Jairo take a left at the next creek entrance. They ride a few minutes upstream to calm water. She announces swimming time. No one wore their bathing suits but that didn't matter. The students take off their long pants and boots, and jump in the river with a life jacket.

Bob laughs. "I think I know you well enough to know you did this as much for yourself as them."

"You know it," Elizabeth shouts as she leaps off the boat to join the group in the cool, silky water.

* * *

In the evening, everyone is slow to pack. Packing makes it real that you are leaving. They shuffle around their rooms, telling stories, laughing to hide the sadness they are feeling inside. The boys are almost finished when Ed pulls out this weird gecko-looking like thing in a ziplock bag. John asks, "What the heck is that?"

"Caught him outside a couple of days ago. He's dead."

Mike adds, "You know you can't it through customs…either side?"

"Well, I thought I'd just have it in my bag, and if they take it, they take it. The problem is I'm afraid it will get smashed in my suitcase, and I don't want it in the inside of my backpack so where to put it?" Ed is trying to figure it out.

"What about that outside pocket? It long and slender like that reptile."

"Oh yeah. Good idea." As Ed grabs the tan backpack, an eerie scream stretches from the middle of the back boardwalk to their bungalow. Ed drops his bag but keeps the gecko in his hand as the boys run toward a frozen Charlene and Alison. Above their heads a two-meter snake is slithering across the inside of the thatch roof with his head lowered in the air, advancing straight toward them. The girls are trying to be still while totally freaking out.

Ed shouts as he runs by the girls, takes the gecko out of the plastic bag and throws it at the snake's head. He has no idea why he did that. The snake ducks and stares at him directly in the eyes. "Shit." Ed backs up slowly. The snake starts to move higher in the rafter when it changes course and slinks down the pole onto the boardwalk to eat the flattened gecko.

Ed is with the girls who all walk backward gently. The snake plops off the side of the boardwalk and curls up. Rey heard the scream but was in the shower. He arrives and asks what happened. Still shaking, they point to the snake.

"Oh nice, a tree boa. About six feet long. It won't hurt you. Actually, you are lucky. Tree boas are getting rarer to see because they look similar to fer-de-lance, so people end up killing them, which is too bad." Rey walks on to the communal hut.

Even though the rescue story wouldn't be about a poisonous snake attack that would have killed them, Ed gets lots of cheers and praises from everyone. Makes his trip, the hero who tamed the snake with a snack.

* * *

It is a sad sunrise. Today is the departure. After a month of living in the heart of the Amazon jungle, the students remark that they don't want to leave. Several of them vow to return. When they packed their bags, they filled the space that held clothes with crafts. Elizabeth suggested bringing clothes they could donate to the families as a thank you for all the instruction and care they provided. The clothes and accessories are piled high on a picnic table in the dining room. Now they have space in their suitcases for all the beautiful artisan work they purchased throughout the trip.

Villagers arrive and wait in the communal hut. The last suitcases are placed on the boats by Juan and Juanito while the students say their good-byes. Elizabeth addresses the group, thanking each staff member personally for the excellent care and service they bestowed. She made them understand that no five-star hotel could have done better. She turns to the mayor and families, embraces them, and tries to hold back the tears. She keeps it together until she thanks Anita.

Anita and Elizabeth have worked together many years to reach the women's goal—the production of exquisite, top-quality baskets unlike any in the world market. Today the first shipment of palm baskets is ready to export to the US. Anita will finally earn enough cash to take her son to a neurologist in Iquitos to get medicine, or hopefully, some type of relief for his seizures. The other women also have plans for the cash earnings, excited since never before have they had this opportunity. Elizabeth bear-hugs Anita, and they both begin to cry. Parting, so difficult even though they will see each other again next year. God willing.

The students ride in the boat in silence. Elizabeth and Bob sit in the front, quiet also, holding hands. On the second to the last day, the sacha inchi farmers finally got the brittle recipe perfect after many, many attempts. Two hundred bags of brittle sit with the baskets, ready to export. The cooperative members will take them to the Iquitos airport next week, giving Bob time to get home to receive the shipment. It should only take three days via FedEx from Iquitos to the US fair-trade store in Pennsylvania.

It is a beautiful cloudless day. The bounty of the rainforest surrounds them. The group takes in their last view of this amazing paradise, so green, so lush, so alive. Groups of birds overhead sing what now seem like sad farewell songs. Forty minutes later, they arrive in Nauta. Two of the town's men accompanied the group to help with the luggage. A small bus waits, engine running, black soot oozing out of the bus' tailpipe. A shock to the senses from the purity just minutes before.

They travel on the new road connecting Nauta to Iquitos, which was completed the previous year. It took ten years to build a road of sixty kilometers or thirty-six miles. The jungle is quite unhospitable to thoroughfares. You cut a small line through her, and she always tries to reclaim that land, most times with success. Several parts of the highway had to be built then rebuilt. When the road was finally completed, immigrants swarmed to grab lots alongside it, burning the jungle as far back as they could to build and feed a few livestock. Now as far as the eye can see, the land is denuded. Again a shock to the senses. Recently built small huts cover the sides of the road. People hawk jungle products, primarily fruits from plastic chairs lined up in front of the homes. A large field of dried up, withering vines in multiple rows marks a failed sacha inchi plantation.

Outside of Iquitos's city limits sits the new black market animal rescue center run by the state of Loreto's fish and game department. The bus turns left and parks at the building's front door. The students enter the small concrete block structure with a corrugated tin roof. Wood chairs line two walls. Cages with an assortment of snakes, a pair of armadillos, a dozen or so tarantulas, and two baby black caiman are stacked against the back wall.

A recent graduate of the regional university, Carolina introduces herself and explains her academic background. Her degree is in biology with another specialization in conservation. Her passion in life is to prevent the marketing of jungle animals. The center is only two years old, constructed to temporarily house rescued animals until they can be released back into the rainforest as quickly as possible. The biologists care for the animals and give education programs in the local schools across the region. The ultimate goal is to stop the trafficking before it begins. They believe to focus on schoolchildren is the best way to achieve this goal just like Pro-Naturaleza does.

"If our work is successful, then one day, we won't even need this center." Carolina concludes her speech with the students.

The group exits the back door to see the mammals and birds rescued. About a dozen blue macaws and various species of parrots screech in a tall cage. Carolina reports that birds only stay a day or two because it is easier for them to readapt to almost any place in the jungle. She says, "We are in luck today because there is a woolly tapir, a very rare species. No one who works in the center had ever seen one before, and they are struggling to figure out where to release it."

Two three-toed sloths cling to tree branches, asleep, of course. Four types of monkeys swing in large cages. A capybara just gave birth to three offspring who nurse in a pen.

The last cage holds a gorgeous baby ocelot with silky orange fur marked with black spots. She paces back and forth, back and forth, in what seems like a large cage but, obviously, not large enough. The cat cries and moans to be free. Tears well up in the professor's and several students' eyes for the ocelot. Elizabeth loves all animals, but she has special soft spot for cats. The biologist explains that they are not really prepared to care for wild cats. They need vast spaces. Cages are suffocating. And relocating them in the jungle is almost an impossible task. The cats need to go deep in the jungle where hunters can't reach them if they are to survive. Poachers kill the mother, who is too dangerous to capture, and steal the baby cats to sell. The kittens grow quickly but are often ill prepared to survive on their own. Elizabeth wishes she hadn't seen the ocelot because she will never be able to forget its misery—the image of that cat pacing.

The rescue center works with the Pacaya Samiria Reserve's park rangers. As the largest of all Peru's protected areas, the Reserve becomes home to most of the rescued species. Unfortunately, only twenty-two rangers oversee the 20,800 square kilometer area. They are paid by foreign environmental organizations in partnership with the Peruvian Wildlife Conservation Foundation. Many endangered species are making a comeback due to the educational programs that teach locals how to sustainably harvest food and other resources, and most importantly, how to protect the area against poachers and loggers.

"I'm so glad we got to see how they protect the turtle eggs, paiche, and dragonfish to make their populations grow in the reserve," Jane tells Carolina, who speaks English well. Jane plans to go to law school and specialize in environmental protection when she finishes her undergraduate education. "Instead of telling people they can't eat turtle eggs, which they love and need, I agree that it is better to allow them to keep a certain percentage and protect the rest. The people seemed pleased with this arrangement and are more willing to release the babies when they hatch, so they can live and reproduce. We learned that the program has had amazing success in just five years. Would you agree?" Jane is interviewing the biologist as part of her research for her paper on endangered species.

The students' spirits are saddened to see the poor, frightened creatures in the cages. To be stolen from their families so young is heartbreaking. "At least they will be free again one day," Elizabeth tells them to lift their spirits as well as hers. Silently, they shuffle back onto the bus.

14

IQUITOS

A restless night. How could it be any other way? The clock is about to run out. One day left. Tomorrow, the Americans fly to Lima. The day after they are on to Never Neverland, and Alberto will never, never see those diamonds again. He dresses, eats some eggs and toast, and hurries to his boat. He needs to get out of his house. Last night, the walls closed in on him as he racked his brain, trying to figure out how to get the diamonds. All night, he paced back and forth. It was impossible to sleep. His mind raced without any results. If only he had someone to share this with someone whose smarts he can trust. He realizes that he has probably judged Juan unfairly who, up to now, has not screwed up. But he has no time to deal with his prejudices now.

Alberto figures the American group will take a trip from Iquitos to see one or several of the nearby tribes on the smaller tributaries.

Anthropology, the study of people and cultures around the world. He looked up the definition in the dictionary after learning the group's purpose here that horrible evening Alberto humiliated himself under the lodge's boardwalk. He must go to work today to keep his cover. Tomorrow is a holiday, and the mine will be half staffed. He also gets the day off. Good thing. That will give him some flexibility although never once in the two previous years would Alberto even have considered taking a day off except Christmas. Everything is different now. Maybe the fresh air on the river will stimulate his thinking.

Alberto must look at his problem from a different perspective. His favorite professor taught him that. Reevaluate. The problem last night, however, was that a different perspective didn't appear.

The only plan he came up with is to wait until the evening when the students arrive at the hotel, tired from a long day. Then he could run as fast as he can toward the group, grab the bag at full speed before the tall kid enters the hotel door. But that means he'd probably have to knock him to the ground to get the bag off his arm or back. A risky proposition, considering the likelihood that he too would fall. Plus, the young man is part of a group. Surely the others would come to his aid. They would try to stop him. Not goods odds for success.

The river is a little choppy, a strong wind blowing in Alberto's face. His piqué pique bounces along the jungle's edge. He watches as birds flutter above him, trying to find shelter from the gusts. The birds flying remind him of little planes overhead. Planes, airport, kids, a plan starts to materialize. Or rather, the ultimate chance in case he can't get the bag before they leave Iquitos. Fresh air. That's what he needed to get the blood flowing better in the brain. Still Alberto ponders as to what he should do tonight and tomorrow. There must be an opportunity to get close enough to the students to steal the tan backpack. He continues this thought as his finishes his journey to the mine.

Alberto slips his timecard in the slot. He feels humiliated every day he does this. He is a professional, a salaried manager. How dare they make him punch in and out like a common wage earner? He tries to shake his anger away and goes straight to his office, takes the clipboard, and begins his morning inspection. Everything is in order. His extra work last week has paid off. The mine operates like a fine-tuned ship. As he enters hall A, he sees Juan's cleaning cart in the middle of the corridor with Juan mopping behind it. For the first time, Alberto realizes what a good job Juan does keeping everything sparkling clean in a place where dirt normally rules. Juan is about to speak, and Alberto gives a quick shake of the head indicating no. As Alberto passes, he whispers, "Later." He still has no idea how to snatch the bag tonight.

At two o'clock, the bell rings for lunch. The mine's owners built a small cafeteria on site because there are no restaurants or quick shops anywhere in the jungle for workers to get something to eat. One meal is served per shift and consists of rice and fish with fruit or sometimes gelatin as dessert. No variety except for the types of fruit or fish. The owners deduct seven soles from the workers' daily wage to pay for it. Expensive by Amazon standards, yet the men appreciate having a hot meal instead of trying to bring some type of cold, pre-made snack. Most of the miners' families live far away, and they have no one to cook for them. They miss their mountain foods, especially potatoes and any type of meat.

When Alberto enters the cafeteria a half hour later, he sees that Juan has already finished most of his lunch. He is still spooning the last of his gelatin into his mouth. Alberto pours himself a cup of coffee and takes a banana, too nervous to eat a meal. He gobbles the banana in three bites and throws the skin into the trash can. He carries the coffee to the table to add sugar, lots of sugar. He has been living off caffeine and sugar the past couple of days. Juan carries his tray to the woman, who washes the dishes. They smile and exchange a few pleasantries. He ends with, "I'm off to clean the bathrooms," loud enough for Alberto to hear. Juan hopes Alberto will get the message. He is anxious for news.

Alberto sips his coffee, speaks to one of the secretaries, who snickers, and then exits the cafeteria. He walks across the hall to the bathroom. Juan is mopping leaving the two stall doors open, so Alberto can see that they are alone. "Your friend?" he asks.

Alberto sighs. "Unfortunately, he is not going to work out."

"You told him about the diamonds?"

"No, of course not. I tested him to discover if he is the type. And he definitely is not," replies Alberto.

"I don't understand. What test?"

"Forget it. This evening, I will simply follow the students around Iquitos and wait for an opportunity to lift the bag. The kid has to get distracted sometime. If not tonight, then tomorrow."

"Oh, great plan," Juan says sarcastically.

"Don't worry. I have a backup plan for the following morning. Meet me at the Anaconda Café tonight after 9:00 p.m., and we'll finish this conversation. I've got to get back to work, so I can leave early." Alberto washes his hands.

"You always say don't worry, but I am worried."

Alberto doesn't reply, just shrugs his shoulders. He cannot worry about Juan too. Just focus on the students. He wishes for the hundredth time that he knew a pickpocket to get some advice. Never mind wishful thinking. He pushes open the door.

Juan used to think Alberto must be very smart to be a manager. Now he is not so sure.

* * *

Monica and Shala are busy preparing for the students' visit. Shala now has a few photographs of their small home village. She has posted them on a wall with straight pins stuck into the bamboo to hold them in place. A simple village dotted with thatched roof platform houses similar in style as those in San Jorge. The Shipibo are a matriarchal society, which are few in the world. The women make ceramics—cooking pots, large urns, plates, bowls, and animal figurines—and textiles decorated with geometric designs.

"They are the roads to the gods," explains Shala. The students crowd around a large cloth Shala is painting on the floor in one of their two stalls. Two old, large water bottles are cut in half and serve as containers for the mud dyes, one dark black, the other a light brown. Beside her are a pile of metal spokes. She dips the spoke into the dye. With a steady hand, she paints the textile, following the design she has faintly penciled onto the cloth.

"Wow, look how she can paint a perfectly straight line free hand," remarks Anne. John is more curious about the metal spoke that serves as her paintbrush. He motions to his professor.

"Ask her," replies Elizabeth.

"Ah, what is that thing?"

Elizabeth can't help but roll her eyes and translates his question with more specificity. Shala explains that they are the metal pieces inside umbrellas. The dye slides down the metal groove shaped like a U at a constant speed, making it easier to control. In the past, they used quills from large birds, but the advantage of the metal spokes is their strength. Often when pushing the quill along the cloth, it would break midstream and make a mess.

Sarah looks at the big pile of spokes and asks in her uncertain Spanish where they got so many spokes. "*Muchas* umbrellas?"

Shala giggles. Smiling, she points to the professor. Elizabeth winks back. "Four years ago, one of the students was a RA in Smith dormitory. She decided to collect all those broken umbrellas residents throw away during spring semester. Bob and I took them apart and brought the spokes to Shala and Monica the next year. I think we went a little crazy in quantity but at least they won't run out of them for the next several decades." Elizabeth smiles and translates what she said in Spanish so Shala understands.

Shala picks up the spokes, "Gooood, goooood." It is the first time Elizabeth has ever heard her say a word in English. Everyone claps.

While Elizabeth and the students learn about Shipibo art, Monica pulls Bob outside the bamboo stall to talk about their current dire financial situation caused by Mr. Wang's usurpation. She explains to Bob that sales have fallen steadily this year as tourists buy Wang's machine-made imitations. Not sending money to their family isn't as problematic as their impending ejection from the artisan market. That is scaring them to death. Bob asks Monica if she can come by the hotel later in the evening, so Lizzie can join in the conversation, and together, they can make a plan. "Don't worry, Monica. We'll figure out something. Right now focus on sales. I think those young ladies over there are searching for pants that fit," Bob advises.

The female students are going crazy over the cotton pants. A simple drawstring at the waist does make sizing easier. Beautiful Shipibo snakelike designs flow down the legs. The guys try on some shirts. Monica made sure to bring all the clothing they have finished. Often they leave a pile in the apartment to hawk at night since the apartment is located between the main square and the market. Carrying around a pile of clothes is arduous, even though both women are quite strong.

They learned from past years that they didn't bring enough variety to the market stalls to show the students. A mistake that resulted in reduced sales and left several students shoppers disappointed. Monica spent the last two nights hemming more pants until the wee hours. If she doesn't find a solution to their current money problems, she may have no choice but to return to live in her native village, a move that makes her anxious to just consider.

Ed comes strolling back from another stall. Grinning ear to ear, he carries a large caiman head mounted on a board.

"Ed, you didn't buy that, did you?" Elizabeth asks.

"Nah. That guy asked me to show it to everyone. He's got an even larger one and a bunch of other wild stuff. An anaconda skin longer than me!"

"I think that man hopes, by you taking it, you're going to buy it. You probably should go and return it." Elizabeth hates the moments when she must take the childlike joy away from a student for his or her own benefit. Part of the professor job.

Ed slinks to the man's stall. He didn't get the attention he desired from the group. Sometimes he thinks Dr. Long is too protective or something. No fun. He holds the caiman head out to the man. The man doesn't take it back right away to make sure Ed won't keep it. Slowly he gathers the head from Ed. A basket full of caiman teeth catch's Ed's eye. Cool. And only three soles, a dollar. He purchases the biggest tooth. The man smiles. It may have not been a big sale like the head would have been, but at least the kid bought something. Maybe he has *buena mano,* meaning the buyer will bring good luck for sales that day. It is associated with the first sale of the day. Kind of late in the afternoon for a first sale, the vendor laments. Only a couple of tourists all day until this group showed up. And they only seem interested in Shala and Monica's stuff, the vendor notices.

* * *

"We have enough money to make it home. Barely. I told you, sister, the European River Cruises are better than going to some god-forsaken third-world county." Helen folds the last of her clothes to pack in her suitcase. One small suitcase, neat and tidy, sits at the end of her bed. On the other bed, wadded up clothes sit in a pile. Baskets, a coconut mask, carved tagua nut figures, seed necklaces, and who

186

knows what else are stuffed in the small case, leaving little room for the clothes. Edith shoves everything inside and resorts to sitting on the top of the suitcase to get it closed. Helen can't help but smile. Her little sister Edith has had a trip of a lifetime.

Edith can't quite understand her sister either. The Amazon, one of the world's last great marvels. She has been full of wonder since the day her foot touched the ground stepping from the airplane. She loves Helen dearly but wishes she could relax, let go sometimes. Her sister has been on guard forever. She smiles at her and replies to her comment with a simple, "Yes, dear." She learned decades ago to never argue with Helen. No point in it. Helen will stick to her opinion like gum on a shoe, a characteristic shared by many people it seems these days, Edith surmises.

"They said we will arrive in Iquitos sometime in the evening. How's that for accuracy? And will drive us to our hotel. We have a day to rest with air conditioning. I can't believe the cruise personnel equated ceiling fans to air conditioners. Really now. You know maybe I can change our tickets to leave for London from Lima to a few days earlier."

"What? Why can't we stay in Lima for a few days as planned? You know how I want to see the city. The Spanish capital of the New World. Lima's gastronomy is ranked one of the best in the world. Many interesting seafood dishes—seafood we've never even heard of before." Edith rarely gets angry but she is perturbed that her sister could suggest leaving early.

"I understand, sister dear, but how do you intend to pay for those marvelous dishes?"

Money, Edith sighs. Always the problem. Money. The hum of the cruise ship's engine sputters and dies. An eerie moment of silence, followed by a long shrill. Finally a "kurplunk" sound and again silence.

The sisters hear feet running on the wood planks of the ship's floor. Down the stairs. *Splash, splash.* Two crew members jump off the stern into the river with no tanks, just underwear and machetes. The propellers must be tangled in some vegetation. The men can hold their breath underwater for ten minutes or more like the shell divers in the Philippines, giving them enough time to cut the vines or branches. Normally a quick fix. This time, however, the problem seems to be more difficult. The crewmen surface several times, yelling to their mates to get or do something.

Helen doesn't have a strong Spanish vocabulary of mechanical terms. Moreover, fluency in Spanish doesn't help when people use local, indigenous words to describe things, much to Helen's annoyance. She prides herself on being trilingual, completely fluent in Spanish, French, and of course English. Yet this trip has exposed her for the first time to colonial expressions of the mother tongues. As she has repeated to several other passengers, she is used to "proper" French and Spanish.

Native tongues don't die a complete death. Isolated words, mostly nouns, or sometimes phrases, are injected into the colonial language, producing regional varieties of Spanish, French, and Portuguese. Helen had taught this fact to her students in the classroom but had failed to grasp what that meant in practice. Now she knows. An hour passes, and the ship still sits anchored. Edith left the stateroom to stare at the jungle again. As if the scenery has changed at all Helen snorts. She loves her baby sister, grateful to have had her in her life all these years, but she will never totally understand her, especially her lack of any kind of protective instinct. Helen worries what will happen to Edith if she dies first. She somehow can't let that happen. Edith is no survivor.

Helen finds her sister in a large chair made from vines with brightly flowered cushions. Edith fans her face with the *chambira* palm fan that she watched a woman make during the artisan cooperative visit. She is humming a Roy Orbison song. Helen starts to make a wisecrack at the engine repair scenario but looks at her sister's tranquility and quietly takes the chair next to her. Ponytail man's cabin door opens. He and Doris, a widow of five years, appear. Looks like cupid's arrow may have struck her in the heart. Doris is glowing. Her arm is wrapped tightly around his with her hand on top, caressing his fingers. So entwined and in their own world, the two don't notice the sisters for a few moments. "Oh, hello." Doris grins. "Herman and I were just going to see why the boat has stopped."

Helen says under her breath but loud enough for Edith to hear, "The boat stopped well over an hour ago, could be two." Edith motions to Helen to button it and replies, "We don't know. Several men are in the river. I don't mind. I just love looking at the rainforest. I'm sad the trip is ending." The couple nod and continue walking toward the stern.

The sun lowers nearer to the horizon, layering yellow, orange, red and blue stripes across the sky. Helen worries about arriving in Iquitos after dark. Edith utters "aha," "yes," and "uh-hum" at appropriate times so her sister thinks that she is listening to her. In reality, her mind couldn't be farther away. She is daydreaming about the pink dolphin city under the mighty Amazon, a wonderful story Jose Antonio told them last night. If she saw a pink dolphin right this instant, she would jump into the water to join him to live in an underwater castle, a perfect end to a long life. Edith still misses Ralph desperately every day. People say time heals all wounds. Well, not hers. The hole in her heart is as big as ever. Ralph would have loved this trip. Together, it would have been heaven. They treasured every moment of traveling, even the difficult ones. Ralph always found a way to see the cup half full in any situation.

She watches the divers reboard and realizes that the engine is humming again. Sister is happy that we are moving. The ship pulls into the port of Iquitos around 8:00 p.m. Some scattered streetlights illuminate the otherwise dark area in front of the docked ferryboats. The numerous vendors who hawk their goods during the day have all gone home. Two small buses await the cruise ship's passengers. When she first arrived in the Amazon, Edith was surprised to find buses made out of wood, but since her voyage, she learned that the Amazon people can make anything and everything out of wood. Trees appear to be plentiful. She must have seen a million of them except near that dreadful mine.

Helen stumbles off the dock, not realizing it is a deep step down. She doesn't fall but drops her travel bag when throwing her arms out for balance. "Darn it. I knew it would be dangerous to arrive in the dark," Helen yells. Edith motions to the bus driver to take her hand so as to not repeat her sister's misstep. Helen tries to brush the mud from her bag. Not an easy task. She takes her handkerchief to wipe her muddy hand and grumbles onto the bus.

The hotel is beautiful. Colorful tropical flowers in large ceramic urns grace every corner of the lobby. The rooms form a square around an open-air patio with a pool and bar on the ground floor. More blossoming plants and flowers adorn the pool area. An instant blast of cool dry air hit the sisters' faces as they enter the lobby. Helen finally smiles.

The sisters check into the modern room, simple but adequate. CNN in English is on the TV. Helen can't wait to take a hot shower in a cool room. Who knew what a luxury hot—not lukewarm—but hot, steamy clean water is. Again she questions the cruise ship's claim of hot showers. "Our customers prefer the water to be a refreshing temperature, not cold but not hot either due to the Amazon climate," the crew member told her when she complained. Henceforth, she would never take a hot bath for granted again. She sees her sister staring out the window in another daze. Helen thought it was just the jungle putting Edith in mesmerizing trances, but now she is not so sure. She worries that Edith's mind will go first.

Edith turns. "I'm hungry."

* * *

The Lizard lifts his sour face. Out flies the forked tongue, zapping the centipede. It curls in his mouth and slides to the stomach. He wretches for the second time. The shaman takes his potent powder and sprinkles it over the vomit. The powder bubbles and shrivels. Is it man or reptile?

The Lizard seeks the help of the black shaman for the second time in his life. The first time resulted in his accumulation of sizeable wealth. The warning to never seek the dangerous magic of the black shamans went unheeded then as it does now. Greed, power, and lust fill his soul. Only these emotions allow him to survive in the black market business.

A vision repeated in his dreams for many nights of vast riches in Iquitos has brought him to the shaman for answers. He drinks the hallucinogenic brew and transforms to his lizard totem to find the information he desires—to clarify the vision, to find the source. He knows something is brewing in the city that he claims belongs to him. The shaman blows black tobacco on his head, in his face, and along his spine. He chants a cursed song. The lyrics speak of white ghosts, tall white ghosts. The Lizard crawls on all fours, flicking his tongue to taste the air. Small leaves glisten in the trees above like diamonds. Yes, diamonds. The vision starts to become clearer.

* * *

Edith orders her new favorite drink, camu camu juice while Helen orders tea.

"Make sure you boil the water a full three minutes," Helen tells the waiter. "I'll also have the roasted chicken. Crisp. I don't want any uncooked meat. No wonder we are starving. It is after nine o'clock. I guess sticking to a schedule is unheard of here. It's so late to be eating. I thought we would never arrive."

Edith smiles at the waiter, who has patiently waited for the old woman to finish her rant. "I'll have the dorado. Thank you." Edith shakes her head at her sister. "Do you always have to be so cross? These people work hard to please the tourists."

"I can't believe that you ordered fish after eating it on the cruise boat every day," she replies, ignoring her sister request for a little gratitude.

"Yes, I love it. I may eat fish every day for the rest of my life. Oh look, Helen, there are those nice students who we ran into a few times." Waving, Edith motions for them to come over. Two of the students walk across the street to the café. "How was your trip today?"

"It is hard leaving the people of San Jorge. Living with them was the most awesome experience in my life," responds Julie. "I'm so sad that we have to go home."

"Yeah and then stopping at the rescue center made me more depressed," adds Betty.

"Rescue center?" Edith asks.

Betty tells them about the center. How important it is to stop animal trafficking. Like her professor, however, she can't get that beautiful baby ocelot out of her mind. "I don't want it to die although the odds are not in its favor."

"All you can do is have faith, dear. I so understand." The thought of losing a young life, be it cat or human, causes Edith pain. Helen almost makes a joke about it making a lovely fur coat but decides against it.

Julie perks up the conversation. "We also met the most amazing Shipibo women who paint with mud dyes. I had learned about mud cloth in West Africa in one of my anthropology classes, and this was similar, only they don't dye the entire textile in a mud bath. They use the different color muds to draw the designs."

Edith is immediately curious and asks where they saw the women.

"At the artisan market on the main road to the airport. It has a name, but I forgot to write it down."

"Oh, we must stop there, sister, before we leave." Edith says to Helen, who shrugs her shoulders in a noncommittal way.

Julie adds, "You might be able to meet them now. They told us that they always sell clothes in this main square each evening near that yummy ice cream parlor with the native fruit flavors: *aguaje, lucuma, coco*."

"Sounds like a delicious walk after we finish dinner, no, sister?" Edith again gets little response from Helen.

"Julie. Betty." Julie turns her head and hears her girlfriends calling their names. "Oh, sorry. We have to go. We are going to a place to dance. Rey told us about a fun disco by the river. Not disco music. They just use that word to mean a place to dance. I don't want to think how our trip is almost over. We leave for Lima day after tomorrow. Then back to the US."

"Oh really. We are also going to Lima for a spell. Can you recommend a nice hotel that's not expensive but clean and safe? Where do you stay?" asks Edith.

The student who wouldn't touch an insect a month ago and now lets bugs crawl on her hands, Betty, reaches in her backpack and finds her journal. In it she stuck the business card of the hotel in Miraflores, a touristy neighborhood filled with shops, cafes, and bars in Lima. The students spent a few nights in Miraflores upon arriving in Peru before flying to Iquitos. "We stay at Hotel Carmel. The rooms are nice, and the people who work there are great. You get a full breakfast in the morning too. First time I ever drank papaya juice. Sweet but really thick. Our professor says it's good for the stomach. Keeps your digestion working right."

"Don't you need this card?" Edith asks.

"Nah. I'll get another one from the front desk. Bye or, as they say here, adios!"

"Have a wonderful time and hopefully we'll run into each other later. If not, may God bless you and have a safe trip home," remarks Edith. Talking with young people makes her feel younger and brings back so many memories of her youth. She glows. Helen snorts.

Two men enter the cafe and sit directly behind Edith and Helen. Only when the students leave does Helen notice them. The one gentleman is unusually tall for a local yet his features look like folks here. The other man squirms in his chair like he has to go to the bathroom or something.

* * *

"So why haven't you gotten the backpack?" Juan asks Alberto. "I thought you said it would be easy. Just slip the diamonds in the backpack, and you'd get the backpack from the kid. What is going on?"

"Shh, keep your voice down, idiot. I'm trying to listen to their conversation. The tall kid has the tan backpack, and he is sitting at a table behind us with a couple other guys."

Juan turns around to see.

"Stop being so obvious," snaps Alberto who is eavesdropping. He overhears something about bugs. He doesn't understand much but catches two words clearly that he knows, Miraflores and Hotel Carmen. That must be where the students will stay in Lima. Alberto figures that he may need to check it out and make a reservation as a last, last chance. He moans at the thought of not having the backpack before they leave Iquitos. Either way lots to do tomorrow.

Juan voices out loud his train of thought, "I can't believe I carried the diamonds right to the welcome center and no one noticed. All those diamonds. I was sure everyone could hear them jiggling in the waste bin. But I did it. I did good, no? Found the perfect bag. A long deep side pocket. I really can't believe that student hasn't found them. Lucky for us."

"Yes, lucky for us, and yes, you did a great job. Now I'm going to follow them around tomorrow and see if an opportunity arises to grab it. Surely, the kid will set it down somewhere sometime. But if I can't get it, I do have a foolproof plan to get the diamonds out of the backpack without anyone knowing it."

"I want to know the plan. How do we get them from that tall gringo? I think he's even taller than you. And remember, I told you, no funny stuff. So what's the plan?" Juan keeps fidgeting and spitting pumpkin seeds shells on the ground by his chair.

"Don't worry. I got it figured out. As I said, if I can't get them tomorrow, we will then let them carry the diamonds through airport security the next morning. Not that there is much security, but just in case. We'll let them take the risk. They must be on the only early morning flight to Lima. I'm going to book us on the same flight. When we board, I'll put my bag next to the kid's backpack in the overhead compartment and when he falls asleep, I'll get up and pretend that I'm getting something out of my bag, but I'll grab the diamonds out of his. No one will even notice," Alberto says confidently.

"Wait a minute. Since when are we flying to Lima? This is getting out of control. I thought you'd sell them to the Lizard here. Get our money and lay low. You said we need to go to work at the mine as usual until some months pass, so no one would suspect anything is missing or different."

Alberto snaps his head around and looks straight into Juan's eyes. "How do you know about the Lizard?"

"Duh. Who else?" Juan replies sarcastically. "Everyone in Iquitos has heard of the Lizard. No one has seen him, but we all know he exists and controls the black market. I'm not stupid even though you think I am. So this Lima thing, I don't like that plan. For one thing, we'll have to miss work. Second, if we leave town, we will arouse suspicion. And then if they check and discover that some of the diamonds are missing, we'll be the prime suspects." Juan shakes his head back and forth. He doesn't want to leave his hometown. He just wants to be rich in his hometown.

Alberto lights a cigarette. He exhales the smoke up in the air. "As I said, tomorrow I'm going to follow them. Wait for the right opportunity. I've been too hasty before. Patience, observation, that's the key. I'm sure we won't need to go to Lima, but we have to have a failsafe backup. After they land in Lima, we are basically screwed. Now if you don't want to go to Lima, that's fine. I find a way to send you your share after I sell them."

"Oh, sure you will. No, I'm not letting you out of my sight. Book me too. Anyway, with your so-called great plan, how do you know the kid will sleep on the plane?" Juan keeps spitting the broken shell pieces.

"He's a teenager and the flight is at dawn. Of course, he'll sleep. They all will. It will work. Besides, if he doesn't sleep, you can distract him by spilling a drink on him, and I'll grab them then. Would you stop that spitting? "

"How much do you think they are worth?" Juan can't stop fidgeting.

"I told you, you'll get your cut, and you will. Enough to never work again, okay?" Alberto raises his beer. "*Salut.*"

Juan ignores the toast. "No. Tell me now how much they are worth or we're not getting on the plane."

"I figure we can get about a million dollars."

Juan chokes on the seeds he is chewing. "You're serious, a million dollars? I want half not what you offered before. As you said, we are partners. Partners split everything fifty-fifty. Besides, now I have to leave Iquitos for a long while. That wasn't part of the original plan. Half is only fair."

"Yes. Okay, okay. Half. Now be quiet. If anyone else finds out that tall, lanky student is carrying a million dollars' worth of diamonds in his backpack, we're done. So keep a lid on it. We've got to stay calm." Alberto sips his beer. What an idiot this guy is. If he had any idea of their true worth, he'd poop his pants. "You haven't said anything to anyone, right? Nobody, right?"

"No, of course not. What do we do now?" asks Juan.

"We wait. We just sit tight and wait." Alberto lights another cigarette and takes a deep drag. Smoke drifts around the café. An elderly lady coughs.

15

NATIVE PEOPLES

Elizabeth advises the students to refrain from using the air conditioners in the rooms or at least keep them at a reasonable temperature. Last night she had to give Rachel some antibacterial cream for the ankle she scraped on the sidewalk on their return from dinner. The girls' room was as cold as popsicles. A good way to get sick is changing temperatures so dramatically. They will be in the hot sun and humidity again today. Better to stay acclimatized like at the ecolodge. But it is hard to convince some students who are so accustomed to modern conveniences and being instantly comfortable.

Ed almost lost his backpack again. No matter how many times Elizabeth tells them to pay attention to their things. Mike found it in the restaurant. Ed swears he put it next to his chair, but when he stood to leave and reached for it, it was gone, or rather, it had magically moved across the floor from the table to underneath the open window behind him. He still keeps his passport in it even though Elizabeth instructed all of them to keep passports locked in suitcases until they need them at the airport. Anything can happen to your day bag at any time as Elizabeth knows well, having lived through too many experiences with students losing their bags. So innocent are these young people. For example, one of her favorite students left her backpack on a beach towel while she parasailed over the Pacific Ocean and expected it to be there when she returned from the sky.

Thirty days is a long time to be on guard 24/7. By the end of the trip, Elizabeth admits that she does look forward to home. She just has to get the students on the plane to New York to release them to anxiously waiting parents. Her job will be done except for the grading of papers and projects. Normally she finds grading the least enjoyable aspect of professor duties, but not so with her Amazon study-abroad students. The papers bring her great joy. Lots of surprises as to what the students have learned about the Amazon and, more importantly, themselves. They change in that one month, grow and mature in an enlightened way.

Everyone is in the breakfast room by seven. A miracle. Elizabeth knew that most of them went dancing until the wee hours of the morning. Yet no one seems too hung over. Maybe the adrenalin of last day in the jungle has superseded lack of sleep. Bob is in the lobby talking with Rey and Rey's younger brother, Julio. Julio is studying to become a certified guide and is struggling with the English requirement. A guide must be fluent in two foreign languages, not counting Spanish and one's native tongue, to get the AAA certificate. Rey asked Elizabeth yesterday if he could bring him along today, so he can practice with the students.

Elizabeth greets them in English for Julio's benefit. Usually, she and Rey quickly discuss the day ahead in Spanish. She forces Julio to shake her hand and say, "Good morning. Nice to meet you" in his timid voice. She winks at Rey. Maria Patricia arrives with two large boxes filled with avocado, tomato, and cheese sandwiches, jungle grapes, bananas, and several large bags of yucca chips. Two *garafons* with five liters of water in each sit on the lobby floor.

The group will venture up the Nanay River to meet two tribes, the Bora Bora and the Yaguas. Lunch will be served on the boat between the visits. The Nanay River flows into the Amazon and is about a quarter the width of the mighty river. A mix of brown waters runs in the faster-moving main current, and black waters full of tannins hug the sides. Many trees hang over the riverbanks, creating refreshing shade in which to eat. There is not much wind today, so the Nanay should be quite smooth.

"Let's load up," Elizabeth instructs. The students file out the lobby door and climb aboard the wooden bus. Elizabeth grabs Ed by the arm and pulls him aside. Quietly, she asks him if he has left his passport in his suitcase. She worries it may end up in the bottom of the Nanay or something worse.

"Ah yeah. I still don't know what happened last night," starts Ed to repeat his account of last night's event. Elizabeth cuts him off. "Don't think about it. Just focus on today. The port is always very crowded." They are the last two to board the bus.

Iquitos has several ports around the city since several rivers flow into the Amazon at that geographical point. It is probably why the Jesuits selected it for their mission. On one side, the water is some thirty meters deep. The big ferryboats, cruise ships, and military boats dock on that side. On the smaller tributary is the Masusa Port, the main port for the river taxis, piqué piques, and canoes. Most of the indigenous people bring jungle products, primarily fish and fruits, to sell to buyers waiting at the port.

Elizabeth has hired a river taxi for the day. Rey's wife's cousin owns the boat and is happy to be contracted for an entire day for good pay. But first, Elizabeth wants the students to learn about the different foods for sale, raw or cooked, on small wood and charcoal fire grills that line the main avenue from the water's edge to the main square. A worn statue of Francisco Pizarro, the Spanish conqueror, sits in the center of the square.

Rey teaches the group the Amazon names of a variety of fruits, most of which are only found in this region, so there are no name translations in Spanish or any other language. Rey slices open two fruits that the students haven't yet tried because they only grow on the Nanay River. Colleen and Jane smack their lips from the unexpected tart flavor of each. A woman calls Rey's name. Whole fish complete with eyeballs and tails sizzle on her grill. Bob pays for a couple of well-cooked fish for the students to try. Mike and Julie, the most adventurous of the group, each eat an eyeball. "The best part," Rey comments as he rubs his belly.

They walk slowly to the riverbank where the river taxi awaits, tasting a variety of fish, fruits, nuts, and insects. Not everyone wanted to sample the different bugs. "When will you ever in your entire life have an opportunity to eat these?" Elizabeth holds a kabob-like thing with a dozen roasted grubs on the stick. "Your last day in the Amazon, make the most of it. Live, right now in the moment."

The hesitant students finally pull them from the stick and put the grubs in their mouths. Charlene gags but manages to swallow it. "Not bad," Betty says, surprised. "Although I can do without the antenna that is caught in between my teeth." She plucks it out of her mouth, laughing.

The river taxi lands at the entrance to the Bora Bora village where drumbeats welcome the visitors to the village. The Bora Bora are not native to the area. Forty years ago, an Iquitos businessman traveled several hundred kilometers to find an Amazonian tribe who he could bribe to move close to his city. He knew tourists wanted to see "real" Amazonians, meaning scantily-clothed people who still fished and gathered as their ancestors did. Three families followed him to the current location. They performed as he requested but never received all the goods he promised. Now, decades later, they call the Nanay River home.

Back on the boat, Elizabeth explains that the Bora's homes are located a kilometer further in the jungle. The traditional compound was constructed for tourists closer to the river for easier access.

"Yes, Colleen, they wear shorts and T-shirts like everyone else and save their bark cloth skirts for visitors. Bark cloth takes a long time to make, and the Bora do not want to tear it working daily in their yucca fields. Plus, shorts protect one's private parts better. The skirts show tourists how their ancestors dressed. Yuclillate, the wife of the chief, asked me several years ago if I could bring T-shirts instead of money to trade for their seed jewelry. She redistributes the shirts to others. A chief and his family's reputation depend on generosity. I'm happy to recycle T-shirts in great condition from thrift stores to give her. People throw away good stuff in America."

They find a lovely spot downstream where the river wants to create an oxbow lake. Straight, then a sharp curve to the right and back left again. The U-shaped spit of land already has a channel forming cross the part where the spit connects to the main land. The boat parks on the riverbank.

"Trees to the left, male. Trees to the right, female," Elizabeth calls to Rey, who nods and watches everyone get off. On shore, Rey has already made sure any snakes hanging around have moved deeper in the jungle. Lunch is delicious. Somehow food always tastes better outdoors. The students devour the last of the yucca chips, their new favorite food. They plan to buy some in Iquitos to take back to the states.

Elizabeth informs them that they a short shelf life. "The home-made chips don't have preservatives. As you know, people eat pretty much everything fresh here. You can find some canned foods in Iquitos because it is a city. But the rest is fresh. So share them as soon as you can when you get home."

One year, a student took home a packet of fresh chocolate with Brazil nuts. It became rancid and made her sick as a dog when she ate it a couple weeks later. Elizabeth doesn't want a repeat.

The boat putters to the Yagua village located up a very steep bank but still quite close to the river. Yaguas wear below-the-knee skirts made of dried palm fibers hung on a string belt. The children wrap solid red rectangular pieces of cloth as skirts. Some of the younger women use the same cloth to fashion a halter-like top. The younger women in the tribe who have attended school are more conscientious of tourists watching them dance topless. Bead and bone necklaces their mothers wear don't cover enough.

The Yaguas' communal hut is like no other in the jungle. Same building materials—wood posts and thatched palm leaves woven together for roofing material—but the height is astonishing. As tall as a three-story building, the hut's steep conical form holds the cooler night air like natural air-conditioning. Amazingly, at two o'clock in the afternoon, the hottest time of the day, no one is sweating.

The Yaguas gather as another small group of tourists arrive and join them inside the tall hut. The Yaguas sing and sway to the rhythm of the bamboo flutes and small wooden drums. The students watch and listen. The tribe invites everyone to dance together. After the musical performance ends, one of the women tourists opens her backpack and pulls out a bag of hard candy. The children push and shove to crowd around her, grabbing as many pieces as they can. The youngsters normally don't behave like that, but they had never tasted candy until tourists starting bringing it the past few years. And each one wants to make sure he or she gets a piece.

Elizabeth pulls the woman aside. "I know that your intention is good, wanting to give the kids a treat, and obviously, they can't wait to eat the sweets, but what you may not realize is that the children here don't have toothbrushes, dentists, or any type of oral care. Next time you may want to bring pencils and crayons, something the children love also and can really use, but won't rot their teeth."

The woman glares at Elizabeth. "A little candy never hurt anyone. How dare you? Besides look at their smiles. They have great teeth." She turns her back to Elizabeth and walks off in a huff.

Elizabeth didn't mean to offend the woman. She just wanted her to think about the consequences of her action. In communities that now have access to premade sugary things, people are suffering from bad tooth decay. Collen hugs the professor, "You did the right thing." Elizabeth smiles and hugs her back. "Thanks."

Rey calls the students together so that the Yagua elders can teach them how to shoot a blowgun. They put the dart without poison on its tip in a long wood tube. Puffing the checks full of air, the elder blows as hard as he can. The dart flies swiftly to strike a carved wooden bird on top of a post. Everyone takes turns trying to hit the target. Most of the darts soar above or below the bird. After a few tries, several of the students hit the bird dead center. Afterward, the students buy some seed jewelry and miniature blowguns from the Yaguas. They snap hundreds of pictures.

Waving good-bye to the families as they board their river taxi, the students grow sad that this will be the last dance in the Amazon with local peoples. As they start toward Iquitos, Elizabeth remembers a beautiful swimming spot that almost has no current, where she swam a couple of years ago. She directs the driver. A refreshing swim in the silky black waters will lift everyone's spirits. With life jacket in hand, one by one, the students jump off the bow. Soon laughter erupts as all enjoy the cool water. Elizabeth loves to swim. Bob calls her his mermaid. She makes a mental note to plan more swim stops next trip. Everyone is happier in the water.

* * *

Alberto rises at 5:30 a.m. as he does every work day even though today is a holiday. For the first time in two years, he is taking the day off due him. His fear of losing his job is irrelevant now. He is up early so he can spy on the students before they leave for their activities. Today, he can dress like any other to be incognito. He didn't style his hair. He needs to get close but not be noticeable, which is hard to do with his height.

The sun's rays peek through the houses. Alberto locks his door and walks in the direction of the hotel. Sounds and smells waft from the homes. Families prepare for work or school. Not many people on the street yet. The noisy mototaxis are minimal. Two fellows on the corner catch Alberto's eye. Really just one of them stands out. The short guy is nondescript with a T-shirt, sandals, and jeans, but the taller guy wears a beautiful leather jacket, unusual for the Amazon. Alberto continues to the Victoria Hotel. He calls a mototaxi to sit and wait with him. As the wood bus loaded with the students pulls away from the hotel, Alberto follows it.

The port. It's a good opportunity, Alberto thinks. Walking in the crowd, he notices how easy it would be to grab one of the young ladies' bags hanging loosely on a shoulder. They are totally distracted by the sights. Unfortunately, the tall kid is more cautious. His backpack is tightly strapped across his back. Being a head taller than the crowd allows Alberto a good view. He is puzzled again by tourist behavior. He knows that Americans do not eat bugs. What on earth makes them risk it here? he wonders.

The group boards the boat. A man paddles his canoe to the right side, and once alongside, he asks if anyone wants to buy a snake. He holds up a four-foot rainbow boa, a gorgeous snake. *Click. Click. Click.* Cameras again. Rey lets the man know no one is interested. Alberto watches from behind a streetlight post. He realizes that it is no use to follow them on the river. It is too obvious. He walks back to the square, hails a mototaxi, and heads to the bank.

Alberto waits a half hour before his turn with the teller. He has never understood why the bank employees are so slow. They should be more professional. When he exits the bank, he takes a one-hundred-eighty-look around the street. He spots him again, the man in the leather jacket. This can't be a coincidence. The guy looks away when Alberto stares straight at him. Alberto gets a creepy feeling, but there is no time to waste.

With most of his savings tucked under his shirt in a money belt, he hurries to his sister-in-law's cousin's travel agency and enters before leather jacket man turns the corner. The distraction makes Alberto's mind go blank, and he can't remember the cousin's name. Maria something. He needs to make her like him yet remain unmemorable. He doesn't want her associating his trip when the news of the robbery breaks. He tells himself, no matter what, not to mention the mine or his work. Talk about the family is best.

"Hello. Busy?" Since he can't recall her name, he thinks asking a question will cover for his lapse.

"Alberto. What a surprise. Maria Carmen."

"Of course, Maria Carmen. How is your family? Boys growing up tall?"

"Not as tall as you, but they are sprouting. What can I do for you today?"

Alberto explains that he needs two tickets to Lima. She starts typing on her computer keyboard and asks about Juan. Alberto says vaguely, "An associate."

"Oh yes. You must meet some powerful people at the mine, being the boss and all," Maria Carmen responds.

Crap, Alberto thinks. So much for not mentioning the mine. Be humble. "No, not really. It's pretty routine."

Maria Carmen shows Alberto the computer screen. A plan of the airplane's seats is displayed. A large block in red indicates occupied. A few more seats interspersed throughout the plane are red also.

Alberto knows the block must be the students and selects the two seats closest to the block. "Marvelous technology," he murmurs. The printer clicks back and forth across the page. Maria Carmen pulls out two tickets, folds the itinerary and puts both in an envelope.

Alberto pays her in cash, not unusual in the Amazon where credit cards are still few. They exchange a few more pleasantries and bid each other a good day. Before he opens the door, he scans the area from the windows. Realizing that may seem odd, he scurries to the door. "Thanks again," he says as he exits. He doesn't see leather-jacket man in either direction. He lets out a sigh and relaxes. Iquitos is a small town really. Leather-jacket man is probably just a bloke doing some business.

Alberto walks to lunch at his favorite *chifa* restaurant. The Chinese-Peruvian fusion is now becoming world renown. Who knew so many Chinese live throughout the country? Alberto is about to take his first bite when he looks up and sees a grinning Juan across the table. "What are you doing here?" Alberto growls.

"I did it!"

"Did what?"

Juan reaches over to lift a large black plastic garbage bag by his feet.

"Garbage, so what?" asks Alberto.

"Not garbage."

Suddenly the light bulb illuminates. Alberto gets it. My goodness, he got the backpack. "How is it possible?" he mutters to Juan. Juan reaches to pull out the backpack but Alberto stops him. "Go in the bathroom and leave it in the stall. Come back and order some lunch. I must see it. I just can't believe it," Alberto exclaims.

A few minutes pass. Alberto returns to his seat. No garbage bag. No grin. He lifts his fork, and chews several bites. Impatient, Juan stands to retrieve the bag before someone else enters the bathroom.

Alberto taps the top of the table with his index finger to make Juan sit down. "Wrong backpack," he states exhaling a deep breath.

"No way," Juan rebuts.

"The backpack is tan. Yours is yellow. Was the tall boy carrying it?"

"Ah, no. One of the girls had it next to her while sitting on the steps of the main square at the port. I went to get guavas for Mom and saw the group. I thought this is the opportunity you talked about. I casually walked by and picked it up while her back was turned and stuffed it in the trash bag. It was so easy. I couldn't believe it. Then walking home I saw you come in here. I figured it was fate. Boy, this is terrible. Now I'll have to give it back to her."

Startled, Alberto asks, "What? What do you mean you have to return it?"

"Well, it's not the right one, so why keep it? Bad karma."

Alberto can't help but to laugh at the absurdity. "So when did you get so religious?" He pauses. "Actually, you are right about returning it. Otherwise, it will increase vigilance on their stuff if one in the group has been ripped off. We can pay some kid a few soles to carry it inside to the hotel's front desk and leave it." They finish the chifa in silence.

A boy delivers the bag to the hotel and runs out before any questions can be asked. Alberto gives him three soles. The boy skips happily across the street. "I need to go to the internet cafe and book a room at the Hotel Carmen where the students will stay in Lima."

Juan is puzzled. "Why? You said that we'll definitely get the bag on the plane."

"One must always be two steps ahead. Prepare for the worst possible scenario. Meet me tonight same place, same time as last night. We may still have a chance to snatch it when the students dine this evening."

Sitting at the computer, Alberto finds the hotel and other information he needs. His eyes glaze over reading the webpages. His head is heavy. His forehead smacks the monitor. He dozed off for a minute. Lack of sleep is catching up with him. He stands to stretch, glances out the door as another customer opens it. Whoa. There outside is leather-jacket man. Juan's words come back to him. "Everyone knows the Lizard." Could it be him? Not likely, but it could be one of his men sent to follow him. But how would the Lizard know about the diamonds? Only he and Juan know. Juan must have told someone. Damn it. He knew he couldn't trust him to keep his mouth shut. Yet Juan swears he hasn't said a word to anyone. Folks say the Lizard talks with demons and spirits, knows everything that has, is and will happen. Alberto never believed what he considers to be pure nonsense, spirits among us. Yet, could it be true?

* * *

Edith enjoys her sister's improved mood. So far, not one complaint, no negative comments. She must be happy now that they are on their way back home, only a few days to London. Edith finds this fact depressing. Cold, rainy, boring London. Helen accompanied her cheerfully to the San Juan Dios artisan market. She even translated enthusiastically Edith's questions and the artisans' answers. Two full hours of fun. Edith wished that Helen could have been this positive during the entire trip.

Showering at the hotel, Edith cannot believe her ears. Helen is humming? Helen had asked nicely the hotel's receptionist where they could eat a gourmet meal. To both of their surprise, there is a four-star hotel in Iquitos with a matching four-star restaurant inside. Normally, Helen would scoff at the idea of spending so much on a meal, but this afternoon, she announced that she wants to try it. Edith agreed wholeheartedly knowing the food will be fantastic.

How could it not? She has loved everything so far. People may not have many material possessions but they sure do eat well. Au naturel.

The four-star hotel is home to the first elevator in Iquitos. The hotel put a guard at the door beside the bellman to stop the flow of curious townspeople who entered just to watch it ascend and descend above the atrium when the hotel opened. The guard never approaches foreigners, so the sisters casually stroll inside.

A tropical paradise complete with a waterfall showcases the center of the hotel. The rooms rise above in a circle with balconies to view the garden below. The hotel has ten stories and is the tallest building in the city. The restaurant's tables are in the rear half of the atrium. It has a clear-glass roof so clean to look above one assumes it is open sky. The maître d' addresses the women in English. Helen is polite, almost delightful, when she speaks to him. Edith wonders if an alien has taken over her sister's body. Two fancy tropical cocktails with a few slices of pineapple on the rims and little umbrellas are placed on the table as the sisters view the menus. Helen sips hers through the straw.

"What happened to only tea, sister dear?" Edith can't help but to tease Helen a little.

"Oh, we don't have to worry about good hygiene here. The maître d' speaks English for goodness sake."

Edith fails to grasp her sister's logic, how speaking English prevents bacteria from slipping into food or drink, but she is not about to waste a beautiful meal arguing with her. They order dishes with recognizable names: shrimp cocktail, poached salmon with dill sauce, and french yucca fries. Helen orders another Tropical Explosion cocktail. Already feeling the "explosion" swirling around in her head, Edith orders a camu camu juice. Remarkably the bar doesn't have any. To Helen's surprise, her sister requests hot tea. Being in the air-conditioning has given her a chill. She prefers the warmth and humidity outside. They end the meal sharing a delicious coffee flan.

Helen orders tea also and laughs. The sun sets as the sisters pay, both pleased with their last dinner in the Amazon.

Even with a very full stomach, Edith still craves a camu camu juice. She will never have the chance to drink this juice again, she explains to Helen. Her new agreeable sister suggests they return to the Anaconda Café. A nice spot to people watch. The main square's trees and bushes help buffer the noisy mototaxis' roar.

At the café, five of the students sit drinking beer. Helen chooses the table next to them and strikes up a conversation. Edith knows, without a doubt, a Martian has indeed invaded Helen's body.

"What did you do today?" Helen inquires.

"It was wonderful. We went up the Nanay River to meet the Yaguas and the Bora Boras," answers one of the students. "The Yaguas showed us how to use blowguns, the real ones that are like six feet long. Everyone took turns shooting at a parrot. I hit it once!"

"My, my, the poor parrot," Edith blurts without thinking.

"It wasn't a real parrot. They had carved one out of wood and painted it. I'd never shoot a real parrot. Sadly, we did learn they use the blowguns to kill monkeys. They dip the tip of the dart with some type of poison that stuns the animal so they can grab it. Fortunately, the younger generation has stopped killing monkeys because of a program in school that said it was bad to do so. This has caused problems though between generations because the older guys kept rubbing their bellies and licking their lips anytime someone said monkey. I guess they really like them."

"See, sister? I told there are still savages here," snorts Helen. Edith sighs and sees that her old sister is back. "They—"

Anne interrupts Helen. "I don't think they're savages. People just eat what they grow up eating. My professor says she loves raw oysters, like salty snot sliding down your throat only tasty, so she can't say anything about what other people eat. It's true we are products of our culture. Although I come from hamburger land, but I don't eat mammals. Cows are so cute. How can anyone look in their eyes and think yummy. And pigs, well, they lie in their own poop. At least monkeys are very clean. They spend hours grooming each other."

"Yeah. We ate grilled grubs from the ladies in the Masusa port. They grill them on the street. Have you tried any?" Sarah adds.

"Oh my, I could never eat insects. How barbaric!" remarks Helen.

"I had to close my eyes and pretend it was something else at first. Then I discovered that they're really good, kind of like buttered popcorn—greasy on the outside, crunchy on the inside. If you get lost in the jungle, you can always find and eat grubs to survive. Only if you eat them raw, make sure to remove their heads. Rey said that would make us sick. But roasted, you can eat the whole thing."

"We also visited the Bora Bora." Anne describes the people, the bark cloth they wear, and other customs.

"Oh yes, we know them. On one of our first days here, the cruise ship stopped there. I loved the dances." Edith reaches into her bag. "I bought this beautiful necklace with four different colored seeds. And can you believe that the white pieces are actually fish vertebrae? Amazing! They can string something so fragile. The red and black seeds are to give the wearer good health and happiness."

Sarah leans over and shows Edith the two necklaces she is wearing both with the same seeds. "Lucky seeds. They told us the same thing, good health and happiness. I hope they work at home! I have felt happy the whole time we have been here."

Helen inquires, "It appears that we all leave tomorrow for Lima. Will you stay there long or are you visiting other places in Peru?"

"No. Unfortunately, we'll just be there a day. Our spring semester starts in a week. We have to go back to write our papers and reports for Dr. Long," Anne replies.

"I don't want to think about leaving," Sarah adds with a heavy sigh. Both tables sit quietly, sipping their drinks for a few minutes. The students soon start chatting then laughing again. Helen motions to the waiter to bring the check. She places some soles on the table. The elderly sisters walk arm in arm back to the hotel.

The students stay enjoying the warm night air, knowing that back home in the states, it is cold. It snowed a few days ago and the temperature remains below freezing. They drink Cristal beer and do shots of 7 roots. The time flies by, and soon it is almost midnight. Elizabeth cautioned them not to stay out after 10:00 p.m. because Iquitos can be dangerous late at night. The girls are pretty wasted and need to walk about six blocks back to the hotel. They pay their bill and stagger up the street. Out of nowhere, a group of four young men cross the street and block their way. At first they seem harmless, just the normal flirting. The boys want to take them to some bar to dance. They don't understand word for word but get the general gist.

"No. No. We go," Sarah says and shakes her hand, trying to motion them out of their way. One of the young men grabs her arm and pulls her close to him. He smells of alcohol and seems drunk. His grip on her arm is strong. She shoves him away, which angers his friends. The boy's friends grab the other girls and push them forward toward an open door on the street. Noises can be heard from inside. Probably a cantina, a place for men to drink.

Julie screams, *"Alto. Alto.* Stop, stop." The boys just laugh. Next thing they know, two older men grab the young men and start speaking firmly. The boys let go of the girls and stumble around the corner. The men say nothing while the girls say thank you over and over again. The men accompany them back to the hotel. The students run straight to their rooms, the adrenaline still pulsing vigorously in their veins. It could have been a bad ending to a beautiful trip. Next time they all agree to heed their professor's warning.

16

THE PLANE

Flights at dawn are never a good idea when traveling with a bunch of college students who like to stay up late and sleep in. Elizabeth knows this, but she had no choice when she booked the flight. Thank goodness the airport is only fifteen minutes away with two commercial flights in the morning. There shouldn't be any crowds or long lines. She counts the students for the hundredth time on the trip as they drag their bodies into the hotel lobby. Three are missing. Which room? Rachel, Alison, and Claudine in room 236. She calls them from the receptionist desk. After five rings, a sleepy Alison picks up and barely says hello.

"We are leaving in five minutes," Elizabeth asserts in her stern, I'm-not-kidding voice.

"Shit. Oh sorry. We're coming," Alison is now fully awake.

"Three MIAs. Probably went to bed an hour ago," Elizabeth tells Bob, who, with raised eyebrows, asked her what's up. He smiles, remembering late nights in his youth. Elizabeth heads up the stairs to room 236 to reinforce the urgency. Five minutes isn't time for makeup, showers, or packing like some students assume—that five minutes equals as long as they want it to be.

Elizabeth knocks three times, and Rachel opens the door. "All right, gals. Pee and grab your suitcases. No time for anything else." The girls are in a frenzy. Suitcases still open, stuff everywhere. "Good grief," she can't help but to say out loud. Elizabeth starts throwing things in any bag. "You can figure out who has what when we get to our hotel in Lima tonight. For now, just stuff your things in any bag. We have to go." The girls look at her like deer blinded by headlights. "Now. I said move." They throw on the rest of their clothes, grab the suitcases, and run out the door. Elizabeth takes one more look around the room, in the closet, the bathroom, and the drawers. She finds a small bag with some necklaces in the nightstand by the bed. She takes another glance. Satisfied, she closes the door.

Bob has directed everyone onto the wooden bus, and the last three students struggle to put their stuff on the bus's roof. The professor had already paid the bill, so she lays the last room key on the front desk. "Gracias. Thank you. Thank you so much for everything," she says, smiling.

"You are very welcome. We look forward to seeing you next year," replies Oscar, the manager, in his heavily accented English.

That morning, the airport is oddly crowded. Only when one is late. If they had arrived early, the airport would have been empty. They get in line behind two men. One of them is unusually tall. Elizabeth knows that she has seen him before but can't place him. "Next," shouts the airline employee.

Check-in goes smoothly. With tears, the students say their good-byes to Rey, Julio, and Patricia and reassure them that they will friend each other on Facebook as soon as they arrive home. Elizabeth looks at her friends, her right hands. Without them she could never do all the things they do in the Amazon. She struggles to hold back the tears and hugs them tight. "See ya next year." She blows them a kiss. Last in line for security, she shows her ID and puts her carry-on on the conveyor belt.

* * *

Alberto rises before the sun. He packs all of his clothes in one suitcase. He has no idea what he will need in Lima. If all goes well that morning, he will not return to Iquitos for years, a decade at least. He has not said a word to any of his siblings to protect them. There is the possibility that things may not go well, and he will return. Return to his current life.

Alberto calls Jacobo, the second in command at the mine, to tell him that he is ill. "The doctor says it is dengue fever. There is a vicious outbreak in several villages upriver from Iquitos. You know how highly contagious the fever is." Alberto continues lying to Jacobo, "The doctor has ordered complete bed rest for several days. I think I'll be better tomorrow." Jacobo freaks out on the other end of the line because of the big bosses arrival. "You can handle it. Everything is ready." He allays Jacobo's worries the best he can and finally finishes the call.

The Lima bosses will arrive early today, and they will realize that some of the diamonds are missing. All hell will break loose. They will probably fire him or maybe Jacobo, since he will be the one at whom they'll bark questions. And of course, Jacobo will have no answers. He feels sorry for him, but there's nothing he can do about it now. Maybe he'll send him some money anonymously after he cashes in the diamonds. Right now, Alberto must get to the airport.

Ironic that he is the thief, but only Juan knows. There is no evidence. No person at the mine can open the vault. The big bosses made sure of that. He laughs. Let them solve the puzzle. If he does return, he will blame the power shortages, the security problems, which he is not in charge of. The bosses brought their man Raoul from Lima to head security. Let their boy deal with it. Anyway, hopefully, he will be far, far away, preparing for a new life, never to worry about that damn mine again.

A knock on the door jolts Alberto back to reality. Juan is punctual. Dressed in clean jeans, a buttoned-down shirt, and tennis shoes as Alberto advised. No huarache sandals. Airline personnel often discriminate against those who appear overtly indigenous. They need to blend in. "Fly under the radar," he told Juan.

Alberto looks around his house, the house he built block by block. He worked hard and has done well by Amazon standards. He knows that his family is proud of him. If only his parents were alive. He pauses and thinks no, better they aren't. They wouldn't understand stealing. They never stole a thing in their lives. He realizes if he doesn't return, he will become the number one suspect and may never be able to see his family again. He hadn't thought about that before. Though money can buy pretty much anything; just look at how each president robs the country blind. They always manage to return after a few years in exile so why can't he? He can change his name.

Juan yells to Alberto, "Let's go," and they climb into the mototaxi. In ten minutes, they are at the airport. Juan carries a simple backpack. "Only one suitcase to check?" inquires the airline employee. Albert nods. He places it on the scale. They get their boarding passes. Alberto hears the students behind him but never turns to avoid eye contact. Under the radar, he reminds himself.

"Flight 645, destination Lima, is now boarding," the voice on the intercom system squeaks. The plane is one of the new Peruvian Airlines fleet. It has comfortable leather seats with lumbar support. Alberto whispers instructions to Juan, who acts like a fish out of water. "I thought that you have flown before?" he asks. Juan starts to explain. It's the first time he has opened his mouth since arriving at the airport.

"Never mind. Just sit here." Alberto barks. He waits to put his carry-on bag in the overhead compartment until he can see which one the tall young man will use. Most of the students are placing their bags under the seat in front of them. Shoot. Alberto assumed that they would all put their things in the overhead compartments. Please, he prays. Just this one favor, he asks the Virgincita. His wish is granted. Ed, who needs all the leg room he can get, opens the bin across the aisle from Alberto's seat and places his backpack in it. Finally a break. Alberto looks to the heavens and says gracias to the saint.

After the students settle, Alberto stands, slides his bag next to the tan backpack, returns to his seat and clasps the seatbelt. He closes his eyes willing the students to do the same. Juan fidgets. Alberto opens one eye. "Sleep like everyone else, and if you can't, just pretend to do so."

The plane appears ready for takeoff, but the flight attendant receives notice that two more passengers will board. While waiting, most of the students fall deep asleep as Alberto surmised. The older couple traveling with the students is fortunately seated in front of the group. Adrenalin races through Alberto's veins. He imagines the diamonds in his possession once again. He slows his breathe to calm his shaking hands while keeping his eyes closed. He hears the last passengers shuffle behind him. The flight attendants give security instructions. The plane lifts off.

The flight is only one and a half hours. As soon as they reach cruising altitude, the seatbelt light blinks off. The flight attendants unclasp their seatbelts to prepare the drink and snack cart. Alberto knows that this is it. This is the moment. Now or never. Alberto looks across the aisle at the tall kid. His mouth is wide open with a bit of drool hanging in one corner. Soft snores are heard. Definitely sound asleep. Alberto rises. He opens the compartment carefully. Quickly, he turns the tan bag on the other side and unzips the treasured pocket. He slides his hand inside and can feel a few of the small stones. He rejoices in his heart.

Just as Alberto fingers the stones, he is suddenly knocked off balance and falls backward into his seat with his arms striking Juan. A loud shriek escapes Juan's mouth. The tan bag falls on top of Ed's head waking him up. Air turbulence. No wait. The plane is fine. An older woman pushed him aside. She continues her path to the bathroom. Alberto glowers, complete disbelief and anger spread across his face. Why in that moment did she have to go to the bathroom? He sees that the tall student is starting to place the backpack under the seat in front of him so Alberto quickly taps his shoulder. He motions to Ed that he can return the bag overhead. Ed hands it to him, says gracias, and falls back asleep in two minutes. Alberto realizes that everyone else on the plane is watching him so he closes the compartment. The professor sits again also, having stood to see what the commotion was.

Alberto returns to his seat, 11C, shaking. He tries to calm himself while the attendants start serving beverages and snack boxes containing sandwiches and cookies. The students wake up long enough to guzzle the drinks and chow the sandwiches. Most of them pass out again soon after eating. Albert waits until the attendants are in the back of the plane and are paying no attention to the passengers. At least now both the pockets on the kid's bag and his are unzipped. He visualizes what he needs to do. Just shoot the hand down the side, grab the gems and throw them in his bag. One quick movement. Juan is sound asleep now which is good. If his falling hadn't wakened the kid, Juan's yelling certainly would have. One more time he visualizes his next move.

Bing. Bing. The seatbelt light turns on indicating the initial descent into Lima. The flight attendant tells the passengers to turn off all electronic devices. Alberto knows he only has a few seconds, his last chance. He rises, opens the bin, and slides his hand deep into the tan bag's pocket. For once his height works to his advantage. The stones must be lying on the bottom and he needs to shift his hands a little to reach underneath. The flight attendant appears out of nowhere and touches his arm. Alberto jumps startled.

"I must close this now. You can get your bag when we land. Please return to your seat. We'll be on the ground in a few minutes," she says with a smile. Alberto freezes with his hand halfway in the bag as the small woman tries to close the compartment. He nods at her.

"Now. I'm sorry. We are landing. You must sit with your seatbelt securely fastened." The attendant pushes on the compartment with Alberto hand still in it. She isn't fooling around. "I said sit," she orders Alberto as if he were a dog.

* * *

Red lights flashing. Sirens wailing. The mine is in an uproar. The GIA inspectors arrived with the big bosses from Lima on the early morning flight. They went straight to the mine, forgoing the breakfast buffet that Mario had lined up for them at the fancy El Dorado Hotel. Mario hopes that the cafeteria women have prepared good food because he knows they will be hungry and demanding, a detail he forgot to check when he visited Alberto the other day. The bosses never appreciate the work everyone does to make sure all their needs are met. They change plans suddenly and expect him to have everything ready at the flip of a switch.

Raoul met the bosses, and the two inspectors about half past nine when they appeared at the mine's front gate. Jacobo stayed at his desk, too nervous to leave the office. The men walked straight to hall A where the vault is located. On the way, Raoul pulled aside the main boss requesting a meeting with him as soon as he finishes his business with the inspectors. His boss muttered yes and turned his back to him. The other boss from Lima dialed the vault's combination and the door opened. The four men entered the vault, and one instructed, Raoul to stay outside to guard the door with the two other armed guards.

The inspectors lifted the bin and dumped the diamonds on a blue velvet cloth that covers a small table inside. The inspectors remove some small equipment from their bag to evaluate the stones. At first the men all smiled and slapped each other on the back admiring the great quality and quantity of gems as if they had something to do with their creation. Those smiles shortly turned into frowns.

"Where is the three-carat stone?" yelled the main boss to Raoul. "I want to know where it is now!"

Raoul poked his head into the vault, not sure what to do. He finally decided to enter and face the fire in the bosses' eyes. One of the GIA inspectors kept writing in the notebook. The other guy counted the piles of stones they had made before they realized the special three-carat diamond was missing. The one counting stated that the amount of smaller stones appeared short also.

The main boss grabbed Raoul by the neck and shoved him into the wall. He repeated his question, "Where is the three-carat stone?" It seemed that he didn't hear the GIA inspectors' last comment, so enraged he was by the missing crown jewel of the mine.

Raoul could only stammer a hundred times, "I don't know. I don't know. I don't know." The boss directed him to sound the alarm, get more guards on the door, and find the manager whose name he couldn't recall. Raoul ran to pull the alarm.

All the red lights flash. The noise from the siren is deafening. He runs to Alberto's office to find Jacobo sitting at the desk. "Where the hell is Alberto?"

Jacobo is totally confused. Panicked, he jabbers about the alarm. "I knew something would go wrong. I told Alberto that this morning. I can't believe this is happening."

Raoul clears his throat and looks directly into Jacobo's eyes. "I'll ask you one more time and you better answer me clearly. Where is Alberto?"

"Alberto has dengue and stayed home today. There is an outbreak just north of Iquitos. He told me everything was fine and the inspection should go smoothly. He'll be back in tomorrow."

"I bet he will," scowls Raoul. He leaves the office to find his security men running all over the place like chickens with their heads cut off. He starts barking orders. "No one leaves. No one. And no one enters. You hear me? We are under complete lock down. You, get over there by the gate. You come with me."

He returns to the vault to tell the bosses that the manager has dengue. He repeats dengue fever when the bosses don't understand. Angrier than a bear caught in a trap, the main boss shouts, "Imbeciles. I need to call Lima. We need extra forces here. Carlos, you stay with the inspectors. You guys can finish your analysis with what we have, correct?"

The inspectors' reply that they are uncomfortable being here when obviously there has been a robbery. The have put the notebook and equipment away in the same case. They ask to be escorted back to Iquitos so they can catch the afternoon flight to Lima. They will reschedule the inspection. The bosses agree that is probably the best plan. Raoul finds one of his men to drive them to the Iquitos port and on to the airport.

Everything that happens afterward is like a whirlwind. A few local policemen arrive, who are useless. All the port officials in and around Iquitos are notified to watch for any suspicious people and boats. Airport security is contacted and instructed to beef up and increase security checks. All suitcases, carry-ons, and bodies are to be searched thoroughly. Two flights have already left that morning, one bound for Lima, which has already landed, and the other to Miami, which is still in flight. The bosses in Lima are working on a way to convince US officials that the Miami-bound passengers need to be detained upon arrival in the US. It's possible a tour visitor stole them.

Raoul discusses the problem with the energy grid that they discovered a few days ago and is reprimanded for not reporting it sooner, but no tracks are found outside the walls. A rare, if not impossible, task for someone on the outside to jump the electric fence, enter the building, open the vault, and get away without anyone noticing. No, the bosses assume it has to be an inside job. But how?

The staff is rounded up and sits in the cafeteria waiting to be interrogated one by one. No one can figure out how the diamonds got out of the vault. Not even a major plot involving every staff person could work. They have state-of-the-art security. Yet the employees so far are all passing the NLDS. Everyone is baffled and soon to be fired.

Raoul calls Alberto several times at his home with no answer. He is convinced that Alberto is the thief although he cannot imagine how he got into the vault. No one has the combination, not even him, the head of security. He views the staff to see if anyone else is missing from work. He feels like someone is missing but can't place who it is. Only when the trash overflows may they remember Juan, the invisible janitor.

Alberto's employee identification picture is faxed to the chief of Iquitos police, who turns around and faxes it to police detectives in Lima. Wanted for questioning flyers with his face are produced and posted. The news media gets wind of the robbery in the afternoon. Soon after, several reporters land on the mine's riverbank only to be refused entry. They sit outside and wait. Reporters in Lima also hear the big news. Headline for tomorrow's national paper reads, "The Impenetrable Mine Is Robbed: Millions in Diamonds Missing." That afternoon, the newspaper staff receives a photo of the number one suspect to accompany the article.

17

LIMA

They have one more day in Peru. Elizabeth used to fly from Iquitos on the morning flight, wait in the airport all day, and then take the night flight back to the US. She had luck for years that the flights went smoothly until last year. The Iquitos–Lima flight was canceled at the last minute, no explanation given. The group ended up missing the connection to the states. The American Airlines flight was full the next night. Trying to get eighteen people home was a nightmare. Live and learn, she thought. So this trip, she decided to give herself some breathing room by scheduling an extra night in Lima, a buffer.

The students yawn and stretch while waiting for their luggage to appear on the Lima carrousel. "Dr. Long, I can't find my passport," shrieks Rachel.

"Don't panic. I'm sure it is in your backpack. You had it when we left Iquitos. Sarah, can you help us a minute? Rachel, let's take everything out and hand it to Sarah." Elizabeth holds her backpack open while Rachel pulls out her scarf. Plop. On the floor is the passport. It was tangled up in the scarf. "Whew." Rachel sighs a breath of relief. Elizabeth smiles at her and pats her shoulder.

The students grab their bags and head to the exit. Marcela, Elizabeth's guide and friend in Lima, is waiting with a private bus. They exchange hugs and greetings, load up their stuff, and drive out of the airport to see a few more historic sites in Lima.

"Today we're heading south to the Fuerte Real de San Felipe, the fort built by the Spanish in colonial times. As you read in the *Peru Reader*, Lima was the capital of the Spanish empire in what they called New Spain. It was the political, social, and commercial center. All the booty they stole from the indigenous people came to Lima to be loaded onto Spanish galleons to make the voyage around the tip of South America and across the Atlantic to the motherland. Gold, silver, gems worth billions. You can imagine the need for a strong fort to protect against pirates and other countries' navy men who tried to seize the treasures too. The fort was later the site of the Spanish royalists fighting against the rebellion for independence in the 1820s. It is still used today by Peru's navy. We'll be visiting the little historic museum inside. Questions?" Elizabeth asks.

The students aren't really paying attention. They chit chat softly, look at the hundreds of pictures of the trip on their digital cameras, or just gaze out the window of the bus. The day is a typical Lima grey day, temperature in the seventies with clouds covering the sky, always threatening to rain but never do. Dilapidated buildings are interspersed with new construction. Empty lots are full of trash. Dogs and cats roam the streets in, and around, people hawking food and goods along the sidewalks. Cars blast their horn at the slow-moving traffic. Billboards fill the sky, announcing a variety of products. Dogs bark from the rooftops. It seems like a different planet from where they have lived the past month. Anthropologists talk about "culture shock" when arriving to a new place to live with people from a different culture, but the shock is just as dramatic returning home.

After a twenty-minute ride, the group arrives at the fort. Peruvian soldiers guard the front entrance. Marcela speaks to the guards, and the students are allowed to pass. They walk along the top the fort's thick walls to the oldest section and enter the museum. Ghoulish maps of battlefields with blood shooting out of the soldiers' hearts as they are bayoneted line the walls of the first room. Military weaponry sits in dusty old cases. The actual museum displays are relics themselves of a bygone era.

As they pass into the room holding artifacts from old ships, the museum guide begins his story of a famous buccaneer who captured one of the Spanish ships in 1714. Out jumps a pirate on the stern of a reconstructed miniature version of a colonial ship.

"Yar," he shouts. "I see a many a beauty. Who wants to be my bride?" He leans into the first row and points his sword at Charlene. She gasps. "Grab her!" Two other young men dressed as pirates appear from behind a curtain and take Charlene by the arm onto the fake boat. "You have a choice. Be my mate or walk the plank." Everyone laughs heartily through the rest of the skit. In the end, Charlene chooses not to be his mate so she is pushed from the plank into the sea. Suddenly cardboard sharks appear and swim around her. Ed and John lean over the fake wall and pull Charlene to safety. The pirates take a bow and pass the hat for any kind tip.

After that show, the next room full of old swords becomes even more boring. Ditto for the ensuing one with a limited taxidermy collection. The students shuffle by the glass cases. Finally, they emerge from the dark, clammy rooms to the daylight outside. The last stop is one of the remaining original towers. They climb the very narrow and steep steps for a 360-degree view of the modern day port of Callao, one of the largest ports on the Pacific side of the Americas.

Large container ships float in the sea as far as the eye can see, each waiting its turn to unload.

By then, the little sandwich and cookies the students ate on the morning flight is long digested and their bellies are growling for food. The students are tired and somewhat cranky.

"We have a wonderful lunch planned at Mariscos del Mar," Elizabeth informs them. "A sampling of seafood and fish dishes that are making Lima famous in the world of gastronomy. It's not really too far from here, but the nearby dock area is a pretty rough neighborhood. Not a good idea to walk. Let's go to the bus. Everyone ready?" The group unanimously nods yes as the idea of eating perks them up. The last photos are shot. The group descends the tiny stairwell, walks past the soldiers, crosses the street, and strolls along the concrete bulkhead where the bus awaits.

* * *

"Now what do we do? Your foolproof plan wasn't so foolproof, eh?" Juan smirks sarcastically. Juan cannot believe his own stupidity for getting involved with Alberto. He shakes his head.

"Come on. We got to follow them. If you want to give up and return to Iquitos, go ahead and fly back. I'm not. I had my fingers on them. The tips of my fingers! That damn flight attendant," Alberto growls.

"Oh, right. And how am I to pay for a flight home? You better figure something out. I didn't go to work today, remember? Now I'm jobless and penniless."

Alberto hails a cab. He doesn't respond to Juan's comment, knowing the same is true for him. No, probably worst. By now the inspectors are at the mine, and who knows what is going on there, but he is sure it is not good for him. No way can he bluff his way out of not showing up. As he closes the cab's door, something familiar catches his eye. He turns his head around to look out the back window. OMG. Leather jacket man stands on the curb. Alberto shrinks down in the seat.

"Where to?" the cabbie asks.

"Follow that bus."

Juan and Alberto stand outside the fort. No need to waste money following the students in a museum with soldiers on guard. Juan constant complaints makes Alberto's head ache. "Would you shut up!" he barks a little too loudly. A couple walking by them turns and stares. Alberto smiles at them, and they continue on their way. "Listen. Help me figure out a plan. We can still get them. We've just had a terrible run of bad luck. We will get the diamonds. Failure is not an option." The two men sit on a concrete bench on the left side of the fort and stare at the monochromatic dark blue sea.

"Gimme your money."

"Huh?" Alberto feels something pushing on the back of his neck.

"Gimme your money now." A teenager in baggy jeans, sneakers, and a black T-shirt holds what appears to be a gun covered by a flannel cloth at Alberto's neck. Juan slowly slides to the end of the bench while pretending not to see the boy.

"St-St-Stop or your friend ge-ge-gets it," the boy stutters. Juan stops.

A burst of laughter streams from Alberto's mouth. Both Juan and the boy are confused. Then the boy gets angry, thinking Alberto is laughing at his stutter. Alberto slowly turns to face the kid. "Go ahead. You'll be putting me out of my misery. This is a perfect ending," he howls. There is no way Alberto is going to part with his savings strapped around his waist in a fanny pack. No way. Again he cannot believe how bad his luck is or rather his complete luck of luck.

"Go on shoot me. You see those guards over there? They're real soldiers. How far do you think you can get before they shoot you down like a rat?" Alberto can see that the boy is no older than fourteen, fifteen tops. The kid glances over at the fort, unsure of what to do. His friends told him to put the piece of PVC pipe in a rag and the person thinking that it is a gun would do whatever he says. Scared, he drops the PVC pipe and takes off running in the opposite direction of the fort. Soon he turns left and disappears into an alley.

Juan cannot believe what Alberto just did. "That kid could have killed you. You didn't know it wasn't a real gun. Have you gone crazy?"

Alberto grins.

"What are you smiling about? You have gone crazy."

"No, not crazy. That kid just gave me an idea." Alberto is unsure if he can really do what he knows he has to do now. No other choice. Still he has never been violent with anyone. He abhors violence. He shakes his head to focus. "Come on, let's get outta here."

"What about the backpack? They'll come out of the fort soon. We can't lose them."

"No worries. It's too open to do anything here but we know where they are staying, remember? I made a reservation for us to stay there too. That's where we'll get the bag. We just need to make two stops first. Taxi!"

* * *

"When shall we eat?" Edith asks.

"For heaven's sake, sister, it's midmorning. All you think about is food. I need to freshen up. They say that our room will be ready in a half hour. Just sit tight, okay?"

Edith props her feet on the coffee table in front of the soft, cushiony couch in the hotel's lobby. She stares at an acrylic painting depicting a group of Quechua women harvesting flowers in the mountains. Her sister has returned to her uptight self. Edith knew the relaxed Helen couldn't last long. She falls half asleep, her mind somewhere between daydream and wakefulness. The hotel is small with two sofa sets in the lobby area and a bar/breakfast area off to the left side of the receptionist's counter. Helen stirs her. A tiny elevator carries the two sisters to the third floor. No room for the bellboy with the suitcases. He waits for the elevator to return.

The room is simple but adequate with two single beds, a round table, two chairs, and a closet with shelves. Another acrylic painting with a mountain scene hangs on the wall above the beds. A small television is attached to the opposite wall, so one can watch while in bed. No tub, just a shower in the small bathroom.

"Good grief. You can barely get the bathroom door closed. You have to stand in the shower to shut it," mumbles Helen, who finally manages to close the door.

Edith opens the window and looks at the busy streets below. In the distance, she can see the Pacific Ocean. Large palm trees dot the streets along with flowering bushes, giving the neighborhood Miraflores its tropical name. She smells grilled chicken and figures that must be the specialty of the restaurant in front. A sign says Pollo Loco, which she is pretty sure means crazy chicken. Her stomach growls. Little wafts of smoke puff out of a chimney in the rear of the restaurant. "Another beautiful day in this lovely country. I wish that we could stay longer," she announces out the window. She notices several short, stocky women with long black braids flowing to the center of their backs topped with derby-like hats kneeling on brightly colored blankets on the street perpendicular to the street in front of the hotel. Small items are spread around them. "Oh goodie, looks like more beautiful handmade creations," Edith exclaims.

"What? I can't hear you." Helen struggles with the door and finally busts out of the bathroom. "Okay that's better. I'm ready. You need to use the bathroom?" Edith understands that it is not a question but rather a command from her big sister. She washes her face and pees, and soon the women descend to the street.

The woman wears a series of three skirts, one layered on top of another, and a sweater even though the weather is warm. Across her back is a piece of fabric tied in the front. It took Edith awhile to realize the woman has a baby strapped in there. She motions to the woman, asking permission to pick up a ceramic pot. The pot has a mountain scene and two llamas painted on it. The woman nods yes, she can touch it.

"Oh, look, sister. How beautiful. Look at the fine lines depicting the mountains. I must have one."

"Edith, you can barely get your suitcase shut now. How on earth do you plan to get it home?"

Edith sighs and sets it on the blanket. "Sorry," she mouths to the woman. The woman shows her another, and Edith shakes her head no. The woman lifts her hand to her mouth, indicating that she is hungry. Edith remembers Jose Antonio talking about the many Peruvians from the countryside have migrated to the nation's capital, searching for work and a better life only to find discrimination and no opportunities. The woman is so beautiful; a tear comes to Edith's eye. While Helen faces the other way, Edith reaches in her purse and gives the woman several coins. Edith places her finger to her lips. Ssssh. She points to Helen and giggles like they are co-conspirators. The woman cups Edith hand in a gesture of thanks and turns to open a black plastic bag behind her as Edith and Helen continue their walk on the street.

All of a sudden, Edith feels someone tugging on her shirt. A little boy holds out a painted ceramic disk on a black cord necklace. "No, I'm sorry. I can't," Edith says. She starts to walk again when the boy grabs her hand, places the necklace in it, and points up the street. Edith sees the woman with the baby waving to her and understands that the little boy must be her son. The necklace is for the coins she gave her. "How remarkable," Edith says out loud.

"What? What's remarkable?" her sister asks.

"Nothing, dear. Nothing."

* * *

"Did everyone get enough to eat?" Elizabeth asks rhetorically. The food seemed never ending. It was one delicious plate after another, especially the *ceviches*, fish and seafood cooked in lime juice rather than with heat. *Ceviche de corvina* and the mixed seafood ceviche are Elizabeth's favorites.

"What is corvina?" Alison asks. "I liked it best."

"White sea bass. Of all the different ceviches you find throughout Latin America, sea bass is considered the most typical of Peru.

"All I can say is that was the best meal I've ever eaten," responds Julie. "I didn't think I'd like the little octopuses with its tentacles all over my plate, but was I wrong. Just shows looks can be deceiving. Can you help me with the names of all the dishes? I'm missing some."

"Sure. Sit beside me on the bus. We must hurry. I have one more place for you to see, and I'm hoping we can make it before sunset. Lunch ran a little longer than I thought it would. Let's load up."

They arrive at La Punta, or the Point, a charming small neighborhood, one of the oldest in the district of Callao.

"The area was almost wiped out by a tsunami in the 1930s. Most people left the area. It was abandoned for decades. In the early 1960s, it became a haven for bohemians, thus the beautiful street murals and colorful houses. They took care to rebuild the places just as they were before. Look up so you don't miss all the hand-carved wood. Now some developers are trying to get the area rezoned to increase property taxes and force the older residents out. With the view of the sea on all three sides of this little peninsula, the developers want to tear down everything and build a five-star resort."

The group crosses the street to see one of the oldest homes in the neighborhood. Elizabeth continues, "The community, with support from some international environmental groups has been able to exert enough pressure on the city council to stop the rezoning for now. They just completed the paperwork to have the area declared both a historic district and what they call *santuarios nacionales*, a national sanctuary. The environmental groups are concerned for several seabird species that are close to being extinct. They live over there in those little saltwater ponds. I don't know exactly how, but the ponds create a unique ecosystem due to the way the land juts out into the sea and how the ocean currents flow. Many neighbors depend on those ponds for a living. Let's walk over there. Our friend, Octavio, is waiting for us. He is the leader of the community's citizen's group."

Octavio waves to Elizabeth. The group crosses the road and step up onto the wide seawall that was built in the 1970s to prevent another tsunami from destroying the place. Only one problem with its construction. The city engineers designed it to be four meters high since the surge in the 1930s tsunami was four meters taller than normal high tide. "Somehow the materials disappeared, and it ended up just a meter tall." Octavio uses his fingers to make the quotation sign around disappeared. He says with a smirk, "I guess some politician at the time needed a new driveway or wall around his home."

Octavio is quiet for a moment. He then gets a very serious look on his face. "Really, this is why we can't advance. We have talent, intelligence, skills, but most of all, we have corruption. We have soooo much corruption."

He tells the students about their struggle to save the little neighborhood and can only presume they will succeed. "You have to believe," he urges. They walk closer to the ponds while he explains their unique biology.

The students take more pictures and watch the pelicans dive for fish. Seashells full of little critters, crabs and other shellfish swim in the ponds. The birds dive for the sea creatures. They break open the shells with their beaks or throw them on the concrete walkway to eat the tasty treat inside. It's low tide, so a thin, pale strip of sand separates the wall from the sea of blue water. The sun lowers on the horizon, casting a warm glow over the bright community. The shadows created make it a photographers dream to capture.

"I love it here. My favorite spot in Lima. Thank you so much for meeting with us and sharing. I know how busy you are." Elizabeth bids Octavio good-bye and turns to see Roberto getting out of a cab.

"Hey, you almost missed us. Just heading back now to the hotel. How did it go?" she asks.

Roberto had left the airport to get a stamp for export approval on a document from the national trade office downtown. It should have taken no longer than an hour but, as if to confirm Octavio last comment, the wheels had to be greased, and it took all day. "I got it but only after buying another bottle of scotch. They invented some new regulation. You know how it is. I'm so sorry to have missed lunch. Bet it was incredible."

"Better than expected." Elizabeth hugs Bob and hears his stomach rumble. "You haven't eaten?" She feels badly that he had to sit some bureaucrat's office while everyone else was dining on marvelous food.

"Nah. Thought I'd grab something here, but I can wait until we get back to the hotel." He looks over at the sun dipping below the horizon. "Nice ending to a great trip, Lizzie. You've done a wonderful job again."

"We've done a wonderful job again. Thank you." Elizabeth counts the students as they board the bus. "To the hotel," she instructs the driver.

* * *

Alberto and Juan make their way across the city toward Miraflores. They make two stops, a plumbing store and a pawnshop. Juan thought maybe Alberto was getting some PVC pipe like the kid had to scare the tall gringo into giving them his backpack. He is surprised to see Alberto's arms full of clothing, overalls and two caps. He starts to ask why but changes his mind and thinks better not to say anything. They jump in the cab that waited for them.

"What's the plan?" Juan asks Alberto for the millionth time.

Alberto bobs his head toward the driver, and Juan settles back into his seat mouth closed. They drive past some newly opened casinos. A two-story tall Lady Liberty graces the entrance to one of them. Soon Alberto spots a large pawnshop. "Stop here," he instructs the driver. To Juan he says, "Stay here. I'll just be a minute." Juan isn't sure he wants Alberto out of his sight, but Alberto leaves his bag so Juan figures it will be okay. Alberto returns quickly with a small brown bag tucked under his arm. "Hotel Carmen in Miraflores." The cabbie nods and pulls into rush hour traffic. It takes what seems like an eternity to get to the hotel.

Alberto stuffs the clothing into his bag and keeps the other small brown bag tight under his arm. He hands Juan the money to pay the cabbie. They enter the hotel.

"Good evening, sir. How can I help you?"

"Reservation for Gonzalez." The hotel clerk asks for ID and hands him a card to sign. They finish up when Alberto gets a funny feeling in the pit of his stomach. He glances around the hotel. Nothing seems out of order, a few tourists in the lobby. The clerk hands him the room key and asks if they need help with their bags. "No, we got it. Thank you." They stroll to the elevator and ride to the third floor. From their window, they can see the front of the hotel. They decide to take turns watching for the students to arrive while each takes a shower and puts on the plumber uniforms. Juan showers first then turns on the TV while Alberto is in the shower. He flips the channels, looking for a soccer game when he pauses at the news channel.

"Their total value is yet to be determined but it is estimated to be over twenty-five million in US dollars. The police are looking for Alberto Reyes Gonzalez Gomez for questioning. Anyone having any information on his whereabouts should call the police immediately. There is a US$100,000 reward for information leading to the capture of those responsible," states the newscaster.

Juan sinks slowly into his chair. An outdated picture of Alberto is plastered on the screen. Not so out of date that one couldn't identify Alberto. He takes a swig of the beer he opened from the little refrigerator in the room. He was just thinking all was going to be fine when he came in the room a half hour ago and noticed that they leave drinks for you. Nice place. Maybe our luck has changed. But now he is in the same room with the most wanted man in Peru. What should he do? It only takes him a minute to realize that he should get the hell out of there. Thank goodness, he didn't sign anything, and only the hotel clerk saw him with Alberto. He thought that she was super cute, so he kept his head down and avoided eye contact, so he wouldn't get a hard on and embarrass himself. Juan doubts she could identify him.

Juan strips off the overalls Alberto bought and puts his jeans back on. He grabs his few personal items and stuffs them back into his bag. He has a toothbrush in the bathroom but he can't risk getting it. Alberto has turned off the water. That lying son of a bitch. Worth a million. Not even close to the real value. Twenty-five million. Wow. He was going to get squat. No time to think about that now. He needs to flee. He looks around, grabs the bottle of beer, and throws it as far as he can out of the window. He regrets doing it as soon as he does it, fearful that it may hit and hurt someone. He doesn't even know why he did it, only the adrenaline is pumping so fast in his veins, he can't think straight. Pure fear washes over his body.

With his sleeve, he opens the room's door so not to leave his fingerprints and quietly creeps out the door. He runs to the stairs and then hesitates. Where to go? He has no idea. He just wants to get out of there and as far from Alberto as possible. He descends the stairs two at a time, keeping his head bent. Fortunately he passes no one. The lobby is small. Only a few steps farther and he is free. He makes it to the front door when a bunch of students push it open from the outside. They spin Juan around, apologize for bumping into him, and head to the couches to wait for room assignments. Juan is half-way down the street by the time all the students enter the hotel with their bags. His last sight is the tall lanky kid with the tan backpack hanging on his shoulder.

Albert is rubbing his head with the towel, wondering why Juan isn't answering him. He hears the TV on and figures it's too loud. He stares into the mirror, thinking about a disguise, wishing he had thought about it before. He should have bought some hair dye and scissors to at least change is his hair color and style. He shaves off his brush mustache, the mustache he grew when Ivonne left him and has never shaved. He admits that he does look quite different without it. The thing kinda took over his face. Now he looks younger and kinder, not as stern. He realizes how much pain he has kept locked inside, only revealed by the grimace on his face. Too release the pain would be to admit it exists. He's not ready to do that yet.

He dresses in the overalls and dons the cap. With no mustache and the cap over his eyes, he figures no one will recognize him, that is, if they are looking for him, which he assumes they must be. He opens the bathroom door to find no Juan. From the window, it sounds like a bus is pulling away. He looks, and sure enough, the students' bus is leaving. Darn that Juan. He's supposed to be on lookout. He needs to know which room the tall kid is in. He rushes out of the room to the stairs and stops. Taking a deep breath, he strolls down the stairs, hearing the students before he reaches the ground floor. He edges closer.

Elizabeth continues handing out room keys. "Betty, Anne, and Colleen, room 102. Rachel, Alison, and Claudine, room 103. The guys in 105. That's it. Remember the elevator is tiny, so if you can carry your bag, it's only one floor." The students shuffle around, gathering their things. Jane and Charlene, with their enormous suitcases, wait for the elevator. Alberto quickly climbs up a flight and a half to spy on them as they take their rooms. He needs to clearly see which one the backpack goes in. Room 105, room 105, he repeats to himself and retreats to his room to hide out until things become quieter. He figures that in a couple hours most of the hotel guests will have returned to their rooms for the night. Maybe he'll go to the bar for a sandwich to go. He hasn't eaten all day.

The remaining students sit in the lobby, waiting to use the computer. Without electronic devices and internet access for a month, they can't wait to see their messages, e-mails, Facebook, etc. They turn when they hear a high shrilly voice saying hello.

"Oh, my goodness. Looka here. Those wonderful students. Hello. Remember us?" asks Helen. She and Edith just returned to the hotel after their long walk around Kennedy Park with an early supper in one of the outdoor cafes. Edith looks at her sister in disbelief. "What? I enjoyed talking with them. Nice to see intelligent young people." Edith just shakes her head and then spots Sarah. She sits beside her on the lobby couch. They chat about their day, the old fort with its pirates and the woman with the ceramic pots. Sarah really got Edith's attention when she told her about their lunch. "Do you hear this, sister? We must go there. It sounds amazing. Sister. Sister? What are you staring at?" Helen turns around from watching several students carry their suitcases up the steps.

"I'm sorry, dear. Had a good lunch, did you?" Sarah answers Helen, but clearly, the old woman's mind is somewhere else. Edith rises and bids Sarah a good night. She grabs a hold of her sister's arm and leads her toward the elevator. Edith is afraid that her sister is having a stroke or something. "Let's take the stairs. I need some exercise after that dessert of churros and hot chocolate, heavy on the stomach," requests Helen.

"Are you sure? I think you need to lie down."

"No no. I'm fine. We'll just walk up one flight." They slowly ascend the stairs. As they round the top, Helen catches a glance of Ed's and John's backs as they enter the room at the end of the hall. "Okay, that's enough. Let's use the elevator. You know, it's probably not good that we are all the way up on the third floor. Maybe we should ask if we can change rooms to the first floor."

"Our room is fine. I don't want to move all my stuff, and I don't—"

Helen cuts Edith off. "I told you to stop buying all those trinkets. But you have to do things your way."

Edith looks up and thanks God that her cranky sister seems to be coming back. She doesn't understand Helen's weird behavior of late. The elevator door opens to the third floor and standing in front is a man vaguely familiar to Helen, a very tall man. He kept his head down, so she couldn't get a good look at him, but instinct is telling her that she knows him. They enter their room and the lightbulb goes on, not only in the room but in Helen's head also. "It's him."

"Who is who, dear? Please come and lie down. I'll get you some bottled water."

"It's the man on the plane," Helen mutters.

"Yes, dear, the man on the place. Now lie down here. Drink this. Let me help you with your shoes." Helen does as told robotically, her mind totally focused on the tall man from Iquitos. After Helen rests for an hour or so and seems fine, Edith turns on the TV to *CNN International News* in English and undresses. She puts on her pajamas, brushes her teeth, and climbs into bed with the remote. The next news story grabs both their attention. "Listen, Helen, isn't that the mine we visited? It has been robbed. Can you believe it?" Helen sits up. She sees Alberto's face and is positive that it is the man she saw in the hallway. She puts her shoes on again. "What is it now?" Helen stands and walks to the door. "Where are you going?"

Helen stops. She wants to tell Edith what she believes to be true but thinks twice since the situation could be dangerous. They have always shared everything, all their escapades, but she won't expose her sister to the possible risk. Better she stays safely tucked in bed. She thinks about the students in the same hotel, knowing that man is after one of them. Who knows what he'll do now that he is officially wanted by the police? She decides that she must do something even though she is unsure of what. "I must have a spot of tea before sleeping. I'm sure they can make me some in the bar." She slips out of the room before her sister can say another word.

Helen creeps quietly down the stairs. She is glad they are made of concrete so nothing squeaks. She gets to the first floor and looks both ways. She hears voices at the end of the hall. Quiet as a mouse, she hugs the wall as she moves toward the voices. The last room's door is cracked open.

"You heard me. Hands up. You there give me your backpack." Alberto holds the pistol steady in his right hand. The three boys are white as ghosts. The fear drains the blood from their faces. The man said something about plumbing, so they had foolishly opened the door for him. Their hands are up, but they don't know what the man is saying. Alberto forgot that they don't speak Spanish. Shoot. Always something. He remembers some English words. "Give me that." He points over in the corner where Ed has his suitcase and backpack. Ed first picks up his jacket on top of the case and hands it to him. "No.

That." He points with his gun again in the same direction. Ed picks up his backpack and Alberto nods yes. "Slow."

Ed moves toward him with his backpack outstretched in front of him. Alberto snatches the pack. He moves to the table, trying to hold the gun and open the backpack at the same time. He fumbles and drops the gun. It's so old, it almost falls apart. He smirks, thinking it is a good thing that the kids don't realize that it is just a prop. It can't fire a single bullet anymore. Not that anyone can buy bullets. A special permit is required. For the boys, the gun certainly looks like it can kill. Coming from a country where anybody can buy guns and bullets in the same store as they do groceries, they are frozen.

Alberto picks up the gun and puts the pack's shoulder strap in his teeth. His left hand unzips the outside pocket. He reaches deep into the bottom and feels the gems. His heart pounds faster. He releases the diamonds to take a blue velvet cloth from the rear pocket of his overalls and places it on the table. He seizes the diamonds and pours them onto the cloth. The boys' eyes light up like Times Square on New Year's Eve. Ed clutches his chest. Pain shoots through his side. He thinks he's having a heart attack. He puts his hands down and clutches his chest tighter.

"You stop. Hands up," Alberto motions with the gun up. Ed does as told. The pain passes. Alberto hears a sound outside the door. He motions to the boys to be silent or else and looks through the crack in the door. No one is in the hallway. Alberto walks back to the table and shakes the bag vigorously to make sure he has recovered all the diamonds. He inserts his left hand and feels no more stones. He throws the bag on the floor and folds up the blue cloth and places it back in his rear pant pocket.

"No speaking. No speaking. You speak, I come and kill you," he says in his broken English. He slips out the door and walks calmly down the hallway. He waits for the elevator, so no one will see that he will ascend the stairs instead of immediately leaving the hotel. In room 105, the boys keep their hands up for several minutes, unsure of what to do.

* * *

Helen sees the man in the wanted photo from the TV in the room with three of the students. He has a pistol pointing at them. Then her eyes spot the diamonds. Beautiful diamonds sparkle on a blue cloth. She stares paralyzed for several minutes before she realizes that she must get help quickly. She tiptoes back down the hallways and pushes the elevator button. Thank goodness, it is already on the first floor. The door opens with a loud pinging sound. Drat. She jumps in, hoping no one else heard it.

As the door opens on the ground floor, she runs to the counter and tells the night clerk what she saw in fluent Spanish. The clerk shakes his head in disbelief. He has been on duty all evening, and only guests have entered the hotel. "He is a guest," she shouts in desperation. "Call the police." Still the clerk is wary, thinking the old lady is batty. The TV in the lobby is on, and Helen points to it. "That's the man." She points to the monitor where Alberto's face is being shown over and over. The clerk realizes that she is serious. He goes to the manager's door to inform him of the situation and finds him gone. He remembers that he and the barman stepped outside to take a smoke. As he ponders what to do, Helen crosses behind the counter and tries to dial the police but doesn't know how to get an outside line. The clerk takes the phone from her hand and calls the police.

In minutes, sirens are heard moving in the direction closer to the hotel. The clerk is explaining to the manager and barman what Helen told him. The manager turns to ask Helen a question, but she is gone.

Alberto hears the sirens from his room. He took off the overalls and put on his suit hoping to leave before the boys called for help. Again time has run too short for him. He shaved off his hair earlier. Bald and without his black brush mustache he looks like a different man. He throws the plumber clothes, the ancient pistol and his national ID card under the bed, grabs his bag and exits the room. The sirens can't be more than a block or two away. He quickly bounces down the stairs passing several people. Surprised to find several people milling around, he mumbles again about his bad luck.

Alberto pauses when he hits the ground floor. There are a few more people entering the lobby after a night out on the town. A drunken guy is trying to hit the button for the elevator but can barely stand up. Greeting Alberto with a big smile. "Hey, amigo. Let's party." He swaggers into him and holds onto his waist. Alberto knows that time has run out and he must make a break for it. He pushes the drunken guy away from him. An elderly woman tries to catch him but falls into Alberto's arms instead. The party dude stumbles and lands on the floor. All eyes turn to Alberto. Full force he runs to the door. Bam! He pushes the door, but it won't budge. Then he remembers to pull the door handle. When the door swings wide open, Alberto faces three cops rushing onto the steps guns drawn.

"That's him," the clerk shouts. The police grab Alberto. Alberto tries to fake indignity. "Take your hands off me this instant," he snarls at the young cops. They look at each other, not sure what to do with the man in a suit. When they hear the clerk shouting, "He's the one who stole the diamonds, the diamonds," the cops order Alberto to stop and put his hands in the air. They take his bag and dump its contents on the steps of the hotel's entrance. They search his pockets for weapons and diamonds.

Nothing in his pockets. Just clothes and toiletries in the bag. No diamonds. The cops had hoped to retrieve the diamonds first. Not only would they be national heroes, but they secretly agreed it was only fair for each one to keep just one diamond as compensation in case the mine owners reneged on the reward. Most likely they would. The policemen compare the granulated copied photo of Alberto to the man himself to try to see if he is in fact the same man.

"ID!" the one cop orders. The other two urgently search through his things again. If the diamonds are there, they better find them fast before more officers arrive on the scene. Alberto ignores them. He pats his chest coat pocket and feels nothing. He looks on and around the steps for his blue velvet cloth with the diamonds. They aren't there. How is that possible? He placed them in his inside coat pocket for safe measure. "ID!" The cop smacks Alberto across the back of his head making it spin. Alberto shrugs and collapses to the floor. On his way down he sees a man stomp out a cigarette with his boot. Leather-jacket man turns away from the hotel and leaves the scene. Alberto can't believe his eyes. "You!" he screams out.

EPILOGUE

SIX MONTHS LATER

Helen is full of cheer. The sisters boarded another cruise ship this morning. The cruise carries guests along the Loire River in France. Edith was totally confused as to how they could afford it until her sister shared her secret that afternoon. During the last six months, they had been pinching pennies, spending less than before their Amazon trip. Edith thought that they were flat broke. Coupled with the cold, rainy days in London, a chilled Edith was on the verge of depression. How dearly she missed the heat and beauty of the rainforest.

For a week or so after their return from the Amazon, the sisters were treated like celebrities by friends and acquaintances who discovered the sisters had visited the famous diamond mine days before the place was robbed. How exciting! Did they see the robbers? "No no," they said. Soon the friends realized that the sisters knew nothing of the robbery. Hearing repeated descriptions of what the mine looked like, all they could share, grew boring and unpleasant, especially as

Edith's descriptions made the place uglier and uglier each time she talked about it. The conversation was dropped. The sisters returned to their normal routines until two days ago when Helen announced a big surprise.

Helen bought tickets for a new cruise. Eight days on the Loire River, eating gourmet food and touring old castles. They packed, flew to France, and boarded the boat before Edith even had time to question her sister how it was possible. All Helen said was "Soon. Soon all will be clear."

Now they sit in comfortable stuffed chairs, enjoying the first wonderful dinner prepared for the cruise passengers by a famous French chef. The boat is small and similar in style to the one they took on the Amazon.

"Pour me another glass of the wonderful Pommard, sister." Helen moves her wineglass closer to Edith. "Simply spectacular this fish dish. The French do know how to cook."

"Just like the delightful fish we ate on the Amazon cruise. All those unique flavors and the marvelous ways to make yucca," Edith smiles at her recollection.

"Really, sister. How in the world can you compare the two? This is haute cuisine, not bait. Anyway, don't you remember what happened to you not heeding my advice? Tea and bread, British basics. But no, you have to taste everything little Ms. Exotic. Throwing up till you turned blue. I thought I was going to lose you," Helen huffs. She pauses to take a deep breath then smiles at Edith, her baby sister. She can't imagine living a day without her.

"I have never gotten used to British basics. British anything to tell the truth." Edith laughs. "Even though I don't really remember Mom and Dad, I still feel like a Southern girl at heart. I wish I could remember Momma's cooking better. It's all faded now. And yes, you were right about having digestive problems, but I was only sick for a little bit," retorts Edith.

Helen mutters, "What I remember about Momma's cooking is that it wasn't very good. Even that old stray cat we had didn't eat her leftovers." She swirls the dark red wine, watching it stick to the glass's sides. Slowly it slides downward. Helen can be more serene now that their finances have improved. Improved dramatically.

"I still cannot believe what you told me this afternoon. It's impossible. A dream, sister. Really." Edith closes her eyes to taste every flavor of the buttery fish dish. "I guess our difficult days are over. And we should focus on the astonishing future we now have. Look at us. Who would have imagined that we'll eat like queens the rest of our lives?" "Yum." Edith picks through the bones on her plate to get every last morsel of fish. "I have always said that you are the clever one in the family, sewing the diamonds in your bra. Brilliant! The way they searched everyone's luggage, purses, pockets, even peeling back the soles in our shoes when we left Lima."

"Thank goodness my hunch that no one will touch an old white British lady's droopy breasts in the middle of a public airport paid off."

"So true. So true." Edith raises her glass to toast her sister. She sips the wine slowly. "But I still don't understand how you knew when he would get the stones from that poor student. I was so relieved to hear that no one got hurt in our hotel. Those unfortunate boys. Imagine to be held at gunpoint. Too scary."

"I'm sure once the students set foot in the states, the holdup became the most dramatic story of their adventure. Young people are way more resilient than we give them credit for. And the young man who had the diamonds all that time in his backpack and never knew. Boy, I bet he'll check his belongings better next time he travels!" Helen exclaims.

"There was nothing in the papers about the young man carrying them. Surely the professor told the police?" asks Edith.

"No, I think she kept her wits about her and decided that since they had the robber, best to keep her students out of it and get out of the country as quickly as possible. You never know what the police would have done, especially since they didn't recover the diamonds that night. And the mine owners were frantic to get them back. Still are, I'm sure. You must remember, sister dear, that some cops are quite corrupt. To cover their own butts, they probably would have tried to implicate the young man. Make him into an accomplice. Send the poor boy to one of their horrific jails and extort his family for lots of money. Remember how the guides always said for any incident come to them and stay as far away from the cops as possible."

"But you had the clerk call the police."

"Well, I certainly couldn't let anything happen to those boys. To tell the truth, I didn't think about it. I just reacted when I saw the gun. When I first heard of the diamonds in the café that evening in Iquitos, I never felt any real danger. The guy was a bureaucrat, and the other one I think was a miner or some other low-paid employee. It appeared to be happenstance how the robbery happened, so I didn't think there was any reason not to try and pinch the diamonds myself."

"But why didn't you tell me? We have pickpocketed wealthy old people on cruises for years now to make ends meet. Why did you leave me in the dark?" Edith reaches across the table to get the wine bottle. She pours another glass for herself and motions to her sister. Helen nods yes. Edith empties the bottle in her sister's glass.

"I thought it best until things calmed down to not involve you. Good thing too because your complete innocence convinced the police. I figured they might come and interview us since we had been to the mine, and we left Iquitos the day they discovered the robbery. The mine owners have powerful friends everywhere, you know."

Edith motions to the waiter to bring the dessert menu. She chooses crème brûlée and herbal tea with lemon. Helen declines dessert but requests tea with hot milk.

Helen continues her reasoning. "I really assumed the whole thing to be a long shot. I just thought I'd keep my eyes open and see if any opportunity appeared. I believed I'd have a better chance of lifting them from the young man while we stayed at the same hotel in Lima, which is why I prevented the robber from getting them on the plane. Boy, was he surprised when I knocked him off his feet!" The sisters laugh wholeheartedly. "You played a key role, sister, just by being your friendly self and establishing a relationship with the students."

"But how did you know when that tall man was going to make his move?"

"When the elevator door opened and I saw him in what I now know was a disguise, instinct told me the jig is up. Even more when we saw his face on TV. I knew he couldn't wait any longer. Anyone by that point would be desperate. He needed to get them and go underground. But I must admit I did almost lose it completely when I spied in the room and saw him pouring all those diamonds into the velvet cloth. My heart lit up with desire, but when my eyes roamed to see the fear in those boys faces, I knew I had to get help. God save me if one of them had been shot. I hid in the stairwell after I heard that the police were on their way. I thought he'd use the stairs, and I could try to pinch them from his back pocket. But then he disappeared. I guess he used the elevator. I stayed on the lobby floor and stood in the shadows, waiting to see how it would play out. Fortunately for us, that drunken guy showed up and gave me the moment for the lift. You know, I only need a few seconds."

"Yes, sister. You were well trained by that ghastly Malcolm. How you tolerated serving with him those years in the West house, only God knows."

"Yes, he was a rough bloke, but I now give him a toast. I have no idea where he is or if he is still alive, but thanks to his initial instruction, we will live very well from now to our deaths. To Malcolm." They lift the teacups in the air.

"Sister, you are a smart one. And to know to wait six months before selling them? Did you see that in a crime show?" Edith still can't believe that Helen managed to steal and sell the diamonds without her noticing anything.

"Probably, but I don't remember. What I do know is that the world moves at an ever faster pace, and people have short memories. Yes, the missing diamonds were on the news nonstop for several weeks, but with our limited attention spans, you know it won't last. The newscasters must find some other disaster or scandal or awful thing to report to keep us tuned in. I figured, by six months, no one around here would remember anything about them. Plus, I couldn't keep it from you any longer. You were slipping back into that depression, and I was about to burst, keeping it a secret, especially when we returned and the robbery was all folks talked about."

"But how did you know dear departed cousin Sid's partner would help us discreetly. He must have known they were hot, and he always seemed so upstanding to me," asks Edith.

"Yes, but Jurrian is Dutch."

"So?"

"He's from Antwerp."

"So?"

"Antwerp, the world's diamond capital, where 80 percent of all rough diamonds are traded," Helen responds.

"Yes, but still, that doesn't mean he would know an illicit trader. I sure most folks who live there know nothing about diamonds."

"Of course. Just because he is from there doesn't mean he is involved in the diamond trade. But I recalled that year we spent New Year's Eve with them, right before Sid died, may he rest in peace. Sid was talking about acquaintances of Jurrian. Said he had many friends in the diamond business. Remember?"

Edith nods but is more focused on her crème brûlée that the waiter just served.

"Sid joked what a shame his partner wasn't in it so they could afford that dream apartment in midtown Manhattan Sid wanted for years. We were all laughing until Sid mentioned the name of some guy, I can't remember now, but Jurrian's face went ash. His smile changed to a frown crinkling his forehead. He cleared his throat and changed the conversation. I thought it odd at the time, and it stuck in my mind." Helen sips her tea.

"And?" asks Edith.

"Well, because of that I went on a little fishing expedition. I called Jurrian and told him that I found several diamonds in the park. Probably a necklace that broke and scattered on the ground. I had dropped my purse and had to kneel in the grass to retrieve my belongings and there they were, right in the grass. Since there was no way to know who their owner is and return them, which is of course what us proper ladies wanted to do, I had put them in a drawer at home and forgot about them, not even sure if they were real or not. But now with our savings gone, I thought I'd see if they had any value and if so, sell them."

Incredulous, Edith shakes her head. "And he bought that story? Come on. There were rough." She makes her I-can't-believe-it face.

"I'm sure he thought it was unusual and that they couldn't be part of a necklace, but I offered him twenty percent for his troubles. I'm guessing that when his contact told him their potential value, twenty-five million dollars, that got his attention. I guess he figured for five million dollars the story was not only plausible but exactly what happened!" Helen laughs.

"How do you know we can trust him?" Edith looks up to the sky. "No disrespect, Sid. But what if he wants more or has a change of heart and reports us?" frets Edith.

"Dear sister, he would be arrested as an accomplice. Plus, now there is no evidence. No documents, no rough diamonds. The diamonds were cut and sold a month ago. Our money safe in a nice quiet Swiss bank account. Besides don't you see in the movies that there is some type of code among high-class thieves? Never rat on one another."

"Especially not ones with millions in their pockets." Edith sits quietly for a moment prompting Helen to ask if she is okay. "I'm fine. I know exactly how I want to spend my half."

"What do you mean? We'll keep the money in the account and draw on it as ours needs dictate. Good Lord, we are old now, and who knows what may happen or what we may need. End of story."

"No, sister, not for me." Edith looks directly into her sister's eyes. Only once before has Helen seen such a serious, thoughtful, and intense look on her face. That was when she told Helen her intention to marry Ralph. Helen knows on the rare occasion that Edith is absolutely determined about something, there is little she can do to stop her. She hopes that Edith hasn't secretly fallen head over heels for some guy she's met on bingo nights.

Edith continues, "I will contact one of the environmental groups that are suing the mine for the ravishing destruction it has caused and will continue to do if someone doesn't stop them. You know when we saw the size of the mining area? Well, it is now four times that size."

Helen's eyes open wide.

"Don't be so surprised. I know how to use Google now, sister dear. There are photos. The mine owners are still clear cutting and searching even though the geologists have told them they are out of the meteor strike's range, and they will find no more diamonds there.

Spreading grey death they are. But the owners' greed is, as always, out of control. I will pledge them my share. Or most of it. Nine million to stop the destruction, the stealing of one of the last remaining rainforests. Stop before you say anything, sister. We are old, so we will never be able to spend all this money. I feel very strongly, very strongly." Edith pauses to make sure she has Helen's full attention.

"We need to help save that beautiful place, the earth's lung, from which we are so fortunate. It has given us everything we need. I won't sleep another night if we don't give back in a big way. I can live off a million dollars, that's over 650,000 pounds for goodness sake for the rest of my life. And you can do whatever you want with your half. I know you have always thought me frivolous and unconcerned about my future, but I'm standing firm on this. Nothing you can say will change my mind. It's the right thing to do."

Helen doesn't respond. She stares off at the beautiful Loire river valley with its chateaus dotting the countryside. "I only have one thing to say." Helen pauses and a big smile spreads across her face. "I can live with that. No, actually I couldn't agree with you more. A grand gesture. Time to give back." Helen again raises her teacup. "Here's to luxurious days and a better world, dear sister."

As their cups clink, the evening light twinkles off the gold rims and the new sparkly rings on each of the women's right hand.

ABOUT THE AUTHOR

 Kimberly Grimes is an anthropologist who has had the pleasure of taking her University of Delaware students to the Amazon rainforest for over a decade. She is also the director of Made by Hand International Cooperative, a fair-trade business. Kimberly has worked throughout the world developing sustainable business solutions to alleviate poverty while preserving cultural and environmental resources. Her books include Crossing Borders: Changing Social Identities in Southern Mexico, A Guide for Retailers: Creating a Successful Fair Trade Business, A Journey in the Amazon (children's book), and is the coeditor of Artisans and Cooperatives: Developing Alternative (Fair) Trade for the Global Economy. She and her husband, Marco Hernandez, live in Fenwick Island, Delaware.

CPSIA information can be obtained at www.ICGtesting.com
Printed in the USA
BVOW08s0417051215

429410BV00001B/5/P